LOVER
COME
HACK

**The Madison Night Mystery Series
by Diane Vallere**

LOVER COME HACK

A Madison Night Mystery

Diane Vallere

HENERY PRESS

To Doris Day

ACKNOWLEDGMENTS

Madison Night's lifestyle provides unique opportunities for research. In some cases, the people who help the books go from idea to page are strangers who may never know of their help, but that doesn't minimize their contribution.

Thank you to:

The staff of *Atomic Ranch* magazine, for curating content that closely aligns to Madison's world and delivering it to me in convenient magazine format four times a year. Your stories have been a constant source of inspiration for her imaginary clients.

Shannon from House-Improvements.com, whose YouTube videos made removing a non-load bearing interior wall seem like something Madison could do herself.

Doris Day, for continuing to be the perfect role model for Madison.

Josh Hickman, who answered approximately 327 of my questions about ceiling finishes, painting, panda-pawing, mudding, sanding, mortaring, patching, and more while never alerting the landlord to maybe keep an eye on me.

Retro-renovation.com, for massive archives of time capsule houses and restoration projects. Madison's new yellow kitchen was designed with resources found on this blog and it's no exaggeration to say I wish it were my kitchen instead.

Lee Lofland, for writing *Police Procedure and Investigation: A Guide for Writers*, which was instrumental in helping me know what would happen if Madison were bleep bleep bleep or bleep bleep bleep, both of which happen in the upcoming pages.

Henery Press and my fellow Hen House authors, for giving both me and Madison a home and a community.

Amy Jolly, for saying yes to my big, fat, last-minute, post-deadline favor!

Subscribers of the Weekly Diva: I have the best readers! Thank you for letting me spend time with you every Sunday, for embracing my different series, and for volunteering to be deceased characters who originally owned the stuff Madison Night acquires. I know that makes you sound a little weird, but I love you anyway.

ONE

I should have expected the letter. In my fifty years, I'd maintained polite and friendly relationships with bosses and employees. Friends and family. Bad dates and good lovers. When I looked at it like that, I guess I was due for a bombshell like this.

Dear Madison, it started, *It's taken me a few days to collect my thoughts. I can no longer be a part of this relationship. When we met, I accepted that we wouldn't always see eye to eye. I knew you had strong opinions and I was attracted to that at first, but after butting heads one too many times, I can't take it anymore. You are* not *always right. You are* not *the most talented person in the room. And we are no longer partners on the application for the Very Important Projects competition.*

The letter continued with a line by line breakdown of my character flaws followed by how fellow mid-mod designer and recent attached-at-the-hip friend, Jane Strong, had interpreted my behavior as a personal affront to her. I stopped reading the list of my faults about halfway through. There's nothing like seeing the carefully thought out dissection of your natural personality in a neatly formatted document to make you consider adding booze to your first cup of coffee.

And did I mention? Jane hadn't just spent time collecting her thoughts. She'd color coded them and provided a handy key at the top of the email to help me understand which of my flaws were the worst.

This is what happens when you collaborate with a friend.

Jane Strong was the one who had first told me about the

DIDI—Design in Dallas Initiative. DIDI was a group of established professionals that recognized excellence in design, decorating, and renovation projects in Dallas, Texas. Their mission statement was to identify buildings within the Dallas Tax Base that had been ignored. Dallas had undergone several transformations in its lifetime, yet for every new hip part of town that popped up on the radar, another one fell into disrepair and in some cases, abandonment. Jane had read about my recent renovation of an old pajama factory that I'd inherited and had told the DIDI about my work.

That was the first job I'd completed on such a large scale, and the wave of positive attention from the design community had been unexpected. The DIDI endorsement had given me massive name recognition overnight, and Mad for Mod, my mid-century focused interior decorating and design company, had gone from booking the occasional atomic kitchen renovation to kitschy movie theaters, novelty restaurants, and even one theme-room bed and breakfast. I had the luxury of being selective about the jobs I took. For a small business, it was a good feeling.

About a month ago, the DIDI sent out an email announcement of a pop-up competition to kick off the Very Important Properties competition, or VIP, as it was truncated to fit into a world increasingly dependent on initials. The lack of pre-competition buzz had been intentional to even out the chances of winning amongst both established and emerging talent in the city limits. Other components of the contest were equally determined: rigid design requirements, capped budgets, and a tight window for execution once applications were approved. Jane asked if, instead of competing against each other, I was interested in pooling resources and collaborating on a joint submission for VIP?

A flurry of emails, an invitation to brainstorm concepts before giving an answer, and a gigantic delivery of fresh daisies to thank me and proclaim there was no way we wouldn't win, and I said yes. It didn't hurt that I was looking for ways to avoid the mess that was my personal life.

Jane and I shared a common design philosophy, an attraction to the mid-century modern aesthetic, and a proximity to the same milestone birthday (fifty, though to be fair, the two years between our birthdays ensured I reached it first). Things like that can lull you into a false sense of compatibility, especially amongst potential friends where the messiness of romance wasn't part of the equation. For an independent woman like me, the novelty of having a new friend who shared my passions was a high. We traded lipstick recommendations, watched TCM movie marathons on Friday nights, swapped out vintage clothing we'd accumulated, and alternated driving the truck we took to the local flea markets to shop for inventory.

Still, after giving up nights, weekends, and paying jobs to collaborate with Jane on our VIP entry, today's email hit a nerve. I'd jumped through hoops for her, and this was the way she thanked me. By attacking my character in an unemotional message she'd needed days to write after "collecting her thoughts."

I steeled myself with a deep breath and called her office.

"Posh Pit, Vonda speaking," her assistant answered.

"Vonda, this is Madison Night. Is Jane available? I need to speak to her. It's urgent."

"Madison. Tell me Jane didn't send the email. Of course, she sent the email. Why else would you be calling me? I am so sorry. You have no idea. She's crazy. The woman is totally off her nut."

"This really is between Jane and me."

"I can't let you talk to her."

"This will only take a moment."

Vonda Quinn was Jane's assistant, but from what I'd seen, her job involved little more than answering phones, data entry, and unsolicited attitude. Her sigh was clear despite the crackling of the forty-year-old mechanisms inside my 1970s yellow donut phone. "She's not here. She went to the DIDI offices to turn in her submission for the competition before the cutoff for entries tonight."

I felt the heat rise over the back of my neck, not an entirely unwanted sensation considering the back door to my studio was propped open and the cold air from outside had entered. "Jane can't submit that application. The designs are mine. The concept is mine. The building belongs to her, but there's more to that submission than the property."

"Don't shoot the messenger," Vonda said.

I wedged the phone between my ear and my shoulder and grabbed an empty file folder. I was so distracted, I almost forgot it was my turn to talk. "I'm going to the DIDI offices right now. If you have any way to get in touch with her, you might want to give her a head's up that I'm on my way. I'm not in a particularly good mood after her email, either."

"That's between you and Jane."

I chose not to mention that I'd already made that point. I straightened my neck and the receiver dropped onto my desk. I didn't waste time on a good-bye. Vonda might not have written or sent the email, but she'd known about it and that was bad enough. As I grabbed a stack of pages off the printer and wedged them into the folder, I wondered how many other people Jane had spoken to about her less than flattering views of me.

I found Effie Jones, a recent college graduate and my first ever full-time employee, in the small storage unit I kept behind the studio. What Effie lacked in knowledge about design she made up for in organizational suggestions and millennial perspective. (It didn't hurt that I'd gifted her with ten Doris Day movies to help her refine her eye. That's how I first learned about mid-century design, and it seemed as convenient a training method as any.) Effie was working on a new inventory database to keep me organized beyond my current if-it-fits, I'll-take-it-home system.

"Effie, I have to go to downtown. Can you lock up the storage unit and cover the studio? There's only one appointment this afternoon—the Bickners. They're going to drop off a list of the items they're selling to me. After we get the list, you can work on inputting them into the new database while you're in the studio."

"Sure, Boss." Effie looked slightly annoyed. "It would have

been more productive if I'd gone out to their house and taken pictures first."

I held up both hands. "This whole system is new to me. When someone says they want to sell me the contents of their never-renovated 1961 ranch house so they can take their family on a cruise for their fiftieth wedding anniversary, I say yes. The details—we can always work them out after the fact."

"Okay, Boss, but I'm telling you, once you embrace this new system, you're going to wonder why it took you so long."

I smiled. Aside from her post-college status, Effie was a former tenant of the apartment building I'd owned. Since getting the job at Mad for Mod, she'd taken to calling me "Boss." I'd learned to accept it.

"Maybe that's true," I said, "but now's not the time to discuss it. I don't know how long I'll be gone, but I'll call you when I'm on my way back."

I fished my car keys out of my tote bag and unlocked the door to my vintage Alfa Romeo. It was my second one in five years, and not in as good of shape as the first. In a perfect world, I'd find the time to restore it. In a perfect world, I wouldn't be on the receiving end of unsolicited emails that attacked my character, either.

The DIDI offices were on the twenty-third floor of Republic Tower in downtown Dallas. Originally built to be the largest building in the city, it battled the Southland Center for that distinction for a few years, even adding a spire to the roof five years after it was first constructed. Like so many small battles, both buildings lost when the First National Tower dwarfed them in 1965.

Republic Tower had started life as a bank, taken a few different turns, and now leased office and retail space. It was the perfect location for the DIDI offices because the building itself spoke of the history of Dallas design and represented what those of us who had an interest in looking to the past for inspiration were trying to protect.

I parked in the underground lot, tightened my scarf around my neck, and walked to the elevators. It was late September, not usually a cold month in Dallas, but with unseasonable rains had come unseasonable drops in the daily temperatures. Fellow residents, as if by unspoken agreement, shifted their wardrobes from summer wear to fall attire along with the flip of the calendar, and I was no different. A welcome chill had arrived a few days ago, giving me a reason to dust off my vintage light pink London Fog coat. I'd accessorized with a white scarf and a pair of vintage Courrèges boots that rarely saw the light of day. White leather gloves with small bows at the wrist completed my outfit. I kept my gloves on all the way through the vestibule, on the short elevator ride, and into the lobby of the building.

"Good morning, Miz Madison," said a rotund black man from behind the security desk. "A little chilly out there, isn't it?"

"Good morning, Delbert," I replied. I pulled off my right glove and signed the visitor ledger. "It's cooler than usual for Dallas, but compared to the summer heat, this feels good."

Delbert Manning had been the security officer at Republic Tower his whole life. He'd gotten the job when he was twenty; that had been 1970. I'd only met him recently, but my obvious appreciation for the building (and numerous questions about its history) had led him to share stories about the various people he'd seen come through those doors, the business that had been conducted, and the celebrities he'd encountered. When I asked him if he'd made them sign in like I did, he insisted he had. "Rules be rules, Miz Madison. Don't matter how important you are. That's the way this whole world works." He was nearing retirement age but had never once indicated he wanted anything more out of life than to greet the visitors of his building. I admired the pride he took in his work.

I glanced at the sign-in log and ran the tip of my left, still-gloved index finger down the list of names in the book. When I didn't see Jane's, I asked Delbert. "Was Jane Strong here today?"

"If her name isn't in the book then she hasn't been here."

"Her secretary told me she was on her way."

"Probably stopped off for something to eat at that little coffee shop under the building. She's always got a cup of joe in her hand." He shook his head and smiled.

Delbert was right. Ever since I'd friended Jane a few months back, I'd learned there were two things she always had: her tablet computer and a cup of coffee. You could always tell when Jane had been present at a job site by a discarded coffee cup with a ring of apricot lip color left behind on the rim. You'd think she would have converted to a more long-lasting formula after all this time, but she seemed to view her lipstick stain as a calling card.

If Jane hadn't been to the DIDI offices, then she hadn't yet filed the application to the competition. Despite the obvious confrontation we were going to have when we were face to face, it was worth my time to wait. The application in question contained months of work on a furnished apartment complex. The city of Dallas had become increasingly popular because of its tax breaks for businesses but relocating meant stress. My concept had been to design a small building of mid-century themed apartments available for short-term rentals. I'd first gotten the idea after spending time in Palm Springs, California, where interest in the Rat Pack style attracted people from all over. Jane had scouted a property and we'd pooled our similar visions for the designs.

"Delbert, if you don't mind, I'm going to wait for Jane in the lobby." Delbert looked uncomfortable, and I quickly assured him that I'd be self-sufficient. "Go about your work like you always would," I said. "I'm going to answer a few emails and return a couple of phone calls. You won't even know I'm here."

"Sure, Miz Madison, go right ahead. If you need anything, you just holler."

Just then, a *bong!* announced the arrival of the elevators. I steeled myself, knowing that *bong!* might be the only warning I got before seeing Jane face to face.

I was right. The doors opened, and Jane Strong strode out. Like me, she dressed in vintage. Jane's vintage was more upscale than mine, and today's ensemble was no different. She wore a smart burnt-umber skirt suit with a blue and umber paisley-patterned silk blouse. A matching scarf was knotted at the neck in a full bow that was slightly off center. The bracelet sleeve length of her jacket exposed powder blue leather gloves that disappeared under her cuffs. Nude stockings and low-heeled brown pumps finished the ensemble.

In contrast, under my pink London Fog coat was a brown, double-knit polyester sheath dress. It wasn't that I didn't own clothes of the same vintage designer status as Jane did, but that I'd found double-knit polyester to be a convenient choice when working in my storage locker. In short, it had a durability factor unequalled in other fabrics, and I could clean temporary stains with a sponge and liquid dish soap.

"Jane," I stood up. "We need to talk."

"What are you doing here?" she asked. She held a white takeout cup of coffee in one hand and a brown leather attaché case in the other. "I thought I made it clear in my email that we wouldn't be working together."

"I called your office and your assistant told me you were turning in the design application. That was a joint concept. The idea was mine." I glanced over my shoulder at Delbert, who was doing a poor job pretending to ignore us. I remembered my promise to be invisible and stepped toward Jane. "What exactly is your problem with me? I honestly thought we worked well together."

She shook her head. "Madison, I don't think you're cut out to work with others. The idea of you converting that old pajama factory into a shared workspace is laughable. What could you possibly know about sharing? Everybody knows VIP is one big job interview. You need me more than I need you."

She pronounced "VIP" phonetically—vip, not V. I. P. It was the shorthand we'd used while working together, a reference to *Lover Come Back*, one of my favorite Doris Day movies. If she wasn't in the process of attacking me, I would have laughed.

I softened my tone. "Jane, I can respect that you want to dissolve our partnership, but there's a better way to go about doing it than stealing my design. That concept includes a lot of resources from the Mad for Mod inventory, and the only reason I agreed to work together was because I expected to have some say in the process."

"I don't want your idea *or* your inventory," she said. She took a long pull on her coffee cup and then deposited the empty cup in the trash bin in the corner. "I have my own plans. This is the perfect opportunity to showcase what I can do. Me."

"You're entering the competition yourself?"

She didn't answer my question. "If you want to win, you need to bring it on, Madison. And trust me. I've seen what you got and I'm not the least bit worried."

See what I mean? This is what happens when you collaborate with a friend.

TWO

The last thing I wanted was to stand in the lobby of Republic Tower while Jane spelled out my shortcomings. It was only a matter of time until someone else joined us, either from the offices upstairs or the parking lot below. And what had started out as one problem—intercepting Jane before she filed the application for our joint design—had now become two: dealing with Jane and submitting an application for myself.

I wasn't about to back down and hand her the prize. Not now.

The application for VIP was available to download from the organization's website, along with a portal to upload the required design concept illustrations. I had the same files that Jane had. We'd shared them via cloud storage. But without knowing what she intended to submit and how much of it might have been pilfered from that original concept, the only true option was for me to start from scratch. And with today being the deadline for application, my chances were already looking less than stellar.

Instead of continuing the losing verbal battle with Jane, I shifted my priorities. I needed a concept—a new concept—and I needed it fast. "Don't get too comfortable, Jane," I said. "I'm every bit the designer that you are."

Jane made a show of looking at her watch, a vintage timepiece she wore on top of her long, light blue leather gloves. "I'd like to see what you can come up with by five."

I felt around in my handbag for my parking ticket. "Delbert, sign me out, would you? I have work to do." I left before Jane had a chance to insult me further.

I didn't want to waste precious time driving back to my studio. I could access my files from a remote access point. I stopped into the coffeehouse to pick up my own takeout cup of fuel. The owner, Paxton Brannigan, was behind the counter. He was tall and on the fit side of trim. He wore his daily uniform of blue chambray shirt, faded jeans, and black Converse hi-tops, with a black apron on top. His brown hair was cut short in the back and foppish on top, a style that reminded me of leading men in movies from the eighties.

Paxton handed a tall white cup to a customer and waved me up to the counter. "Hey, Madison. You just missed Jane. You two planning some big design coup?"

"Not exactly," I said. "I'm a little short on time and caffeine. What's the strongest thing you can make in a hurry?"

He looked at the cups on the counter and spun two so the descriptions of the beverages faced him. "Tall vanilla latte. How's that sound?"

"Isn't that someone's drink?"

He opened the lid and peered inside. "Pretty sure they wanted soy milk and to be honest, I was talking to Jane when I made it, so I can't guarantee I didn't make a mistake." He winked and handed the cup to me. "Don't worry. I'll give the other customer a free scone."

"Great," I said. "You didn't happen to make it a doppio, did you?"

"You're pushing your luck."

I paid for the beverage and left. The Dallas Public Library, only a few blocks away, had computers available with a valid library card. It would be faster to walk than drive, so I left my car in the garage and called Effie on the way.

"Mad for Mod," she answered.

"Effie, it's Madison. I'm not going to be back at the studio for a couple of hours."

"Are you okay? Did you see Jane?"

"I don't want to talk about Jane. We have"—I checked my watch—"five hours to submit a proposal for the VIP competition.

I'm headed to the library to work on the application, but I need access to that inventory you've been working on."

"I thought Jane submitted the application."

"I don't want to get into that right now. Let's just pretend there is no Jane. It's me." I corrected myself. "Us. Mad for Mod. We have as much going for us as anybody else does, but we can't win if we don't enter."

"But the deadline is tonight. You've got plenty of time."

"I'm not taking a chance on someone saying our application didn't arrive. Jane submitted hers in person and so will I. The DIDI office closes at five and I intend to have our application stamped 'accepted' before then."

"Don't you need a property? The collaboration with Jane used her building, right?"

"Right. But this is round one of the contest. We have to submit a concept to be approved by the vetting committee. As long as we stick to designing whatever we say we're going to design, there's flexibility in the choice of properties."

"What are you going to submit?"

I thought over what I remembered about the design requirements. "We need to hit three points: interior design, exterior design, and one renovated element. I'm going to stick with furnished apartment rentals. Every unit will be different. We'll turn one unit into a common room for residents to use—that'll be our renovation. I can design mid-century apartments with my eyes closed, and frankly, this is not the time to bite off more than I can chew."

"What do you need me to do?"

"Get me the login credentials for your inventory. I'll call a realtor for a list of available properties. Might as well keep things in the neighborhood."

"Okay!" Effie sung out. She was peppy and enthusiastic, exactly the combination I needed. "It'll take me a couple of minutes to reconfigure the sign-in so we can both work on it at the same time."

"That's fine. It'll take me a couple of minutes to sign on to a computer."

"Remember to use your phone as a hot spot instead of using the library internet. It's more secure and way faster."

"Got it."

There was something about having a twenty-four-year-old employee that made me feel young and old at the same time. Effie pushed me to modernize the way I conducted my business. She respected my design aesthetic and promised me that she would never suggest something that undermined the decorating values I was committed to maintain. Learning her new systems kept me feeling plugged in (no pun intended) while also letting me see just how much existed that I didn't know about. She wasn't the best salesperson in the world, but what she lacked in natural customer service, she easily made up for in organization, shortcuts, and dedication. If she would come to work in something other than yoga pants, I'd make her employee of the month (a distinction formerly held by my Shih Tzu, Rocky).

I called Kip Bledsoe's office on my way to the library. Kip was the local real estate agent who handled many of the commercial properties in the Lakewood/White Rock Lake suburb of Dallas. In the past I'd worked with a different agent who had recently retired. Kip was on the board of directors of the DIDI, which I hoped would work in my favor.

Kip's receptionist put me through to his service and I left him a message. "Kip, this is Madison Night. I'm a local designer. I'm interested in acquiring an apartment building." I paused to more closely focus on my needs. "A vacant apartment building." I left my phone number and hung up.

I arrived at the library and set up camp at an isolated computer lab. I switched on the hotspot on my phone, bypassed the library internet and connected to mine, and downloaded the design competition application from the DIDI website. I completed it quickly. When I signed into my email, Effie's instructions were waiting for me. I logged into her inventory portal and filtered the results she'd entered until I reached a desirable outcome.

I spent the next several hours completing my application, mocking up the required concept files using online design software, and building a digital mood board to round out the vision. I worked much better with a sketch pad, scissors, fabric, and a glue stick, but if ever there were a time to relent to Effie's push toward technology, this was it. At quarter after four, I clicked print and retrieved my files from the vacant librarian station. I bundled back up in my coat, scarf, and gloves and returned to Republic Tower, stopping briefly at the CVS on the way to purchase a report cover for the documents to make them appear a little less last-minute. I climbed on the first available elevator. I had twenty minutes to spare, and even though I had to pee like nobody's business, nothing was going to stop me from turning in the application before five.

Twenty-three floors up, I exited the elevator and entered the clear glass doors. In front of me, a receptionist sat behind a curved white laminate counter. I gave her my biggest smile. She held up an index finger and turned her head to the side. "No, Mr. Rose. Not yet. I know he said he would. I can stay for five more minutes, but I have to pick up my girls from their soccer game. I'll lock up when I leave. Of course. I'll let you know." She pulled her headset off and tossed it onto the counter in front of her. "Sorry to keep you waiting. The boss has been particularly high maintenance today. Can I help you?"

"Yes. I'm Madison Night from Mad for Mod. I'm hand-delivering my application for the VIP competition." I held out the tan folder. "The requested materials are inside."

She took the folder and set it next to a stack of professionally bound reports that made mine look like a sixth grade "How I Spent My Summer" essay. The report on top of the stack had a brushed steel cover with a die-cut rose in the center. Below the flower was the name Sterling Webster.

Sterling Webster's name wasn't unfamiliar to me. I'd never met the man, but he was legendary in mid-mod worlds for his blatant disregard of the style we all adored. The year before I'd inherited a house for the low price of the annual taxes, he'd flipped a property on my street, destroying the building's humble integrity, and netting a cool half a million-dollar profit.

"Are those the other applications?" I asked.

"Those are the ones that were dropped off. Some came through the portal. Gerry asked me to print and bind the materials so everything would be neat and organized."

"Gerry? Do you mean Gerry Rose?" I looked into the offices to try to catch sight of the man I knew by name only. "Head of DIDI, right? Is he going to look over the applications tonight?"

She studied me for a moment, her lips pursed, and then, as if I'd passed some sort of secret assessment, she relaxed her expression. "Let me guess. You don't trust technology and you're here to make sure your application was received."

"Something like that."

"You're not the only one. I've met more local designers today than I knew existed and everybody wants five minutes with Gerry Rose." She tipped her head toward the stack. "Most put more effort into the packaging than the concepts. I bet half of those haven't even secured the rights to the buildings they're proposing to renovate."

I thought about Jane's proposal. If she'd gone with what we'd discussed, our concepts would be remarkably similar. But if she'd used a different design, then nothing would stop me from pushing forward with what we'd planned all along. If only there were a way to see her entry—

"I can't," the receptionist said.

"You can't what?"

"I can't let you see anybody else's proposal."

"Was I that obvious?"

She smiled. "You're not the first. The boss's ex-wife just offered me fifty dollars to look the other way while she went through the submissions."

"But you couldn't."

"That's right. I got the feeling she was looking for someone specific. Of course, you're a little subtler than she was, but rules are rules."

Just like Delbert. In a world that seemed to reward rule breaking more and more each day, it pleased me to know there were still people whose bad behavior couldn't be bought. Especially since I already knew Gerry Rose's ex-wife was Jane.

Jane had spent more than half of her forty-eight years in a marriage built on security, not attraction, to one of the most successful architects in Dallas. Post-divorce, she was enjoying the perks of being newly single, something I knew because of the night she'd called me in tears. I'd picked up two gallons of ice cream and went to her house thinking she'd been hit with a wave of post-divorce regression. Turns out she was crying over a new lover. She'd expected too much from a rebound relationship and he'd broken off their affair. Any details I knew about their fling came without his identity. A true friend knows when it's more important to listen than to pry.

I thanked the receptionist, noting her coat, a tan suede hip-length style trimmed in white shearling, sitting on her desk. Her handbag and keys sat in the metal inbox tray next to it. The clock mounted to the wall over her head indicated I'd had plenty of time until their offices closed at five, but if I'd dawdled one iota more, I would have been on the unfortunate receiving end of the result of the receptionist leaving early. Of all days! But today, not my problem. My work here was done.

"Can you direct me to your ladies' room?" I asked her.

"Sure. Out the doors, to your left. It's clearly marked."

"Thank you."

She stood up and shrugged into her coat, buttoned the top two faux wooden buttons that were shaped like tiny ram horns, and switched off her monitor. The building was silent, and I guessed the receptionist wasn't the first person to leave early.

I found the ladies' room easily. It was like most office building restrooms: spacious, with a row of stalls along the back wall and a row of sinks along the front. Two of the five stall doors were closed.

I reached for the door on the far-right stall and heard the sound of someone getting sick.

My stomach clenched in an unconscious reaction to the sound. I stepped back and bent down, looking for shoes. I recognized a pair of legs in familiar low-heeled brown pumps pointed the wrong direction inside the middle stall.

I pushed aside my own needs and my battered pride and tapped on the door. "Jane? Is that you? It's Madison. Are you okay?"

The toilet flushed. Seconds later, the door opened. Jane faced me. She looked like a piece of chalk that someone had gotten wet. Her normally alabaster skin was pale and ashen, and a ring of moisture had broken out on her forehead and temples. Dark, purplish-black circles were pronounced under each eye.

"I don't feel so good," she said. She stepped toward me and this time, when Jane Strong let loose on me, it wasn't in email form.

THREE

I backed away to avoid being hit by Jane's tossed cookies. Jane stumbled forward. Her eyes rolled up into her head and her legs gave way underneath her. As she fell to the floor, she grabbed my arm and brought me down too. We landed on the soiled brown and taupe ceramic tiled floor.

There wasn't time to think about the condition of the floor. I pulled myself up to a sitting position and cradled Jane's head in my lap. Her eyes were closed. "Jane," I said. "Jane! Can you hear me?"

She didn't respond.

Think, Madison. I scanned the bathroom. The door to the stall closest to me was still closed. I slid down and stretched my leg out to connect with the dark brown metal, and then kicked the heel of my Courrèges boot against it. "Help! Is someone in there? Please, we need help!" From my angle on the floor I saw no feet. The stall had probably been locked after being deemed out of order.

I looked back at Jane. Her body was still. I felt for a pulse—it was weak. I had to get help, and fast, but I didn't want to leave her alone. Not here, not now, not today, not like this.

The restroom was equipped with the least practical hand-drying option: a loop of white fabric that self-sanitized with each pull to rotate the fabric. My coat and bag lay in a pile by the far-right stall. I unzipped my dress and pulled it off over my head, balled it up, and eased it under Jane's head. In my vintage ivory slip, I crawled to my handbag and dumped the contents to find my phone. I'd forgotten to turn off the personal hotspot, and after hours of working at the library, it was dead.

I threw on my pink coat and pulled open the door. "Help! Is someone there? Please! We need help in the ladies' room!"

I was met with silence. I ran down toward the DIDI offices and yanked on the solid chrome handles. The doors were locked. I moved farther down the hall, making as much noise as possible. The elevator doors *bonged!* behind me, and an attractive gray-haired man got off. He wore a gray wool suit, white shirt, and narrow patterned tie and held an expensive briefcase in one hand and a coffee cup in other.

"Help!" I called. I ran forward and grabbed his arm. "There's a woman in the restroom who needs medical assistance." I turned and ran back to the restroom. The man overtook me in the hallway and reached the door first. "The floor is slick," I called. "Be careful."

When I re-entered the powder room, the man knelt beside Jane. Something dark discolored the floor by the man's shoe. At first I thought it was my dress. It wasn't. When I realized it was a gradually expanding puddle of blood coming from the back of Jane's head, my cookies joined hers on the floor.

To my credit, I didn't pass out. The man in the suit stood. He dumped the contents of his coffee cup in the sink, filled the now-empty cup with tap water, and held it out to me. "Drink this," he said.

"Give it to her," I said.

He knelt down next to Jane. "Did you call the police? 911? Building security?"

"My phone is dead." Immediately I cringed at my choice of words. "The battery died." Again. Why did we insist on morbid expressions to describe the status of our cell phones?

"Was she like this when you found her?"

"No. She stumbled out of the stall and threw up and then collapsed."

"She was alive?" he demanded. "You should have gotten help immediately. That could have saved her life."

"I couldn't just leave her."

"Go down to the lobby and alert building security. Now."

I didn't like this man's attitude, but I'd had enough experience around crime scenes to know that it was more important to deal with the tasks at hand than to worry about politeness. There was a directness to his instructions, and for better or worse, I knew he was right. Still, I wasn't comfortable leaving Jane alone with him.

His expression softened. "I'll call the police. Delbert is closer than they are, and we'll need his help too." He stood and lifted Jane's body off the floor. "She doesn't need to lay in filth."

I picked my dress up off the floor and tossed it into the sink under running water. "Use that to clean her up a bit. I'll be right back."

By the time I reached the front lobby, I was out of breath. The immediate adrenaline rush of encountering Jane and needing to find help had waned, and my legs were shaking with the trauma of what I'd seen. I kept one hand on the wall for stability and approached Delbert. He seemed surprised to see me.

"Miz Madison! What are you still doing here? I thought you left hours ago."

There wasn't time to explain that I'd returned. "Delbert, we need your help. Jane Strong is upstairs in the ladies' room. She's—she's not well."

"She's sick?"

"She needs our help."

Delbert froze. I didn't know what I'd expected of him, but the terror in his eyes was something I hadn't anticipated. Outside the building, I heard the faint sounds of sirens. There was no way of knowing if they were headed our way or toward another emergency. "There's a man upstairs with her. He asked for you."

"I can't leave the lobby unattended."

"You can't ignore the woman dying in the building either," I demanded.

The sirens, as it turned out, were for us. A small emergency vehicle parked in front of Republic Tower and several men in white uniforms climbed out. They pulled a collapsible gurney from the back of their van and approached the building. I pushed the door open and let them in.

"She's on the twenty-third floor," I said. "I'll take you up."

As we waited for the elevators to reach us, I kept an eye on Delbert. He remained behind his station, his eyes shifting from our small group, to the doors, to the clock on the wall. I didn't know what caused his apparent discomfort, but something had rattled him more than I'd ever seen before. When the *bong!* sounded, I pushed thoughts of Delbert's panic out of my mind and prepared to lead the men to Jane.

But when the elevator doors opened, the man in the gray suit stepped off. He held Jane's body, though her head and shoulders were hidden under my newly-rinsed brown dress. Her arm dangled toward the floor, exposing her delicate wrist and burnt umber bracelet sleeves. I flashed back to the blood on the bathroom floor and couldn't begin to imagine what she looked like under my garment.

One of the EMTs stepped forward. "You shouldn't have moved her," he said. "Any movement can make her injuries worse."

"Her injuries don't matter anymore," the man said gently. He moved past the technician and laid Jane's body on the flat gurney.

Reality hit. "She's dead?" I asked. The nausea returned.

He nodded. "She passed away right after you left."

The technician with the shaved head spoke directly to the businessman. "How did she die?"

The man looked at me. "You said she'd been sick," he said. "When you left her in the loo, she probably tried to stand and fell and struck her head. Accidental death—not uncommon, but unfortunate all the same."

I stood riveted to the ground, staring at the carpet runner that protected the Italian marble floors. No, I thought. Jane can't be dead. We had unfinished business. We had to make amends. It couldn't be. It just couldn't.

Immediately a reel of events played out in my mind: hearing Jane getting ill in the bathroom, knocking on the door to find out if she was okay. Her chalky, damp appearance right before she threw up on the bathroom floor, and the moment she collapsed and knocked us both down. She'd been alive after that. I'd checked her pulse, and I'd felt it—weak, but there. Something about the scene, from when I'd left to when I'd returned with help, felt off. I squeezed my eyes shut and forced myself to recall details that my self-preservation instinct wanted me to block: the locked bathroom stall, the gray state of Jane when she opened her door. The lack of blood on her head when I'd sat with her and the presence of blood when I returned. Precious few moments had passed in that window of time, but it had been enough for someone to do the worst.

"Jane was ill. When I went into the bathroom, she was throwing up in one of the stalls. But that's not what killed her," I said. I looked slowly from one face to the next. They were waiting for me to continue. "Jane's death wasn't accidental. Somebody knew she was incapacitated in there. Jane Strong was murdered."

FOUR

Half an hour later, the lobby of Republic Tower was swarming with police officers. Jane's body had been removed from the building shortly after my statement. The only information Jane could contribute would come via the medical examiner when he determined the actual cause of death.

I wasn't unfamiliar with police procedure, though I tended to blur on the specifics of what the officers were required to do. The businessman in the gray suit gave his statement to two uniformed officers. Delbert had locked the doors to the building and led a photographer, a detective, and another several uniforms to the twenty-third floor. And I sat by myself in an uncomfortable brown leather chair by the windows that looked out on Thanksgiving Square. Despite my familiarity with more than one of Dallas's finest, including their captain, Tex Allen, I didn't recognize any of the men who were working the scene. I might have considered calling Tex if my cell had been operable. Fate made that decision for me.

A blond man with a ruddy complexion approached. "Are you Madison Night?" he asked.

"Yes."

"Detective Henning." He held out his hand. I rose and shook it. "You're the one who claimed this wasn't an accident," he said. "I'd like to ask you a few questions if you don't mind."

"Of course," I said.

He gestured toward the chairs and I sat back down. He sat across from me. We were separated by a large chrome and glass coffee table that held an assortment of Neiman Marcus catalogs. The flagship location of the luxury retail chain was two blocks away, making the catalog choice feel more like support of a local business than the profiling of potential clients.

"Tell me about what happened earlier today."

"In the bathroom? When I went in, I heard someone getting sick. I recognized Jane's shoes under the stall door and asked her if she was okay. She opened the door and said she didn't feel very good and then got sick again." Detective Henning's eyes moved from my face to my buttoned up pink London Fog coat. "I stepped out of her way, but she didn't make it to the sink." I said. "She threw up on the floor, and then her legs gave out and she fell forward and knocked us both down."

"What makes you suspect she was murdered?"

"When we fell, we were closer to the row of stalls than the sinks. I checked her pulse and it was there—faint, but there. She was laying on her back. I took off my dress and put it under her head. There wasn't any blood. Another one of the stall doors was closed and I thought someone might be inside. I kicked at the door—I was able to reach it with my foot, but nobody answered or came out to help."

"Why did you leave Ms. Strong?"

"I didn't know what was wrong with her, but I had to get help."

"You knew she was ill and you left her."

"I called for help and nobody came. The receptionist to DIDI locked up early and the rest of the floor was vacant."

"DIDI?"

"The Design in Dallas Initiative. It's an organization that's focused on the beautification and revitalization of the downtown area."

"What was your business with them?"

"I'm a designer. Today is the cutoff for the Very Important Property competition. I wanted to make sure my application was accepted on time, so I dropped it off in person."

Detective Henning didn't say anything at that. He sat in the chair opposite me, watching me, listening to me. I wished I knew something about him, but I didn't.

While we sat off to the side, an officer in a baggy uniform approached us. It wasn't until he was a few feet away that I recognized him. "Officer Clark?" I asked.

"Madison, I mean, Ms. Night. I was looking for you." He stood awkwardly by us, as if he needed something but couldn't find the words. I glanced down at his hands and saw he was holding my purse.

"I think that goes better with my outfit than yours," I said with a smile. Clark looked embarrassed. He held my bag out to me, and I set it on my lap.

Officer Clark had been part of the Lakewood Police Department for years. When I'd first met him, he'd been on the portly side and had been partnered with Donna Nast, a bombshell officer-turned-private-sector security company owner who had become something of a nemesis. Since I'd last seen Clark, he'd transferred from the LPD to the Dallas Police Department, and in that time, it appeared he'd lost about thirty pounds.

"You lost weight," I said.

"High blood pressure. Gave up beer and butter. Not sure it was worth it."

"Just think of all the bad guys you can catch now."

Clark laughed.

Detective Henning asked Clark, "You two know each other?"

"Sure. She's Captain Allen's..." his voice trailed off while he seemed to search for the appropriate word, "friend."

Henning turned back toward me. "How well do you know Captain Allen?"

"Fairly well," I said. I didn't add any qualifiers. Henning's tone changed when he asked that, and I didn't know why. "Do you need anything more from me?"

"Not now." He stood up and turned to Clark. "Get her contact information and then walk her to her car."

"I don't need an escort," I said.

"Ms. Night, while I have no conclusive evidence to back up your claims, according to your statement, a woman was murdered. You were the last person to see her alive. You're a 'friend' of a police captain. All things considered, I'm assigning you an escort."

"But I wasn't the last person to see her alive," I protested. "He was." I pointed across the lobby to the businessman. "Who is he?"

"That's Gerry Rose," Clark said. "He owns the DIDI."

"And he's Jane's ex-husband," I said under my breath.

Detective Henning's mouth drew into a tight line and he glared at Clark for a moment. "I'll see to it that Mr. Rose gets an escort too. Thank you, Ms. Night." He held out his hand and I shook it again, this time feeling less comfortable.

Officer Clark and I walked to the elevator wells. Despite my protests to Detective Henning, I was happy to have company on the way to my car. The reality of Jane's death was too fresh in my mind. Her lifeless body. Her blood pooling on the ceramic tiled floor. Her glassy eyes staring upward. I'd left to get help for such a brief amount of time, yet it had provided enough opportunity for a killer to take her life. That same killer could be anywhere now. In Fort Worth, on their way south toward Mexico, or hiding in a car in the parking garage to watch the fallout. Either way, I felt exposed, and not just because I now wore little more than a slip under my coat.

"Where's your dog?" Clark asked.

"He's spending the day with his family." The police officer looked confused. "Rocky was responsible for a litter of puppies back in March."

"I thought he was a boy."

"He is."

"You didn't have him—you know?" He made scissor motions with his fingers.

"No. I consulted with the vet when I adopted him, and he said if I was planning on being a one-dog household, as long as I kept up with Rocky's health checks, it wasn't mandatory. I guess in the back of my head, I always thought it would be nice to have the option of puppies."

"You left a litter of puppies alone at home?"

"No. They're at the twelfth precinct."

Clark laughed out loud. "You're the only person I know who could get Captain Allen to agree to that."

"'Agree' might be overstating things."

We reached my car. I found my keys in my handbag and unlocked the door, but paused before climbing in. "Detective Henning...he's new, isn't he?"

"Transferred from Amarillo. Nice guy. Came with a good reputation. Didn't Captain Allen tell you about him?"

"These days, Captain Allen and I limit our conversation to paint colors."

"Yeah, I can see how he might not want to encourage you." Clark put his hand on the top of my car door, and after I'd tucked my coat in around my ankles, shut the door and leaned down to the window. "I'm sorry about your friend, Ms. Night. We'll catch whoever did this."

The condolences took me by surprise. I'd spent the better part of my morning angry with Jane, but few others knew that. Until I'd received her email, I'd considered her a friend too. If I'd gone a day without checking my virtual inbox, everything would have been different.

I thanked Clark and left. It was after six and I was late picking up Rocky. And while my overactive Shih Tzu couldn't (and wouldn't) complain about the extra time he spent with the litter of Shi Chi puppies he'd sired, the puppy sitter would. Even I couldn't overlook the massive favor the police department had done by agreeing to let the puppies join the officers for Kids Day.

I charged my cell phone with a cigarette lighter adapter. After it had enough juice to power back on, I called Effie at the studio. She didn't answer. I left a vague message on the answering service to let her know the application had made it in on time and drove directly to the police station.

The Lakewood Police Department was a small precinct that oversaw the Lakewood/White Rock Lake suburb of Dallas, Texas.

I'd had more than one reason to become familiar with them, first when I'd found a body under the wheels of my car a few years ago and the crime had led them to believe I was a target (they'd been right), and most recently after a criminal investigation involving the very pajama factory that had caught the attention of the DIDI committee. My familiarity with the police had led me to a different set of complications as well—ones involving my love life. The less said about that, the better, at least for now.

I parked my Alfa Romeo in the visitor space by the front of the small red brick building and entered the front doors. An unexpected wall of heat filled the room. Two officers, one man and one woman, stood inside by the water cooler. The faint sound of happy barking came from somewhere deeper in the building.

"Hey, Madison," the male officer said.

"Hi." I fanned my hand in front of my face. "Is it hot in here?"

"Broken thermostat. The gauge malfunctioned two hours ago, and it's been like this ever since. You might want to tread carefully. Captain Allen's on the warpath."

"That's not why he's on the warpath," the woman added. "Wojo ate his burrito."

"Thanks for the warning." I turned to the front desk. Officer Garcia, a young Mexican who I still doubted was in police work for the long haul, sat behind the desk. He dangled a pencil over the head of a small white puppy, who hopped on his hind legs while trying to snag the writing instrument. Garcia looked up, temporarily distracted by my presence, and the puppy's teeth clamped onto the eraser end of the pencil. He yanked it loose from Garcia's hands and then followed the fallen object to the floor, snarling at it the whole time.

"Chano?" I asked, pointing at the dog.

"Yemana." We both watched the dog attack the pencil. "Sure was nice of you to let Rocky spend the day here. The kids went crazy over the dogs."

"I'm glad it was a success." Just then, a small, furry white Shih Tzu charged out from the back hallway, fur flying. He had a navy and white striped bowtie clipped around his throat. "Captain Allen dressed Rocky up as Inspector Luger?"

"He wanted Rocky to be Fish, but the fedora wouldn't stay on his head."

About eight months ago, after Rocky had made friends with a female Chihuahua, a litter of puppies arrived. The Chihuahua had been left with no owner, and the Lakewood Police department had adopted the lot of them. Thanks to either the department's new diversity policy or an appreciation for classic seventies cop shows, they'd named the Chihuahua Wentworth, after the female police detective of the 12th precinct on *Barney Miller*, and the puppies after the officers. Several members of the police squad adopted puppies and kept the names, which made reunions that much more fun.

"Get back here!" boomed a familiar voice from the back of the building.

"Is he talking to me?" I asked Garcia.

"I don't know," Garcia said.

A door slammed, and a small white puppy sped toward my feet. He stopped short and lifted a leg next to a worn, wooden chair that was pushed under a round table.

"No!" Garcia and I said at the same time.

The puppy ignored us and peed on the table leg and then looked up and yapped like he deserved a prize. The owner of the booming voice, Captain Tex Allen, stormed after the puppy like he had just escaped his parole officer.

"Garcia, take Wojo outside."

"I'll take him out," I volunteered.

Captain Allen slowly shifted his gaze from Garcia to me. The air in the small building grew even hotter, and I wished I could take off my raincoat. The lack of anything other than undergarments kept the coat in place.

"What are you doing here?" Tex demanded. "You're violating the terms of...the agreement."

"I came to pick up Rocky."

"Garcia said you'd pick him up in the morning."

"Captain Allen, can we talk about this somewhere else?"

Garcia scooped up Wojciehowitcz and carried him to the door. As soon as the door closed behind him, Tex addressed me. "We don't need to talk, Night. I get it. We gave it our best shot, but this is never going to work."

"Don't be hasty, Captain."

He held out his hand, palm-side up. "I don't see things changing anytime soon. Now give me back my key."

FIVE

Perhaps I should back up for a moment. Before finding Jane's body in the bathroom of the twenty-third floor of Republic Tower, before submitting the proposal for the VIP competition, before going to my studio and reading the critical email that triggered the trip to downtown to confront Jane in person, I'd been in Tex's bedroom.

Not *his* bedroom. His spare bedroom. He'd hired me to decorate it and I'd painted it lilac. Apparently, he had a problem with that.

"I left you a note," I said. "The color dries darker than it looks."

"It's purple. You painted my spare bedroom purple."

"I painted one wall. And what's wrong with purple? It's a manly color."

"It's the manly version of pink."

"What's wrong with pink?"

He glanced at my trench coat. I glanced down too, to make sure the buttons were all secured.

"It's not going to be bright purple. It's going to fade as it dries, and the room will have a soft, soothing, lilac glow."

Tex glared at me. "When I hired you to decorate my bedroom, I had something different in mind," he said.

Now what was I supposed to say to that?

Tex and I had a combustible relationship. I'd always written the heat off to circumstance. His job in law enforcement and my narrow escapes from the criminal element often kept us working on similar problems from opposite angles. Only recently had I acknowledged (to myself) that the attraction, though highly out of character, wasn't going anywhere. That acknowledgment came on the heels of my boyfriend, Hudson James, pointing out his own awareness of the situation. Just shy of six months ago, I'd turned fifty, yet I felt like a seventeen-year-old deciding who was going to take me to the prom.

I hadn't liked it then and I didn't like it now.

I'd told both men what they were giving me for my birthday: six months. Six months of man-free life. Six months when I didn't have to make a decision. It was the most self-indulgent thing I'd ever asked for, but I was fifty. I'd earned the right to be self-indulgent.

Those had been the most productive six months of my life.

Once I'd stopped worrying about my love life, I'd made other necessary changes. I told the manager of the local theater that I'd be shifting my role of support from volunteer to patron (a marathon of late seventies Scorsese movies was announced on their promo calendar shortly thereafter). I hired Effie to bring my business practices up to twenty-first century standards while respecting my mid-twentieth century aesthetic. I bid on jobs I'd formerly considered to be too large for a one-woman company and even booked a few.

It was during those six months that I met and became friends with Jane. It had felt like a sign. Arguably the biggest deficit in my life were female friends and here was one who was just like me.

Jane Strong and I were two peas in a vintage pod. Women who had built up our own businesses through hard work and determination. Caught between the boomers and the millennials, we'd both forged our own paths to smaller but laser-focused audiences. The only reason I hadn't met her earlier was that she'd spent a fair portion of her life working for a company that designed McMansions in the cities on the outskirts of Dallas. A company that happened to be owned by her ex-husband.

Jane's divorce from Gerry Rose at the age of forty-nine had provided the impetus for her to strike out on her own. Her husband had seen to offer little more than a lump-sum buy-out of her claims to their estate. She'd been with the company long enough to have a guaranteed pension, but the soul sucking work of cranking out house after house with no individuality had given her the motivation to start Posh Pit, her own design company. Where I was looking to work on larger, commercial properties, her business model was aimed at clients with tiny apartments and small spaces.

But right now, it was neither a commercial property nor a tiny apartment that gave me trouble. It was an angry cop with a townhouse.

"You agreed to my terms," I said. "I have complete creative control over the room you hired me to decorate and my work goes unchallenged and uninterrupted. That's why you gave me a key, remember? Or do you need me to pull up the contract and show you?"

Tex shook his head. "I agreed to give you a key so you could work when I wasn't there. I agreed to let you make informed decisions on my behalf. I never agreed to purple walls."

"Maybe you need to expand your boundaries."

"I haven't seen you in almost six months, Night. I gotta tell you, I had an entirely different fantasy about how this was going to play out."

The only way to honor the decorating job Tex had hired me to do was to schedule my working hours during his shifts at the police station. Ever since Tex had been promoted to Captain, he held office hours, which is how I ended up at his townhouse early this morning. It's also how I knew he hadn't come home last night. It might have had a little bit to do with the choice of lilac on Tex's wall. The man had cad tendencies, and in my world, a little lilac was the perfect antidote to cad.

Tex turned around and headed to his office. I followed. He moved behind his desk and tapped the space bar on his keyboard a few times. Whatever he saw on the screen made him mad. He picked up his cordless mouse and tossed it in the trash. I remembered something Garcia had said.

"Are your computers still down?"

He nodded. "The internet company was supposed to have

them back up by five." We both looked at the clock on the wall, which indicated it was almost seven thirty. "It was as good a day as any for it to happen. When they weren't up after fifteen minutes, I arranged for the DPD to cover our calls. We spent most of the day out back with the kids."

"That explains it," I said.

"What?"

"Why you're treating me like this."

"I'm treating you like I always treat you." His eyes glanced at my pink coat again. For the first time since I'd entered his office, he seemed to focus on something other than his anger over my lilac paint job. "Why are you still wearing your coat? It's seventy degrees in here." Slowly, his expression changed from scowl to the lascivious grin I'd become accustomed to since we'd met. "Wait. Did you make a decision? Did it go my way and this is how you wanted to tell me? Is this one of those visits I like to fantasize about? You're not wearing anything under that coat, are you?"

"I'm wearing a vintage slip."

"I guess that's more you than the garter belt thing." I rolled my eyes. "Hey," he said. "You're the one who wanted me to treat you like I always do."

He was. And that's how I knew he had no idea what had happened earlier today. Tex had cad tendencies, but he wouldn't flaunt them if he knew about Jane.

"What's going on, Night?" He asked, his tone of voice more serious than it had been.

"It's not what you think."

"I think something happened."

"It did. Remember my friend Jane Strong?"

"Sure. Why?"

"She died this morning." Just saying the words out loud triggered the release of adrenaline that I'd felt when I'd tried to help her earlier today.

Tex sat up. "How? Was she sick?"

"Yes. I don't know if it was food poisoning or the flu—"

"That's not what I meant. Was she ill? Was it unexpected?"

"She was murdered, Tex. Assaulted in the powder room at Republic Tower. Blunt force trauma to the head."

"How did you find out?"

"I was there." Tex's brows pulled together in an unasked question. "I just was, okay? It was a simple course of my day-to-day business."

"You said something about her being sick?" He prompted. "Walk me through what happened."

Talking to Tex about my day forced me to view the events through an objective filter. I described my trip to the restroom and Jane getting sick.

"She threw up on you?" His eyes went back to my coat. "That's why you're not wearing anything but a slip."

"I told you it wasn't what you thought."

"Go on."

I finished my recap, ending with the blood on the floor. My stomach flipped with the sight and scent memories.

"You left her, and she came to. She tried to pull herself up by the sink and lost her balance again, struck her head, and died. Accidental death."

"No."

"No?"

"No. Her face, forehead, and hair were all unmarred. The wound was on the back of her head."

"She struck her head on the floor when she fell."

"I don't think so."

Tex studied me for a few moments. "You usually call me when this sort of thing happens."

"We agreed. Six months, no pressure."

"I'm a cop, Night. Calling me about a homicide doesn't fall under that six-month umbrella."

"I spoke to a Detective Henning. Do you know him?"

"Yes. Dallas PD. What were you doing at Republic Tower?"

"I was turning in an application to the DIDI offices. The cutoff is at midnight tonight and I wanted to make sure it was accepted."

"That design competition?" he repeated.

"You know about VIP?"

"Give me some credit."

"I was there right around five. The receptionist left early, so between me dropping off my application and Jane being—Jane dying, probably about fifteen to twenty minutes passed. If you don't believe me, call Henning." I pulled the detective's card out of my coat pocket and laid it on the desk in front of Tex. "Or call Officer Clark. He was there too."

"You talked to Clark?"

"Yes. I talked to both of them."

Tex picked up Henning's business card and held it toward me, pinched between his index and middle finger.

"I heard about the murder over the police wire. I didn't know you were involved." His voice was gentle, but his attitude was reserved. He was acting as a cop, not a confidante. "I'm sorry for your loss."

I took the card from Tex but didn't say anything. A new feeling of unease came over me. That statement was like what Officer Clark had said. I'd been so mad at Jane this morning, but to the rest of the world, we were friends. To the people who knew me well, we were *close* friends. And now she was gone, and our argument would never be resolved. I wanted to unburden myself, to tell someone how she'd picked a fight with me and I'd been at Republic Tower to defend myself, but what was more self-centered than needing to twist the circumstances of Jane's untimely death to my need for an apology?

"Thank you," I said mechanically, taking the card from his fingers. "Did you hear anything else?"

"Not my case."

"So that's it? You won't discuss this with me?"

"I'm honoring the terms of your birthday present." He smiled. "It's the gift that keeps on giving."

SIX

I stood and put Detective Henning's card back into my pocket. Tex was right. I'd asked him to give me space, and he'd honored my request. The only reason I was here at the police station was because Officer Garcia had called to tell me about Cops and Kids day. When I'd heard their idea to let the neighborhood children interact with the puppies, I'd volunteered to drop Rocky off. Him being here had probably been a surprise to Tex.

"Thank you, Captain Allen." I clipped Rocky's leash to his collar, pausing to run my fingertips over the smooth Charvet bowtie around his neck. Instead of removing the accessory, I left it on. I set Rocky on the floor and we left.

As I drove home, I couldn't help feeling like an untethered balloon. I didn't lack direction, but the changing winds of today's events had scrambled my emotions. Anger? Sadness? Remorse? Guilt? I felt a combination of all of them. So I did what I always did when my emotions were in flux. I drove to my studio to work.

Mad for Mod was my port in the storm. I'd chosen the physical location because it was close to the apartment building I'd invested in when I first moved to Dallas. Greenville Avenue, Mad for Mod's address, was a five-block walk from home at the time, and although I'd been recovering from a knee injury, I knew how important it was not to treat myself as a victim. I'd forgone formal physical therapy and used my fledgling business startup as the incentive to get out of bed each day and make something for myself. It had worked. Mad for Mod had a loyal client base, good word of mouth, and produced a steady stream of income, and the walk had done wonders for my spirit. Since those early days, I'd sold the apartment complex and moved into a house that I'd acquired from a generous stranger. That house, which I still (and would forever) call Thelma Johnson's House, was on the opposite side of Greenville in the M streets.

I headed to Mad for Mod, parked in one of the three dedicated parking spaces behind the building, and let Rocky lead me inside. I unclipped his leash and he took off for the showroom while I headed toward my office.

Effie had tidied up before she'd left. The surface of my desk was clean, with active projects filed in folders along the credenza behind my desk chair. It appeared as though she'd even taken time to condition the custom wooden desk with a moisturizing oil. The well-sanded surface glowed with a soft radiance that was easily hidden under Post-its, colored pencils, and eraser dust. She must have viewed my hours working at the library as an opportunity to get me organized. Why was it people believed their own form of organization was better than someone else's? It was one of the major conundrums of our time.

I flipped through the file folders until I reached the one with my original application to the VIP competition, and then sat down and leafed through the contents. Inside were printed out floorplans of Jane's apartment building overlaid with sheets of acetate paper where I'd sketched possible fixture configurations and notations about electricity, lighting, and storage in colorful markers. Jane, who was familiar with the interior design software of her ex-husband's company, had provided her own set of floorplan ideas after inputting the measurements of the building. Her way was more efficient than mine, since the program allowed her to drop and drag with the click of a mouse and mine demanded I started from scratch.

The biggest difference between Jane and my working style hadn't been technology. It had been vision. My own decorating process started with an item. Find one item that represents what the client wanted and design from there. Sometimes that item was a flea market find. Sometimes it was a cherished inheritance. Sometimes it wasn't discovered until we spent a day digging through the contents of the extensive inventory I'd accumulated since starting Mad for Mod. But people who loved mid-century design were emotionally connected to the aesthetic. It wasn't like fashion, when a widely-respected industry source could tell you that for the next three months, your life would revolve around mint green. Mid-century modern enthusiasts didn't change their interiors like trendy outfits. Once an atomic lamp lover, always an atomic lamp lover.

When Jane and I first had the idea to collaborate, I'd offered up my inventory of fixtures and furniture accumulated over years of making bids on estates sight unseen. She'd been enthusiastic and had run with the concept. I'd fast-forwarded through my collection of Doris Day movies to find the best interiors for inspiration, and Jane had pored over vintage design magazines she'd collected from eBay. The process had felt collaborative and organic—or as organic as sputnik lamps and futuristic white laminate pod chairs could feel. We probably should have written up a contract to define who was going to do what, but it hadn't felt necessary.

I had no interest in revisiting Jane's email, so I set to work my usual way, with sketches, markers, and lists.

I found a blank floorplan printout at the back of the folder and taped it to a large sheet of white oak tag. I taped a fresh piece of acetate to the top, grabbed a purple Vis-à-Vis erasable transparency marker, and sketched on the ideas that I'd submitted to the competition. Along the side of the oversized board, I wrote a list of items from Effie's inventory database.

The design challenge would be easy, but not having access to Jane's apartment complex was a problem. I needed a vacant building to renovate, and no property owner would agree to the loss of income without some form of compensation.

I called the realtor again.

"Kip Bledsoe," he answered.

"This is Madison Night. I'm a local designer and possible

client. I left you a message earlier today." I explained my need for a vacant building to use in the VIP competition.

"You want to buy an apartment building for the competition?"

"No, I want to *rent* a vacant building for the competition. Vacant buildings aren't collecting rent, but I would be happy to cover the mortgage on the property during the time in question."

"I'll ask around, but I can't promise anything. Most of my sellers are looking for the sale so they can infuse the cash into the next property."

"I'm well acquainted with the concept of house flipping."

"Then you already know what you're suggesting is a long shot."

"Kip, I'm in a bind. My original property fell through. I've got one week to find a property and redesign it per the application the DIDI committee approved."

"You're cutting things pretty close. You really think you can pull it off?"

"That should be for the judges to decide."

He chuckled. "Okay, Madison, I'll see what I can do." He took down my contact information and enough details to either steal my identity or run a background check to ensure I was worth his time and promised to be in touch.

I turned back to my sketchpad and lost myself in the project. Twice Rocky ran into the office, noisily lapping up water from his bowl the first time and bringing me a "gift" that looked suspiciously like a pom-pom from the coverlet I'd draped over the bed displayed in the street-facing window. I traded the pom-pom for a faded Hacky Sack from a bowl on my desk (a collection recently acquired after I won a bid on the contents of a disbarred fraternity house in the SMU off-campus neighborhood).

When I finished, I felt good about my design. It was close to what Jane and I had brainstormed, but without her clear focus on a primary color palette, I pushed the whimsy factor. I scanned the sketches and switched on my computer to print out the contest confirmation and keep everything together.

That's when I saw the second email from Jane. It had come

through sometime after the first—between receiving her initial note and finding her body in the restroom room. The subject line said, "design files."

I steeled myself and opened the email. It was a simple message that appeared to be an afterthought. *Attached find my files for our collaboration. I'm submitting an entirely unique proposal and won't be needing these, but in the interest of professionalism, it seems appropriate to let you do with them what you wish.* -JS

The gesture was unexpected. Again, I felt the emotional cocktail of anger, hurt, loss, and guilt. I'd spent my entire day trying to outdo whatever Jane might have used on her application, and here was evidence that, despite her feelings toward me, her generosity had triumphed.

I clicked on the attachment. While I waited for the files to open, a small part of me questioned if I should scrap my new plans and design Jane's in her memory.

No. That's not what this was about. This entry was to represent Mad for Mod. There was no need to print out Jane's files. I'd submitted an entirely different concept, colors and all.

I hovered my mouse over the X in the top right corner of the computer screen and clicked. Nothing happened. I clicked again, and then hit the escape key. The internet wouldn't close. I tried a few more times, unsuccessfully. My computer was frozen. I tried Ctrl+Alt+Del to open the task manager. Nothing. Time for a hard reboot.

I pressed down on the glowing blue button on the top of my PC and held, waiting to hear the engine shut off and the see the screen go dark. I didn't like closing the computer in this manner for fear of losing work, but at least the only files that had been open were the ones Jane sent. After the tower went silent, I sat back and watched the sweeping hand of my clock make a full rotation before powering the computer back on. The monitor flashed through a series of boot-up screens, finally replaced with my screensaver, the same Mad for Mod logo on my business cards and the sign atop the front door. Satisfied that the files were now closed, I prepared to put the computer in sleep mode for the night.

That's when it happened. The image of shattered glass appeared superimposed on top of my screen saver. One by one, virtual glass fragments broke away from the screen and fell to the bottom in a pile, revealing solid black. When all but two of the computerized glass fragments had left my screen, blurry words appeared, slowly coming into focus. I feared the worst before those fears were confirmed by the text on my screen.

You've
been
hacked.

SEVEN

I hit the escape key. The screen went blank. A second later, a daisy appeared in the middle of the screen, and one by one the virtual petals fell off, much like the glass shards had from the previous image. When all but two of the petals had fallen from the daisy, an evil smiley face appeared in the center. The same words as before came into view in a circle that rotated around the daisy's depetaled stem.

Driven more by panic than common sense, I tapped the space bar. The daisy disappeared. I held my breath to see what came next, but nothing happened. With my index finger, I tapped a random sampling of letters. Each time I hit a key, the words *You've been hacked!* zoomed toward me from a different spot on my screen. It was like the machine that sends tennis balls to someone practicing by themselves. *Zoom! Zoom! Zoom!* Except there was no way to strike back, no way to beat the system. I was getting pummeled by words on a computer screen and I felt the impact each time. Even the power button did nothing. My last resort was to pull the electric cord out of the socket.

As if my computer were possessed with an evil force, I looked around for something to cover it with. There was nothing. I unbuttoned my coat and used that, and then dropped back into my chair to think. I didn't know much about computers, but I knew enough. What I'd just experienced had been a virus. Computer viruses weren't spontaneous. They didn't just show up out of the blue (in this case, they did, but only because the background of my screensaver was a pleasing shade of aqua). Two immediate possibilities came to mind: Effie's new inventory system, and Jane's attachments.

I didn't know enough about how Effie had set up the inventory website to understand if a virus could find its way from the new database to my computer, but if it could, then there were bigger issues. My entire inventory was on that database thanks to her efforts. Not only would we lose months of work, but my insurance estimates were based on the values in there. It had been the biggest argument in Effie's arsenal and ultimately, the reason I'd caved.

The other possibility was Jane. She'd been mad enough to send me that original email. Had she been the kind of person who would follow up that email with corrupt files on purpose? And if she'd sent them to me, had she sent them to anyone else?

I'd known Jane for six months and we'd gotten along so well that I'd overlooked the anger that clouded her face when she spoke of her ex-husband. But now, after everything—everything!—that had happened today, I was forced to see that maybe I'd never known Jane as well as I'd thought. And if she was capable of actively destroying my professional files after a six-month friendship went south, was she also capable of doing something that had brought on her murder?

The clock told me it was almost ten. It was on the cusp of being too late to call an employee under normal circumstances, but today could hardly be considered normal. Besides, Effie was twenty-four years old. Ten o'clock probably wasn't all that late in her world.

She answered on the third ring. "Hey, Madison," she said. "Did you like what I did to the computer?"

Tentative relief flowed over me. Was this simply a stunt Effie had played? I didn't begin to understand half of the tricks being done with computers these days. I considered myself lucky to have figured out my drag-and-drop website design software after watching an hour of YouTube tutorials.

"You're saying it's a joke? I can undo it?"

"It took me a lot of time to do that," she said. For the first time since she'd started working for me, she sounded annoyed at my lack of technical knowledge. "If you want the company to grow, Madison, you're going to have to stop questioning my work."

The problem with her attitude was that it didn't match the hacking message I'd seen on the screen. I chose to proceed with directness. "Effie, did you or did you not program some sort of screensaver that appeared to take over my computer and make my screen imitate broken glass?" Effie was silent. "Effie? Are you still there?"

"Tell me you're joking. I mean, how do you even know about that?"

"I'm not joking. What's going on, Effie? Did you do this or not?"

"No, Madison, I didn't do that. What you're describing is the personality animation virus. It infects your hard drive, builds a profile of your business, and then animates images to fit that profile and inform you that you were hacked."

"That's it? This was all an elaborate joke?"

"No, that's not all, Madison. In the time it takes for the virus to cycle through a couple of different hacking messages, your files are either corrupted or deleted or both. But you only saw the glass, right? So that means you might be okay. The virus didn't have a chance to build a profile for the customized hacking message."

"After all the pieces of the glass broke away, a daisy filled the screen and the petals fell off one by one. That's bad, isn't it?"

"Don't go anywhere. I'm on my way."

Effie didn't arrive empty-handed. She came into the studio from the back door and dumped a bag of premade sandwiches on the corner of the desk. "Take whatever you want," she said. She glanced at my slip but didn't comment on it. "I know you. When stuff happens, you forget to eat." She sat down in my chair and tapped the space bar, much like Tex had done to his computer earlier today.

I pulled my coat back on. "I turned it off," I told her. "It seemed like a good idea. Actually, it was more of an instinct, like slapping away a bee. When I shut the computer off, the images went away."

"It was a good instinct," she said. "The virus is automated, so once it has access to your computer, it can feed off your files indefinitely. It's kind of like somebody made a copy of the key to your back door and now they're stealing from you at their leisure."

"Great." I tore the wax paper off a sandwich and took a sizeable bite out of the sourdough bread. The salty taste of ham blended with the acidic flavor of Dijon mustard. I chewed with the pent-up aggression I needed to release. The sandwich was as good a target as any.

"The good thing is turning it off was like barricading the door."

"But whoever did this still has a key, right?"

"Yes, but when the computer is off, it's like you put an armoire in front of the entrance. Just because someone can get past your locks doesn't mean they can get in."

"What happens when we power it back up?"

Effie looked uncomfortable. "That's the tricky part." She leaned forward. Her fingers hovered over the power button, and then she pulled them away. "I'm sorry, Madison. If you want to fire me, I'll understand."

"It's ten o'clock on a Friday night and you're in my studio trying to help me. Why would I fire you?"

"Because this never would have happened if I'd remembered to reinstall the firewall on your computer."

I remained calm. I trusted Effie enough to know she hadn't done this on purpose. Since meeting her years ago, I'd watched her go from being a shy college student to a focused computer whiz. It was after her then-boyfriend had been exposed as an opportunistic employee of a local security company that she'd realized the value of not being dependent on anybody but herself. She'd broken up their relationship, moved into a new apartment, and continued her education with a series of night classes while she spent days working the registers of Best Buy. Two years had passed since then, and Effie had been prouder of that training certificate than her college degree.

"I don't blame you," I said. "If anything, my systems were so out of date it's a wonder this didn't happen sooner. I'm used to doing business without these bells and whistles, so Mad for Mod can continue to function while we get this worked out."

"You're sure you're not mad?" Effie asked.

I put my hand on Effie's shoulder to comfort her. "It's been a long day, and far worse things than this happened."

"That's right!" she exclaimed. "I forgot to ask you. What happened when you saw Jane? Did you two have it out? I bet you really put her in her place. The word is out on you. Don't mess with Madison Night—she will take you down."

As Effie spoke, a sickening realization hit me. Whoever had accessed my computer might have known about the email. They might have known Jane and I were no longer on good terms. My first thought had been that the new inventory database had been corrupted, but after talking to Effie, I now believed this had been done with malicious intent. But what did I have that a hacker would want?

I had a relationship with the victim of an unexpected homicide, that's what.

After telling Effie about Jane's murder, we went our separate ways. It was too late to do anything about the computer, and I was reassured by Effie that the best thing we could do was to leave the system powered off. I wanted little more than to change from my raincoat into pajamas. I collected Rocky and headed home. It wasn't the sort of night where I wanted to be alone, and as it turned out, I wasn't.

A blue pick-up truck was parked parallel to my property line. The branches of my overdue-for-a-trim hedges reached out into the street like the limbs of skinny green zombies trying to make contact with the truck's paint job. The oddness of the thought made me realize how dark my day had been and how my usually sunny outlook had been compromised.

The truck wasn't unfamiliar. It belonged to Hudson James, the most reliable and talented handyman I'd ever met. He was equal parts craftsman and artist, and the early years of Mad for Mod had benefitted greatly from his skills. About a year ago, we'd shifted gears from business associates to romantic partners, a step I'd long avoided out of fear of changing the status quo. Hudson, it turned out, had his own thoughts on the matter, not entirely in sync with mine. After a working vacation out of town, he'd remained in California to help his sister find stable footing while I'd returned to Dallas and Mad for Mod. The distance between us had helped me see that rushing a possible relationship was just as bad as ignoring it.

He'd also grown increasingly aware of the third person in our life: Tex. Hudson had been the one to suggest that perhaps I needed to take a long, hard look at what I wanted out of life (and who I wanted it with). When you're paying someone a contractor's fee, they tend not to offer unsolicited advice on your love life, but I couldn't blame Hudson for having an opinion. My indecision affected him too. Him bringing the subject up was a darn good way to let me know he wasn't going to hang around forever.

I'd requested the same six-month hiatus from Hudson that I'd requested from Tex, so while I wasn't unhappy to have his relaxed and familiar company, I was curious of the timing.

"Hey, Lady," Hudson said as I walked up the sidewalk. He opened his arms and I stepped into them for a hug. Rocky, free from his leash, tore off into the yard and ran circles around the maple tree.

I closed my eyes and leaned my head against Hudson's chest. He smelled like wood shavings and musk. The familiarity of the scent overwhelmed me, and I started to cry.

"Hey," he said. His calloused hand stroked my blonde hair. "I was hoping you wouldn't be mad at me for breaking the terms of your birthday present, but this is a little more than I expected."

I pulled away from his embrace and looked at him. With

Johnny Cash's looks and Joey Ramone's wardrobe, Hudson put off a bad boy vibe that kept a lot of people from getting to know him. Circumstances in his past had categorized him as that bad boy and, after being judged by the court of local opinion, he'd worn it as a protective barrier. But Hudson was one of the kindest men I'd ever known. The night he confided in me about his past was the night I knew my life would be changed forever.

"Let's go inside," I said.

Hudson tapped the outside of his black jeans and Rocky came running. I led the three of us up the concrete steps, through the screen door and the solarium, and into my kitchen. Hudson hadn't seen the house since I'd torn out the original kitchen. I replaced the old countertops with an uninstalled (formerly built-in) yellow tile kitchen counter that I'd acquired from a now-demolished cafeteria in Casa Linda Plaza and replaced the outlived (possibly original) tan and ivory rolled linoleum floor with new yellow Johnsonite Cortina Grande Solid Vinyl Tile in Sunny Day. (I told you those six months had been productive.) Big Chill appliances—my one concession to new over true vintage—in Buttercup Yellow, whitewashed cabinets, and the original hardware rounded out the overall transformation. All completed with a white iron pendant lamp with lemon yellow and celery green three-inch metal daisies mounted to the frame. If I had to decide between the two men in my life by which one would fit in a newly renovated yellow kitchen with daisies hanging overhead, I might as well choose single life.

I switched on the light and the soft bulbs glowed from under the daisy chandelier. Hudson's eyes widened, and he took in the room. "You've been busy."

"I've had some spare time on my hands."

"Do you want me to leave?"

"No."

I turned away from him and pulled two vintage glasses out of the cabinet. "Can I get you something? Wine, beer?"

"I didn't come here for a drink."

I pulled a chilled bottle of Sauvignon Blanc out of the

refrigerator and poured the wine into my tumbler. I didn't care that it wasn't the appropriate glass for wine. I was tense, agitated, and uneasy, and I needed something to take the edge off. Hudson's presence in my kitchen offered a different option for working off stress, but I knew I'd regret that choice in the morning. I could sleep off a hangover.

I raised the glass to my lips and took a long swallow. I felt the combination of the cool beverage and the alcohol slowly flowing through my chest, my arms, and my legs. I pulled out a wooden chair and sat on the floral cushion. "Why did you come here?" I asked.

"I didn't have much of a choice. You still have my house keys."

"Did I know you were coming back to Dallas?"

"You should have. I was expecting you to pick me up from the airport."

EIGHT

"Hudson, I think I'd know if I agreed to pick you up at the airport," I said.

"Do you want me to show you the email?"

"There's an email?" We stared at each other. My mind raced, wondering how I could have made such an agreement and completely forgotten. "Didn't that strike you as odd? That I said I wanted you to give me a six-month break but then said I'd pick you up?"

Hudson's expression changed from relaxed to angry. "I thought—never mind what I thought."

He thought I'd made my decision. He thought I'd volunteered to pick him up because I'd chosen him. He was here in my kitchen because he thought I wanted him here.

My surprised reaction must have spoken volumes and not the volumes he wanted to hear. "I—I am happy to see you but I'm—I'm still—I'm not ready."

He pointed to the entrance. "You're sending mixed signals, Madison."

"I know. It's been a long day—a long, overwhelming, crazy day, and when I saw you, I just—it was nice to feel you with me."

He put his fingers under my chin and raised my face. "Whether or not we're in the same city, I'm with you. Say the word. We can leave Texas behind and start over. I'm ready."

"I'm not."

Hudson stepped back. "I'm not going to wait forever, Madison. I can't. I let too much of my life go by without paying attention to it and I want to make up for lost time. I want you in my future, but not if you're pining for him."

I got angry. "That's not fair. I asked you both to give me six months. You and Tex. You're here, and he's not. What does that say about respect?"

Hudson didn't get a chance to answer. The pregnant pause that filled the room was interrupted by a knock on my front door. I looked over Hudson's shoulder.

I should have known.

I pushed past Hudson and yanked the door open. "What are you doing here?" I asked Tex.

"I came to get my keys. You forgot to give them to me earlier today." He glanced over my head. "Nice kitchen, by the way. When did you have the time to do this?"

I glared at Tex. He wasn't at my house at eleven o'clock at night to get his keys and we both knew it. He'd driven past. He'd seen Hudson's truck. He figured all bets were off.

"Get out!" I shouted, pointing at the door. Tex looked at me, past me at Hudson, and back at me. I turned around to Hudson. "You too. Get out of here! I've had a bad day and I want to be alone." Outside, I heard a window slam shut. Hudson strode past me and Tex toward his truck. Tex watched him leave and then turned back to me. I pointed to his car. "Go!"

He threw his arms up in the air. "I'm leaving!" He let himself out seconds after Hudson. And as the two sets of headlights and taillights pulled away from my property, I realized alone was the last thing I really wanted to be.

"Come on, Rocky. Time to go to bed." Rocky yipped and led the way upstairs.

Despite my exhaustion, I stared at the ceiling long after I'd finally traded my pink raincoat for pajamas. It had been awhile since I'd experienced insomnia, but based on the day I'd had, I wasn't entirely surprised. The hacking message on my computer had temporarily pushed thoughts of Jane's murder out of my mind, but now that I was alone, with no distractions other than the infomercials shown in the middle of the night, my mind wouldn't settle down. Correction: I had distractions in the form of the two men who I'd just kicked out of my house.

I didn't really want to think about them either. Not right now.

Except two things bothered me. Hudson claimed I'd sent him an email that I had no recollection of sending. Our conversation had taken an awkward turn right about that point, and Tex's arrival hadn't helped.

That was the other thing. Tex hadn't expected to see me at the police station earlier today. We'd worked out a schedule where I could get into his house to work like I would for any other paying client while honoring the terms of my birthday request. He'd been the one to point that out, not me. And when I'd told him about Jane's murder and showed him Detective Henning's card, he'd had an odd reaction: nothing. For all the other times we'd been thrown together during homicide investigations, he'd always heard me out. He might not have encouraged my involvement, but by now he knew me well enough to know I wasn't capable of turning my back on the horrible situations I occasionally stumbled upon.

It occurred to me that Tex had had other things on his mind when I'd shown up, specifically, the computer systems being down.

If there'd been even the slightest chance of me falling asleep up to this point, the thought of computer problems eradicated it. Was it possible that the Lakewood Police Department had been hacked as well? No doubt they had a firewall in place. But would an attempted virus slog down their network and cause the problems they'd had? If just one infected file found its way onto their computers, would it act as a Trojan horse?

I ran my hand over Rocky's fur and thought back to earlier this week. I'd emailed Tex with some decorating concepts for his room. Attachments. I'd used Jane's interior design software to create the renderings. I was right back to thinking that Jane was somehow responsible for my problems. It seemed petty to find reason to be mad at her in light of her murder, but it felt hypocritical to pretend I had a loyalty to her based on friendship.

I drifted off to sleep somewhere around two thirty, and when my alarm went off at six, I slapped the snooze button and rolled over. Several hours later, I woke naturally. It took me several minutes to shake off disorientation. Rocky, who had burned off enough of his excess energy with the puppies at the police station to sleep through the night was already awake and trying to get me to play. He nosed his head into my hand repeatedly, and then bit the fabric of my sleeve and tugged on it as if he could get me out of bed with his sheer Shih Tzu will. I didn't doubt he'd keep at it until I got up, so I did. It was eight thirty but might as well have been eleven. I felt like I'd already missed half my day.

It was too late to go to the Gaston Swim Club for my typical morning swim. By this time, the lanes would be jammed with people and I'd barely get a workout. I showered, dressed in my bra, panties, and a fresh nylon slip, and returned to the autumn section of my closet.

Early success with Mad for Mod had been contingent upon me having enough era-accurate inventory to design a room for a true mid-mod enthusiast without expecting them to take out a second mortgage. I'd solved that problem by reading obituaries regularly and reaching out to the next of kin of women of a certain age who had passed away. It was often less hassle for the family to accept my lump-sum bid on their mother's estate than to take the time to sort through belongings they'd long since seen as outdated, and by buying entire estates, I'd amassed a sizeable collection of vintage clothes and accessories. Living in Dallas, Texas as I did, I had only a limited window of the year to indulge in the heavier weight fabrics in my closet. I'd spent last October in Palm Springs, so I was due.

Much of my wardrobe swung toward a kitschy sixties look: mod shift dresses, double-knit polyester dresses like the one I'd sacrificed yesterday, and colorful Orlon ensembles that showed off the latest in synthetic weaves that were popular during that decade. The far right of my closet was filled with clear, plastic garment bags that held complete ensembles once worn by LeAnne Sheley, wife of an oil baron. The clothes showed barely any signs of wear, and when I'd first inspected them, I'd wondered if they'd been worn at all. It wasn't until I discovered a scrapbook that showed LeAnne in a series of publicity stills with her wealthy Texas husband that I realized she'd had the money and the reasons to only wear each outfit once.

The weather showed no signs of changing from the previous day, so I dressed in an early sixties orange, coral, and pink silk blouse with a bow at the neck and a coral tweed skirt suit. I added chocolate brown tights and flat brown leather booties. My knee injury from several years ago was mostly healed, but in that time, I'd realized how much easier life was when I wasn't teetering around on heels. I pulled on a coral turban-style hat, transferred my wallet, keys (mine and Tex's, which I hadn't given back), reading glasses, and phone to a brown lizard handbag, clipped an orange leash onto Rocky's collar, and headed to work.

I wasn't surprised to find Effie waiting for me by the back door when I arrived. She seemed anxious. "Madison, don't be mad, okay?"

"Good morning to you too, Effie."

"Yeah. Um, you know what happened to your computer last night?"

"The hacking? Yes, I'm well aware. Let's get inside and make some coffee and come up with a plan." I fitted my key into the door, but the knob turned easily as if it was already unlocked. I looked questioningly at Effie.

She put her hand on the doorknob. "I have a key, remember? You told me to take the one Connie used to have when she started working from home."

"Then why are you standing out here?"

"I have to tell you something before you go inside."

I stood straight and gave Effie 100 percent of my attention. "What did you do?"

"I kept thinking about you being hacked. And it didn't make

sense, you know? Like, why would someone hack a decorator? So when I got up this morning, I called somebody who had experience with computers."

"Why would I be mad? That sounds like exactly what we need." I put my hand on the door, but Effie grabbed the knob and pulled it shut. "What is it Effie?"

"Um, remember how my old boyfriend was really into computers?"

"Effie, tell me you did not use this situation to invite that troublemaker back into your life."

"I didn't. I, um, I called his old boss."

I pushed on the door and Effie relented. Rocky ran ahead of me into the studio, but the leash kept him from arriving in my office much before me. Effie was close on my heels. I turned the corner and confirmed what Effie had been trying to warn me about.

Help had arrived in the form of former police officer Donna Nast, aka Officer Nasty.

NINE

Donna Nast looked far too pleased by my arrival. She pulled a set of
rose gold earbuds out of her ears and tossed them onto my desk.
"About time you showed up. Isn't this your business? I thought you
were a morning person."

Donna Nast, or Nasty, as I (and everybody else who knew her,
as far as I knew) called her, was the kind of smart, confident, and
gorgeous thirty-something who made fifty-year-old women like me
invest in expensive eye cream. (I'd been blessed with a fair
complexion that I protected with high SPF sunscreen and looked
younger than my years, but still, thirty trumps fifty no matter how
you slice it.) As if her perpetually sun-kissed complexion wasn't
enough, she had rich brown hair that hung past her shoulders,
streaked copper courtesy of a pricey Park Cities salon that had
exchanged services with the security company owner.

Nasty and I had a history, as did Nasty and Tex. I suspected
she trusted me about as much as I trusted her, though for the
moment, the balance of power was entirely in her favor. If Effie was
right, then Nasty was here to help.

"Hi, Donna," I said. "Effie said she told you about my
problem?"

Nasty's eyes narrowed for a moment, as if she'd been
expecting worse. I pulled off my gloves and hat and set them on the
corner of the desk and then poured myself a mug of coffee.

"Somebody hit you with the personality virus. You're not the
only one. It's being targeted at businesses all around Dallas."

I leaned against the counter and blew on the black coffee. "Is that normal?"

"Depends on the hacker's endgame."

"Meaning..."

Nasty leaned back in my chair. "How much do you know about hacking?"

"Talk to me like I'm five."

She smiled. "There are different categories of hacker. Black hat, white hat, elite, script, the list goes on. Different categories hack for different reasons. Some good, some bad."

"Good hackers? Like Robin Hood? He's a thief, but he's a good thief because he stole from the rich and gave to the poor?"

"Something like that," she said.

"Is there a way to tell which type hacked me?"

She tipped her head and assessed me. Her glossy brown hair swung down to the side. She reached one hand up and fed it between her hair and her neck, and then swung the sheath of it to the front of her shoulder. It was the kind of gesture that gave her the subtle air of Victoria's Secret Model she maintained, though it was wasted on me. As soon as she did it, she seemed to realize the same thing. She pulled a gold and silver braided elastic band off her left wrist, pulled her hair back, and knotted it into a ponytail. "Let's see if we can find out."

Once I got past the unease of having Nasty in my office, I found myself oddly interested in watching her work. In the time we'd known each other, she'd annoyed the heck out of me more than once, and not always by accident. Despite that, I'd never known her to be incompetent. She'd told me once that leaving the police force and starting her own security business was the best decision she'd ever made, and, frankly, in that way, we were a lot alike.

Nasty's fingers danced over my keyboard like a concert pianist might play a well-rehearsed concerto. I had no idea what she was doing, but I could tell she was confident about whatever it was. The screen to my computer was black with white words aligned on the left side, much like the screens that flashed on the monitor when I first booted it up. Text scrolled over the screen as she typed new commands. To me, the words were gibberish. I had an urge to enroll in a computer class myself just to prove what she was doing wasn't all that hard. The mature part of me already knew any plan rooted in pettiness was probably a waste of time.

"What's this?" Nasty asked. I glanced at the screen. "Not the screen. Those sketches." She cut her eyes away from the screen and looked at the sketchpad I'd left open on the desk.

"Concepts for a local design competition."

"Where's the property?"

"I don't know yet."

"Kinda risky entering a competition when you don't have a building, isn't it?"

Something about Nasty's questions seemed more on point than I'd expected. The decorating and design community was close knit, and if one of my colleagues had asked the same question, I wouldn't have thought twice about it. But Nasty wasn't part of this world. I felt the same as I'd felt when Tex had brought up his familiarity with the VIP competition—like outsiders were infiltrating my life.

"I guess this VIP competition has gotten a lot of press already," I said. "First Tex mentioned it, and now you. I'm not used to anybody outside the design community paying attention to my work."

She looked up at me. "Tex told you about VIP?"

"Tex didn't have to tell me about VIP, but I thought I'd have to explain it to him. Turns out he already knew about it."

She studied me for a moment but didn't say anything. A moment later, she turned her attention back to the screen and started clicking the keys again. She was holding something back and it bothered me, but I wasn't going to let her know that. I'd gone the past twenty minutes without getting into a verbal sparring match with her. I didn't need to break down now.

I refreshed my coffee and this time added a healthy dollop of half-and-half to cut the bitterness. Effie had branched out from my usual cannister of Chock full o' Nuts and talked me into a dark roast and my taste buds were still adjusting.

"Madison?" Effie said from the doorway. "There's a man here to talk to you."

I looked up from Nasty's work. "A walk-in? Are we already open?" I glanced at the clock.

"Not exactly," she said. "His name is Detective Henning."

Prickles rose up along my arms and the back of my neck. I shouldn't have been surprised by the visit from the detective, but the hacking crisis had made Jane's murder seem like it had happened weeks ago, not yesterday. Expecting a reaction from Nasty, I looked at her.

"Don't mind me," she said. "I've got enough here to keep me distracted from whatever you're involved in this time." She fed her earbuds back into her ears.

I followed Effie out front. Detective Henning stood by a wall of red kitchen appliances I'd acquired from a local bakery that had recently closed for good. The owner had kept the oven, range, stove, and broiler in use for fifty years, and while the functionality was A+, the appearance was about what you'd expect after fifty years of cupcakes and pies. After taking possession of the various pieces, I'd consulted with a local powder coater who agreed that sandblasting and paint would bring the units back to life.

Not wanting to damage the equipment, we disassembled the units and protected the electrical and gas hookups with industrial grade plastic. I arranged to pick up the completed pieces a week later and hadn't even recognized them when I returned to the showroom. The dull metal had been replaced with glossy red dry powder, applied electrostatically in a sealed room and then cured under hot temperatures. What I rarely admitted to clients was that I'd first learned of the technique during an episode of *American Choppers*.

"Hi, Detective Henning," I greeted the man in front of me. Today he wore a modest, forest green plaid blazer and dark trousers, white shirt, green tie. There was neither style nor sloppiness evident in his choice of clothes. I guess that's why the department enforced a dress code—to keep citizens from judging the order of the law by ill-fitting low-rise jeans.

"Ms. Night," he said.

"Call me Madison."

"Okay, Madison. I have a few follow-up questions about yesterday. Is there a place we can talk? Your office?"

"I'm having some work done on my computer this morning," I said. "Why don't we get a cup of coffee? My employee can watch the studio."

"I think we'd better stay right here," Henning said.

"Okay," I said slowly. "Follow me." I led the way toward a small love seat and club chair arranged around an Adrian Pearsall coffee table.

Henning surveyed the contents of my showroom. "My wife's into IKEA," he said. "Everything we own is square and white." He leaned to the side and looked at the walnut table base under the thick slab of tempered glass. "She wouldn't know where to begin with something like that."

"It's a coffee table, Detective, not a Mensa quiz."

"Right. It's just—those pieces fit together, but they don't. How do you know when you did it the right way?"

I couldn't tell if the detective was honestly curious or if he was playing me in his version of Columbo. I was in no mood to humor him. I smiled. "I really do have pressing issues, Detective. You said you had questions about yesterday?"

Henning nodded. "I have your statement, but there are a couple of things that don't add up. What were you doing at Republic Tower?"

"Yesterday was the deadline for entry in a design competition. I was there to turn in my application."

"Do you usually cut things so close?"

"No. I thought my submission had already been filed, but it wasn't. I worked on a proposal offsite and delivered it by hand to make sure it was accepted."

He nodded along with me as I spoke, as if our conversation was a technicality. "I thought maybe it was something like that." He scanned the studio. "This is your only studio? You don't have a satellite office anywhere?"

"This is it," I said.

"You live near here?"

"I used to."

"What about storage? You have more than what I see in here, right?"

I felt my eyebrows draw together and forced my features to relax. These weren't questions about what had happened yesterday. They were questions about me. I knew enough about how the police worked to know they needed to establish a rapport to get a sense of what a witness was like when they were telling the truth so they had a frame of reference against someone they suspected was lying. A truth baseline, I think it was called. What I didn't know was why Henning was treating me like I had something to hide.

"I have a storage locker out back, additional storage in my garage, and an off-site unit."

"How do you manage all that inventory?"

"Detective Henning, not that I don't enjoy talking about my work, but what do these questions have to do with the Jane Strong murder?"

He stared me straight in the eyes. "You claim to have spent your day working on a proposal for the VIP competition. What would that involve?"

"My employee, Effie Jones, has been working tirelessly to get my inventory entered into an online database, which turned out to be very good for my circumstances. I spent my day working on a proposal at the Dallas Public Library and returned to Republic Tower to deliver it in person. No, it's not ideal, but in this case, it worked."

"Did it?"

"I'm not one to beat around the bush, Detective, and I'd appreciate if you didn't either."

He looked down at his tie and smoothed the fabric with his hand before looking up at me again. "I'm trying to understand why you say you left Republic Tower for several hours, but the security log shows you never left the building."

"What about the security cameras? Surely they show me leaving."

"The building security is hooked up to a network and it was offline yesterday. We asked the security guard and he said he couldn't say for sure if you'd left the premises. You claimed Ms. Strong was ill, but an early analysis of her blood and stomach contents indicate there was nothing unusual in her system. You left her alone to get help, but a witness places you in the powder room with her when she died. Do you see where I'm headed with this, Ms. Night?"

I saw exactly where he was headed, and I wanted off the train right now. Because while the facts Detective Henning was working from weren't inaccurate, they painted a picture that put me in a position I hadn't experienced before.

The position of Person of Interest.

TEN

Detective Henning watched me while I processed what his line of questions meant. I had left Republic Tower to work at the library, but Delbert hadn't signed me out. He knew I'd left but instead of backing me up and admitting he'd let me leave and come back without enforcing protocol, he stood by the visitor log which said I'd been there the whole time. I'd used my phone as a hotspot while at the library, so I hadn't needed login credentials to sign onto their internet. I'd printed and picked up my application from the librarian station, which had been vacant.

And then there was Jane. My friend. Who was no longer my friend. And while the majority of the world didn't know that, a few people did: Vonda, her assistant. Effie, my employee. Delbert, the security guard for Republic Tower. Anybody else who had heard us argue in the lobby of the building. That was just the people I knew. Why had she been to DIDI when she claimed to have already turned in her application? She must have had other business, and that business may have included badmouthing me.

It was one thing to be on the receiving end of Jane's email, but an entirely different one to realize our dirty laundry might have been aired publicly without my knowledge. And if someone else had murdered Jane in the bathroom of Republic Tower like I suspected, had they seen how easy it would have been to pin the crime on me after Jane's and my public argument? I had to remain calm. I'd done nothing wrong, even if Henning was making me analyze my own actions as if I had.

Before I could think of the proper way to proceed, Nasty came looking for me. She'd removed the metallic ponytail holder from her hair and the long brown locks now hung over her shoulder. I'd never imagined a situation when I'd be happy to have her hijack the male attention in the room, but there's a first time for everything.

"Madison," she said. "Sorry to interrupt you, but I have another appointment and I was hoping we could finish up with that consultation."

Consultation? "Of course. I'll be in my office in a moment." I turned to Henning. "Detective, I don't want to rush you, but I'd rather not keep my client waiting any longer." I looked back at Nasty and she gave me the tiniest nod.

Henning stood. "I didn't realize I took you away from a client meeting." He pulled out his card. "Call me if you remember anything else."

"And if you have any other questions?"

"I'll be in touch."

I walked the detective to the front door. The Bickners, the elderly couple who was selling off their belongings to fund their anniversary cruise, entered as the detective left.

"Such attractive suitors," Mrs. Bickner said after the detective passed her. "I wouldn't want to pick one either." She winked.

"You don't have to pick one," Mr. Bickner said. "You have me."

She kissed him on the cheek and they entered. Effie came into the hallway and directed them toward the same sofa where the detective and I had been seated, and Nasty followed me to my office. When we arrived, she pointed to my computer.

"You're back up and running," she said.

"You really called me back here to talk about my computer?"

"That's why I'm here, right?"

"Sure."

Nasty picked up her phone and wound her rose gold earbuds around it. "I uploaded some malicious software removal code that restored your hard drive. The problem was a temporary virus that distracts you while a hacker gains back door access to your files."

"Effie told me it was like a hacker stole my key and made a

copy so he could steal from my computer when I wasn't around."

"Something like that," she said.

"Can you tell where the virus came from? I've started using an online inventory database—"

"It came from an email attachment. These things always do. Haven't you ever heard not to click links in emails?"

"I don't click links in emails. Not unless I trust the sender."

That's when I realized the last time I'd clicked a link in an email. Last night when I'd received the second email from Jane—moments before my computer had frozen. She'd returned the files we'd been working on and I'd opened them before changing my mind and trying to shut down for the night.

"What do I owe you?" I asked.

"You don't owe me anything."

"I'm not looking for a handout, Donna. You provided a service and I'm prepared to pay you for it."

"Consider it a gift. That call I just got was a city job. Same problem as you, so because you were my guinea pig, I now know my antivirus code works. Besides, you've got more to worry about than my bill."

"I thought you said my computer was fixed."

"It is." She pointed to the back of my computer. "This thing hit a bunch of other people today. You were my practice run. The way the jobs are coming in, I'll bill ten thou before six." She flung her hair over her shoulder and left through the back door.

Rocky chased her halfway down the hall and then came back to the office. I sat down at my desk and tapped the space bar to wake up the computer. I assumed Nasty had closed out of the active windows she'd opened to test my computer, but I'd assumed wrong. Not only had she left the internet open, she'd opened my email and left that up as well.

And the email in question was the one from Jane Strong—the very one I suspected contained the virus that had infected my computer. Nasty now joined the short list of people who knew the truth about Jane's and my friendship.

* * *

Despite Nasty's reassurances that my computer was back to normal, I spent my day working with clients in the studio. Effie's online inventory management system was part of a long-term plan to shift my focus from small jobs—a kitchen here, a rec room there—to bigger ones like houses, furnished apartment rentals, and quirky business offices. I didn't expect the executive set of Dallas to suddenly flip for mid-century modern design, but the recent success of shows like *The Marvelous Mrs. Maisel* had made people hungry for the style without knowing what it was they wanted. It was a fine line, and I much preferred working with clients who were motivated by passion and not trend, but if I could contribute to the retro-ification of my corner of Dallas, then by golly, I was going to do it.

Shortly after, my consultation with a couple looking to convert their newly married son's basement apartment to a Polynesian paradise was interrupted by a phone call. Effie took and delivered the message.

"Captain Allen just called. He's getting caught up on paperwork at the station, and if you wanted to repaint his townhouse, now's a good time to do it."

I rolled my eyes. "The man acts like a proximity to lilac is going to counter his testosterone."

Effie looked up at me. "You painted Captain Allen's spare bedroom lilac?"

"What's wrong with lilac? My living room is lilac."

"Yes, but most people aren't as colorful as you."

I rolled my eyes, clipped on Rocky's leash, and we left.

Tex's townhouse was in the Uptown neighborhood of Dallas. It was on the end of a six-unit building with three floors plus a rooftop deck. He'd lucked into the last available unit when the builders were looking to close out their sales and offered him a special price with a ten-thousand-dollar deposit. Tex, being a lifelong bachelor whose biggest monthly expenses were the dinners he bought while wooing potential female companions, had built up a tidy savings account, and he wrote out a check. I'd known Tex for three years, yet he'd only recently invited me into his home. That was the day he laid his cards on the table and told me he was interested in a relationship.

The day that started the ticking clock of analysis in my life and led to my six-month, decision-free zone.

I came up with the idea after Hudson asked what I wanted to celebrate my half-century milestone (though in fairness, Hudson hadn't called it that. Tex, who'd clocked the same mileage a year earlier, had.) Growing anxiety over facing my attraction to a man who had exhibited an entire catalog of behaviors I disliked since we'd met drove me to my breaking point.

Hudson, who wasn't exactly surprised by my, "we need to talk," statement, said he'd give me six months, but that he wasn't going to remain in limbo forever. I could respect that. He'd called me three times since then and I'd let each call go to voicemail.

Tex, on the other hand, said the idea was never going to work. I'd sprung it on him right after we signed the contract for his decorating job (I'm no dummy). "I just hired you to decorate my spare bedroom. How do you plan to work in my townhouse without seeing me?"

"That's not why you hired me, is it?" I asked innocently. "I thought you knew I'm not the type of woman you pay to get into your bedroom."

"You know what I mean."

"We'll arrange a schedule. You'll give me a key. You told me you had no idea how to decorate and wanted me to handle the entire job. I assume you weren't lying when you said that, correct?"

He'd mumbled something about unorthodox business practices and left. Come to think of it, that might have been the day I bought the lilac paint.

But Tex had stuck to the agreement. Yesterday, at the police station, was the first time I'd been in the same room with him since last March. If my vital signs had a say in the matter, the decision might have been made right then and there. But I wasn't going to let a litter of puppies and a dead body lead me down a path of impulse. This decision required careful thought and the deadline wasn't here yet.

I parked in Tex's two-car garage and let myself in through the back door. Wojciehowicz met Rocky and me on the other side. Rocky, delighted to visit with his friend, strained his leash and then doubled back to me, hopping on his hind legs and begging to be freed so he could play.

I unclipped the leash. "Be nice to Wojo," I told Rocky. "And if he offers you brownies, just say no." Rocky yipped like he understood, and the two dogs took off.

I changed out of my tweed suit and silk blouse and pulled on a T-shirt with "Be Kind to Animals or I'll Kill You" printed on it and a pair of white overalls that I'd left hanging in the closet of the room I was decorating. I put my brown crocodile booties in the closet and laced up a pair of old white Keds and then got started.

I'd already selected the furniture I wanted to bring into the room when it was complete: a walnut Broyhill Spectra Queen-sized bed, nightstands, low dresser, and tall armoire that I'd acquired on my first estate buyout after moving to Dallas. The legs of the furniture showed wear, but nothing a little sanding and stain hadn't fixed. Effie had gone over the wood with a conditioning oil and the legs looked as good as new. But until I decided on the color of the walls, the furniture would sit in storage. And, based on Tex's reaction to the lilac, it was going to be a while before I reached the furniture portion of the job.

I pulled out a clean tray liner and jimmied the lid from a can of Lemon Twist, a soft yellow shade I'd endorsed for the local paint store, and then stirred the paint with an old drumstick. You'd be surprised how many old drumsticks you acquire when you buy out estates. The world, it seemed, was filled with failed percussionists.

I poured a stream of Lemon Twist into the tray, loaded up a

roller, and set about covering the lilac. Despite everything else, Tex was a client. Even if I walked away from the life I'd built in Texas and relocated to Palm Springs, California to be with Hudson and his family, Tex deserved a room he liked. And since yellow was the color-wheel opposite of lilac, he certainly couldn't complain about my new direction, could he?

A blob of paint dribbled from the roller and landed on my foot. I glanced around and realized I'd jumped right into painting and had no rags to dampen for cleanup. I set the roller in the tray, pulled canvas booties on top of my sneakers, and left the room for the kitchen.

I hadn't anticipated two dogs hovering on the outside of the door waiting to get inside. Wojo nosed past my feet, and Rocky, who seemed instinctively to know he wasn't supposed to be inside a room that smelled of wet paint, paced back and forth by the door barking at the Shi Chi puppy. I ran into the room after Wojo. He ran right through my paint tray and then made a dash for the door, leaving behind a trail of yellow puppy pawprints to mark his path.

"Wojciehowicz! Get back here!" I chased the small puppy through the living room and up the stairs.

Into Tex's bedroom.

It was the first time I'd been in Tex's bedroom. Off and on, I'd wondered if it matched the minimalist aughts bachelor vibe he maintained on the first two levels of the townhouse. But now that I was here, I barely noticed the tangle of sheets, the book on the side table, or the framed Leroy Neiman print on the wall.

All of which I might have seen if my attention wasn't otherwise focused on the rose gold earbuds and pile of metallic silver and gold braided ponytail holders sitting on the nightstand next to the bed.

ELEVEN

I stepped around the bed to the nightstand and stared at the items like a detective might stare at evidence he's afraid to corrupt. The pile sat on top of an invoice from Big Brother Security. Across the middle of the invoice, a message had been scrawled in red lipstick: *Thanks for last night. Totally worth it. xo, Donna*

My fists balled up and a charge of heat propelled me out of the room and down the stairs. No wonder he'd been so patient with me! Here I was, maintaining professionalism on the job while he invited Nasty back into his boudoir. If I needed a sign to know what kind of a man I was really dealing with, this one was bold and outlined in technicolor neon tubes. Tex had crossed a line.

You know what? I could cross a line too.

I marched back into his spare bedroom and yanked the plastic drop cloth up from the floor, pried the lid off the lilac paint can, and dumped the colorful shade directly onto the hardwood floor. I dropped onto my hands and knees and rolled the color out until the entire floor was covered. The lilac clashed with the yellow walls in a manner that would wake up even the most sleep-deprived guest. At least the ones who hadn't occupied Tex's bed.

"Ooooooooh!" I exclaimed. Wojo, who had returned to the scene of the crime, turned around and ran back out. I followed him, this time leaving a second trail of paint-covered footprints—these lilac—myself. "Rocky! We're leaving!" I grabbed my handbag and keys from the kitchen counter and, when Rocky joined me, yanked open the door to the garage.

I was halfway to my car when a door on the other side of the house opened and shut. "Fair warning. I'm home."

Tex's footsteps scaled the staircase. Did I want to have this confrontation? No. I was done. Except at the fringes of my anger was the increasing awareness that I'd just painted Tex's hardwood floors lilac and tracked yellow and lilac footprints throughout his townhouse. And while technically it was all Wojo's fault, I also knew the little puppy's pawprints would be a dead giveaway to which part of Tex's house we'd been in, how far it was from the location of the room I'd agreed to decorate, and what I'd discovered while I was there.

I set Rocky inside the car and cracked the widow. As soon as I opened the garage door, Tex would come looking for me. As I aimed the garage door opener at the ceiling mechanism, I heard his voice behind me. "Nasty! Are you still here?"

Oooooooh!

If I had any doubts, Tex had just confirmed them. That was it. If I walked out of this garage now, I'd never come back. I slammed the remote down on the baker's rack that held tools and rags along the rear of the garage and stomped back into Tex's townhouse.

"We are so done!" I yelled at him.

"Night? Are you okay?"

"No, I'm not okay. I will never be okay. This was a mistake. I'll pay for the damage done by the paint and will compile a list of recommended decorators, but we are through!"

"Geez, woman. You're taking your birthday agreement a little far. I left you two messages to tell you I was on my way. Pretend you never saw me. I came home to get something, and I'll be gone before you know it."

"I know *exactly* what you thought you were going to get when you came home. Don't take me for a fool, Captain Allen. Neither one of us is that stupid."

I whirled around and left.

The drive home was fueled by anger and humiliation. And if anybody was a fool in this situation, it was me. From the first time I'd met Tex, in his white T-shirt and jeans and straw cowboy hat—

what a cliché!—he'd done nothing to make me think he was anything other than a bachelor playboy. When I'd resisted his advances, he'd upped his game. And while a part of me knew what he was all along, I couldn't help thinking I'd been fooled by his wolf in sheep's clothing act.

And talk about clichés. It had happened in more than one classic rom-com and I'd fallen for the stunt all the same. Had I learned nothing from a lifetime of binge watching Doris Day and Rock Hudson?

I'd had it. I'd had it with everybody. My life had been fine when I was alone. Personal growth was overrated. I was going to go back to being comfortable in my own little world where nothing mattered but my work and my dog.

My car practically drove itself. I didn't know where I was headed when I left Tex's house, but as I drove, my destination became clear. I crossed the highway and turned left on Ross Avenue and followed it to Skillman. At a break in traffic, I turned left and left again, into the parking lot of my old apartment building.

A For Sale sign was nailed to the exterior. It seemed somehow poetic that this building was on the market. The sale was listed by Kip Bledsoe, and it seemed we were destined to do business together. Did I want to go back in time and reenter those doors after everything that had happened inside?

I let the engine idle in the narrow driveway and called the number on the sign.

"This is Madison Night. I need to speak to Kip about the twelve-unit apartment building on Gaston Avenue."

"One moment please," a woman said.

Seconds later, a man came to the phone. "This is Kip."

"This is Madison Night. We spoke yesterday about finding me a vacant apartment building," I said to jog his memory. "I'm at a complex on Gaston Avenue and it fits my needs perfectly."

"Yes, I remember. I contacted the seller and told him someone wanted to rent out the property for a month and he wasn't interested in anything but a sale. My office is working on finding you another property."

"What is his asking price?"

"I don't think you understood. He's not interested."

"You just said he's interested in a sale. I'd like to make an offer. What's his asking price?"

Kip gave me the number. It was considerably more than I'd gotten when I'd sold the property, but considering I'd sold it while recovering from one of the most traumatic experiences of my life, I probably hadn't been at the top of my negotiating game.

"I'll take it," I said.

He paused. "Don't you want to conduct a walk-through? See the condition of the building? It's been vacant for over a year and the former owner tore out a lot of fixtures."

"I'm familiar with the property and I'm not concerned by the condition. I'd like to make an anonymous offer. If you feel better about the sale, then you can meet me at the property."

"What time?"

"As soon as you can get here." I hung up and pulled into the lot behind the building.

Twelve spaces were painted out on broken concrete under an overhang of rusted, corrugated metal. A dumpster sat to the right of the last space, next to a six-foot-tall wooden fence that separated the property from the alley behind it. A door on the fence was padlocked shut.

Butted up against the building were visitor spaces. I parked in the one next to the handicapped one and turned off the engine. Rocky, who seemed to recognize where we were, stood on his hind legs with his paws on the inside passenger window and stared outside. He dropped back down to all fours, padded across my lap, did a one-eighty, and went back to the window.

"I know, Rocky. There a lot of memories bundled up in there."

Unpacking the first box of personal belongings that I'd brought with me when I left Pennsylvania. Setting up the food and water bowls for a wriggly Shih Tzu puppy. Restoring the bathroom fixtures to their original shade of Mamie Eisenhower pink. Having a chenille pillow pressed down on my face by a killer intent on suffocating me.

I never said the memories were all good.

But they represented my independence. I'd sold this building to Hudson, who'd been transitioning between the role as my handyman to the role of my boyfriend, and moved into a house involved in the case that brought Tex into my life. I hadn't moved on. All I'd done was find a new way to tangle things up. If Life had an Undo button, I was about to activate it.

A silver BMW coupe pulled into the parking lot and eased into the space on the other side of the door. Rocky pawed the window, leaving puppy streaks in the condensation.

"Let's go, Rock." I clipped the orange leash onto him and we got out of the car.

Real estate, like decorating, was a business of opportunity. On most days, I dressed in vintage attire to be a walking business card for Mad for Mod. When prospective clients entered my studio, I'd know within five seconds if we could work together based on their reaction to my clothes. But I was still wearing the painting clothes I'd changed into at Tex's, now stained with lilac and yellow paint. I doubted I'd make a strong first impression.

Kip Bledsoe, on the other hand, was the sort of man who seemed to know at any moment of his day he would be faced with a potential client, and his appearance had been cultivated for that purpose. He wore a camelhair topcoat over a suit and tie, and freshly polished brown wingtip oxfords. His hair, dark blond, was on the longish side for a man, but I secretly guessed the cut was courtesy of a stylist, not laziness. He reached up and smoothed his hair back with one hand, exposing a cleanly shaven face and mischievous hazel eyes.

"Madison Night?" He asked.

"Yes." We shook hands. "Thank you for meeting me, though I assure you, it wasn't necessary. I'd like to make an offer on the building."

"Humor me."

Kip fed a key into the back door and pushed it open. Rocky, who'd grown up in this building, pulled me toward the stairs. Until I knew the extent of the damage to the interior, I didn't want him running around unsupervised, so I held his leash tightly. Kip flipped a switch on the wall and a couple of exposed lightbulbs lit up the hallway.

"There's electricity?"

"With no one living here, the bill's almost nonexistent. We thought it was better to keep it on for prospective buyers than to shut it off. I come in once a week and check the place, make sure there aren't any vandals or squatters."

I walked down the hallway and surveyed the rooms. Fixtures had been torn out and left mid-replacement. A few electrical wires protruded from a hole in the hallway. Apartment-grade carpeting had been installed throughout. This didn't look like Hudson's aesthetic, and it certainly wasn't left over from when I'd owned the place.

"I'm surprised by the condition," I said.

Kip shrugged. "The owner's desperate to unload. I can probably get him to come down on the price."

"He said he was desperate?"

"My words."

I ran my hand over the wall. The paint in the hallway was flat eggshell. And while I could appreciate the value of every color in the rainbow, I considered the choice of flat eggshell to be uninspired. "Why is the building half finished?"

Kip sighed. "This building is never going to be the moneymaker the owner wanted. He was going to get the units up to code and rent them out, but he ended up pulling his team to work on something bigger."

"And he listed it for sale without saying a word. No sentimentality, no nothing. Just like a man."

"You say 'man' like it's a curse word."

"Today it is."

Kip looked to the left and then to the right. "It's a good thing there aren't any men around here," he said with a grin. I didn't feel much like smiling, but Kip couldn't know the reasons why. "Madison, I'd feel a lot better about this sale if I knew you walked the building first. I'll watch your dog if you want."

I handed Rocky's leash to Kip and climbed the back staircase. My old unit was on the second floor and overlooked the parking lot. I turned the knob, bracing myself for whatever memories would come back to me when I entered. But the apartment had been whitewashed like the hallways. The carpet had been torn out and fresh—albeit dusty—padded floor insulation had been exposed in its place. I walked through the apartment, down the hallway, and into the bedroom. The place was like a blank canvas that had a couple of tears here and there. And because of that, because the memories had been painted over in uninspired eggshell, it had even more potential than if it was how I'd left it when I walked away.

Kip found me in my old bedroom, staring out at the parking lot. "It's a dump, right? The agency can find you another property. I know of at least five different listings for apartment buildings twice this size."

"Draw up the paperwork," I said softly.

"You're sure?"

"I'm sure. This building has everything I want—or it will once I make a few modifications." I walked back to the living room and pushed the toe of my paint-stained sneaker under the foam carpet padding. "It's the perfect property for what I need."

"I'm afraid you lost me. Why do you need a rundown apartment building?"

"So I can win the VIP competition."

Kip's eyes narrowed. "You're going up against some very qualified teams. You really think you can win with this building?"

"I'll never know if I don't try."

"It's going to take more than a new coat of paint."

"I know exactly what it's going to take, Kip. It won't be easy, but I have resources too. And you can't make an omelet without painting over a couple of eggshells."

TWELVE

"I wish all buyers were as decisive as you," Kip said. "Tell you what. Fill out a mortgage application and bring it to my office. I'll notify the seller that you're interested, and we'll go from there."

"Anonymous bid," I said. "I don't want anybody to know I'm buying this building until it's a done deal. I'm willing to forgo negotiations to protect my identity."

"Understood," Kip said. "I have copies of the paperwork in my car. As soon as you drop it off, I can get to work."

"Do you want me to follow you to your office now?" I asked.

"No point. The computers have been down since yesterday. The only way to speed this thing through is going to be with phone calls, faxes, and a good old-fashioned notary."

"Let me guess. You got hit with the personality virus?"

Kip looked at me suspiciously. "How did you know that?"

"They got me too. My business."

"You're fairly calm about it," he said.

"It's fixed now." I was about to sing the praises of Nasty—odd in and of itself—when I remembered her Jungle Red lipstick love letter on Tex's nightstand. Both of them were being exactly who they were. But Nasty had nothing to do with my situation with Tex. As far as I was concerned now, she could have him.

"Call Donna Nast at Big Brother Security. She can fix it."

"We already tried. She's booked. She said she can't get to us for another two days. Something about her former employer getting hit bad. She didn't work for you, did she?"

No, but she'd worked for the police station. And when she left my studio this morning, she'd told me a fat city job came in, the kind that would give her ten grand by the end of the day.

"I have to go," I said. Because a new thought was tickling the back of my brain. One that involved the computer hackings around town. I'd been hacked. Kip's real estate agency had been hacked. And if I was putting together the puzzle pieces of intel from Nasty, the police computers had been hacked too.

The parallels between the hackings propelled me to a conclusion I might not have normally considered. Yesterday when I was at the police station, Tex said the computers had been down all day. I'd already considered that a virus might have slowed down their network, but what would happen if someone had gained backdoor access to police files? I had a feeling it wouldn't be good.

I took the paperwork from Kip and we went our separate ways. I assumed he went back to his office. I went to mine. It was closing in on six, and the sun was heading toward the horizon. I wanted to get a status report on the inventory project and the state of our computers from Effie before she left for the night. Now that I'd decided on my former apartment building as the setting for the Mad for Mod entry to the VIP competition, the clock was ticking on the execution of my design. I'd lost valuable time today already. I needed to get to work.

It was less than a mile from the apartment building to Mad for Mod, but I wasn't motivated to walk, and Rocky didn't have his sweater. I drove the short distance and parked next to Effie's new white Ford Escape. If not for her vanity plates: Eff U, it would blend in with every other white SUV in Dallas. Ah, the millennial sense of humor.

I found her in the display area with Joanie Higa, a local thrift store owner who oftentimes beat me to the sidewalk finds around Dallas and then sold me the items I could have claimed for myself if only I'd forgone my morning swims. Despite her ruthless business practices, we were friends. And to file under turnabout being fair play, on more than one occasion, I'd collected a paycheck from her for boxes of oddities she could sell in her shop, Joanie Loves

Tchotchkes.

Joanie was Japanese-American. Her personal style was rockabilly with a jet-black beehive, cat eye glasses, cuffed jean, and platform stilettos. A few months ago, she'd twisted her ankle and had to rethink her choice in footwear. I'd gifted her with the vast collection of bowling shirts and shoes in my inventory. We'd both been delighted with the transfer of ownership: her wardrobe had quadrupled overnight, and I'd made some room in my closet. Today she wore a purple and white bowling shirt that said Ed's Bakery on the back, slim jeans, and black and white bowling shoes.

"Madison!" Effie said. "Check out this collection of original 1950 Blendo Joanie brought us!"

Joanie smiled. "I didn't tell her that's what they were. She recognized them on her own."

I smiled at the two women and picked up a small, round neon green glass. Blendo, produced by Anchor Hocking, was a popular choice of drinkware in kitchens of the era and was the cornerstone of many mid-century enthusiast's glassware collections today. It was at its peak production in the fifties and sixties and was instantly recognizable by its vivid, opaque colors at the base that visually faded into clear glass at the opening. A thin stripe of shiny gold accented the rim of each piece. Often it was the gold rim (or lack thereof) that indicated how much use a set had seen.

"Madison's been teaching me the classics," Effie said to Joanie. She turned to me. "The Bickners' grandson emailed me digital photos of everything they're selling to us so we're all up to date. I can't wait to show you. I'll be right back."

"Emailed?" I called after her.

She turned around and smiled. "Don't worry, the computer is still fine. I ran a virus check every hour on the hour just to make sure. The firewall is doing its job." She disappeared into the hallway.

"Computer problems?" Joanie asked.

"Yep. Did you get hit?"

"I've been unpacking boxes all day. If there's a computer

problem, I don't know about it yet. Why? What's the deal?"

"Apparently there's a hacker attacking businesses in Dallas. I got it after opening an attachment."

"Mads, everybody knows not to open suspicious attachments."

"It wasn't suspicious. At least at the time, I didn't think so. It was from Jane Strong—"

"That's different. I'd trust my bestie's attachments too."

"Aren't we too old to say things like 'bestie'?"

"Speak for yourself. I've turned forty-nine seven times so far. I don't exactly live by the rules. What did Jane say when you told her?"

"I didn't tell her."

"Why not? She might not even know her computer is infected. Who knows how many emails she's sent." Joanie was looking at me funny. We stared at each other for a couple of seconds while fragmented thoughts pummeled my brain. The timing of Jane's email and her murder. We'd had words in the lobby of Republic Tower, so I knew the email hadn't been a hoax, but what if? What if the person who murdered her was the person who'd loaded the virus onto her computer? I'd found her throwing up in the bathroom stall. She'd been sick. She said she'd been sick for hours. But Detective Henning had said there were no signs of anything unusual in her stomach contents or bloodwork. Had stress or a panic attack made her ill? What if someone had found a way to make her sick to get her out of the way so they could upload the virus to her computer, knowing she'd unwittingly distribute it to her own network?

I could understand her emailing me. We'd emailed multiple times daily since becoming friends. And Kip Bledsoe. It wasn't a stretch for an interior decorator to have reason to contact a real estate agent. But the police? Why would she contact them? What attachment would she possibly send to the Lakewood Police Department that they'd be motivated to open?

I dropped onto a pink square-backed sofa. In my desire to complete my own application to the VIP competition and my anger with Tex, I'd kept one obvious thought at bay. Only a handful of people knew about my fight with Jane. When news broke that she'd been murdered—and that I'd been there—the questions would start. Why wasn't I mourning her death? Why wasn't I trying to find out the truth about what happened like I had with other similar situations in the past? Why wasn't I broken up? And then the finger pointing, the judgment, and the whispers would ensue. My own community would be torn apart by the subject, especially if I chose not to discuss it. There was a short window of time until the news went public.

"Madison, are you okay? You look like you're about to have some sort of breakdown," Joanie said.

I looked up at her. "Can you stick around after Effie leaves? I could use a friend."

"Sure." She dropped onto the sofa next to me. "This isn't about those men, is it? I knew this six months thing was going to blow up in your face."

"I'm done with men," I said.

"You're switching teams?"

"I'm done playing the game."

Effie rejoined us. She held a yellow file folder on top of a pile of mail. "Here's the inventory list and the pictures. I didn't realize how late it was. I'm meeting my parents at Texas Land and Cattle for dinner and if I don't get there soon, I'll miss out on the free sourdough bread."

I took the pile of files and mail from Effie. Joanie nestled into her corner of the sofa. "Madison does not want to be responsible for keeping one of the few remaining bread eaters from getting free bread, right?"

"Right. See you tomorrow."

"Tomorrow's my day off."

"That's right. Have fun and eat a slice of bread for me."

I set the pile on the sofa next to me and stood up. I picked up two Blendo glasses and carried them to the bar cart by the front door, where I uncorked a bottle of Pinot Noir and poured a healthy amount of wine into each of the tumblers. I carried the glasses back to Joanie and handed her the purple one. "To birthdays, business, and life getting less complicated."

We clinked glasses, and each took a sip. When I lowered my glass, Joanie raised hers. "To your life *never* being less complicated, because I live vicariously through you and less complicated would be boring."

We drank to that too. We were half way through the bottle before Joanie said something other than "hit me."

"You know, Madison, I have no problem sitting here drinking your expensive wine, but you said you wanted to talk."

I raised one eyebrow. "It's not that expensive."

She finished her glass. "It's more expensive than the stuff I keep in my store."

I finished my own glass and set it down on the coffee table. There was a reason I'd asked Joanie to stay and it wasn't because I didn't want to drink alone. She'd known me for a few years, and I knew I could confide in her.

"Jane and I weren't friends anymore. Yesterday morning she sent me an email to let me know what she *really* thought of me and destroyed any chance of an ongoing friendship."

Joanie refilled both of our glasses but said nothing. I continued. "I know, we became friends pretty quickly. Too quickly. Who expects to find a new bestie after they're fifty?"

"Word." She raised her glass and clinked mine.

"But it was like we were the same person. We had so much in common. We were both mid-century modern decorators in Dallas. We were both self-taught, me from watching Doris Day movies and her from reading old copies of *Better Homes and Gardens*. We both wore vintage clothes. We both started our businesses later in life. We're both Aries."

"Yes, but she was two years younger than you, right?"

"So what?"

"Japanese horoscope is based on birth year, not birth month. Two years makes you very different people."

I picked up my glass, stared into the smooth garnet surface, and then set it back down. Whether the alcohol or the security of hanging around a different friend had loosened my tongue, I didn't know. But talking about Jane felt like letting go of a cumbersome parcel of day old groceries that were past their freshness date.

"Jane Strong was murdered yesterday morning. I found her body in the bathroom at Republic Tower. Almost everybody thinks we were still good friends, but we weren't. She sent me a nasty email yesterday morning and when I saw her at Republic Tower we had a fight. The last words I said to her were vile."

"Why have I heard nothing about this?" Joanie said. "This should be all over the news. What did Tex say? Wait, he doesn't think you killed her, does he? Is that why you're mad at him?"

"This has nothing to do with Tex. He wasn't the officer called to the scene and when I saw him yesterday, he refused to discuss the case."

"Whoa! Back up. You saw Tex yesterday? What about the whole six-month birthday present?"

"Rocky was at the police station and I went to pick him up."

"You saw Tex. How did he look? Was there chemistry? Did he look hot?"

I stared at her. "Joanie, I just told you a woman we both know was murdered in a bathroom in a famous building in downtown Dallas and you asked if Tex looked hot."

"I know."

"You're focusing on the wrong part of the story."

"Jane is dead, right? She was mean to you, and now she's dead. You could spend your time focused on all that negative energy, sure. All the things you want to say to her, the reaction you had to her email. You could stay awake at night getting mad about how you thought you had a friend who wasn't a friend after all. And then the guilt over the anger because you're alive and she's dead. Or you could think about the two hot men who are waiting for you to make a decision."

"But she's dead. A woman died. Someone murdered her. I

wasn't even supposed to be there, but I was, because I was so angry."

"Yes? But you didn't put the knife in her back, right?"

"What knife?"

Joanie waved her hand back and forth like someone had served her stinky cheese. "Don't focus on the knife. You were not responsible for her murder, right?"

"Right."

"That means somebody else was. Jane Strong, lovely as she may have been, did something that made someone else—not you, the friend who she attacked via email—do something far worse than engage in a verbal battle in the lobby of Republic Tower."

I picked up the bottle of wine and checked to see how much we'd gone through.

Joanie stood up and tucked her legs underneath her. "You've heard of Confucius, right?" she asked.

"Sure."

"Confucius said, 'Be not afraid of mistakes and thus make them crimes.'"

"Meaning…"

Joanie leaned forward, suddenly very serious. "Stop. Close your eyes. Inhale. Exhale."

I did all of the above.

"Now listen. 'Be not afraid of mistakes and thus make them crimes.'"

I opened my eyes. "You're saying it's okay to make mistakes."

"That's right. And you're punishing yourself by focusing on her death. But you being self-centered did not kill Jane."

"I'm self-centered?"

"Every single woman over fifty is self-centered. It's a badge of honor."

I leaned back against the pink cushions and thought about that. "How come you can quote Confucius?"

Joanie considered the contents of her wine glass for a moment. "I'm half Japanese. I've been quoting Confucius from the womb."

"You never quoted Confucius to me."

"Until tonight, grasshopper, you were not ready." She drained her glass.

We finished the bottle. Joanie called Connie, a former client turned former part-time employee turned Etsy businesswoman who crafted and sold one-of-a-kind sleeves for old vinyl record albums. Yes, that's what I thought too.

Connie lived in the neighborhood, which is why I wasn't surprised at the knock on the door a few minutes later. I stumbled up from the sofa, flipped the lock, and pulled open the door, ready to greet Connie to our party.

But my day wasn't destined to end on a high note. Because the person who had shown up to join our impromptu girls' night in was Nasty—Donna Nast.

THIRTEEN

"Hey, Nasty," I said. "What's happening?" I swayed while speaking and put my hand on the doorframe to keep my balance.

"Madison?" Nasty said. Her eyes moved from my face to the overalls I still wore from Tex's apartment, down to my sneakers, and back to my face. I tried to look her up and down too but felt dizzy. Joanie and I had been sitting for most of the night, and the effort of standing up and walking to the door had been more difficult than I'd expected. Maybe we didn't need Connie to bring reinforcements.

"Come on in," I said. And then I remembered I was mad at her. "Go away. Take him. I don't want him. He's yours."

"I don't believe this. You're drunk? I didn't know women like you *got* drunk."

"What do you mean, women like me? I'm not the kind of woman who has women like me." Did that make sense? "You are. Women like you. Women like you sleep with other men. Other women's men." I stopped speaking for a moment and over enunciated the thought I was trying to verbalize. "Men other women are considering."

Nasty pushed past me and came into the showroom. Joanie still sat on the pink sofa, and Rocky was curled up next to her. Rocky stood up and growled at Nasty.

Good dog.

"I cannot believe I'm here," Nasty said. "Have you two eaten anything?"

"Not really."

Nasty turned to Joanie. "Give us a chance to talk. Maybe go find some food?"

"Do you have any food?" Joanie asked me.

"I have a box of Cheez-It crackers in my office."

"I love Cheez-Its!" Joanie said. She jumped up and headed down the hallway, leaving me alone with the enemy. Rocky followed Joanie.

Bad dog.

After Joanie disappeared, Nasty turned back to me. "This is unbelievable. If I didn't believe it would bite me in the ass, I'd film you and use it for blackmail. Perfect Madison, who never colors outside of the lines, is drunk on," she picked up the empty bottle, "a five-dollar bottle of Pinot Noir."

"What's your damage, Heather?" I said.

"Just when I thought things couldn't get any better. Damn those anti-surveillance laws."

"I don't remember inviting you." I said. (slurred). Nasty sat down on the pink sofa, crossed her legs, and draped her arms over the sofa back on either side. "Why are you here?" I demanded.

She pointed to the chair opposite the sofa. "Sit. Listen. I'm only going to say this once."

I purposely chose to sit on the beanbag chair instead, and then struggled to establish some form of dignity in the goofy lime green vinyl blob. "You have something to say? Say it."

"I'm trying to." She pulled her arms in from the sofa back and leaned forward. "I'm not sleeping with Tex."

"Don't lie to me. I was in his bedroom. I saw the note you left on his nightstand."

She narrowed her eyes. "I thought he hired you to paint his spare room. Why were you on the second floor in the first place?"

"Wojo ran through my paint and took off. I ran after him, up the stairs and into the bedroom."

She smiled, and then her smile turned into a laugh.

"What's so funny?"

"Wojciehowitcz. That dog is going to cause more trouble for

Tex than a whole room full of ex-girlfriends."

"I don't follow."

"You did. Yesterday. And that's why I'm here."

I sat back against the beanbag chair and tried to make sense of Nasty's cryptic conversation. There was a very small possibility that the wine was making it hard for me to focus. I would have paid good money for one of Jane Strong's never-ending cups of takeout coffee.

"The note you left on Tex's nightstand said something about 'thanks for last night' and it totally being worth it. You wrote it with lipstick." Details of the note were tattooed on my brain. I did not mention the X or the O above her signature.

"Tex's computers were hacked. He asked me if I could do anything about it and I said I'd bump another job if he paid a surcharge. He did. Now I can buy that Louis Vuitton handbag I've had my eye on."

I narrowed my eyes. "You mean the *police department* was hacked. You left here to do some work for the city. That was them, right?"

"The police department's computers went down because of the virus, but that's not what I'm talking about. Tex was hacked. Personally. Same virus that hit you. I've made a boatload of money in the past two days. I wish I could find the hacker and thank him."

"Him? Isn't it sexist to assume the hacker is a man?"

"Most hackers are men."

"You're not a man."

"I'm not most hackers."

We were silent for a moment. Joanie reappeared. She had a folded newspaper under her arm and a TV tray of Cheez-It crackers, sliced *Saucisson D'Arles*, and a couple of Greek yogurts. It was an odd assortment, but considering I'd had half a bottle of wine on an empty stomach, I wasn't complaining. If I remembered any of this in the morning, though, I'd up my grocery game the next time I went shopping.

Joanie set down the tray, handed me the newspaper, and

picked up the tray. I unfolded the newspaper and separated out the obituaries, and then opened the rest of the paper at the bifold and spread the pages on top of the coffee table. We'd picnicked in the showroom before and this had proven to be a good system. After covering the table surface, I leaned back and switched on the ball lamp that dangled over our table. Just as Joanie was setting the tray onto the table, I noticed a page of the newspaper that looked different than the rest.

"Hold it!" I said. Joanie jumped. A couple of Cheez-It crackers fell off her tray and onto the floor. Rocky left the sofa and ate them like they'd been intended for him all along. He looked up at Joanie expectantly. Joanie looked at me. Nasty looked at me.

And I looked at the newspaper spread out on the table.

In general, newsprint has a look about it. Column sizes, article fonts, the occasional ad to fill space. Graphically, the density of words on a page gave it a patterned quality. It's why Joanie had a whole bookcase filled with items that had been decoupaged with newsprint. As a material, it was both cheap and easy to use, which made it a cornerstone of the trash-to-treasure look. But the page I stared at was none of the above. It was largely empty, with an open letter printed in a font so big it could have been used above the fold on an eye chart.

Dear Residents of Dallas,

The design public is deeply troubled by the death of Jane Strong, leader of the modern design aesthetic revival movement in our downtown district. Her loss will be felt throughout the community. As a gesture of respect, my company plans to dedicate our entry in the VIP competition to her memory.

Jane, may you rest in peace.

The note was signed Sterling Webster, Founder & CEO, SterlingCo.

"That man is a disgrace to the profession," Joanie said. "He's blatantly taking advantage of Jane's death to get attention for his building. I can't believe he's stupid enough to try something like that." She picked up a pink velvet pillow from the end of the display and tossed it onto the floor, and then set up camp on top of it.

I agreed with Joanie that the stunt was in poor taste, but I didn't believe for a second that someone had struck Sterling Webster with the stupid stick. This felt less like an opportunistic business move than an act of diversion.

I kept my eyes on the newspaper and read it four separate times. Sterling hadn't said that Jane was murdered. He hadn't said her body was found at the DIDI offices. He'd kept the letter short and sweet, and to anybody not plugged into the news, it would sound like her death, though unexpected, was part of the cycle of life. Sterling had chosen these words carefully.

Too carefully, in my opinion.

"I thought you were collaborating with Jane Strong," Nasty said, interrupting my train of thought.

"How'd you know that?"

She tossed her hair behind her shoulder. "I saw something about it when I was on your computer this morning."

I didn't doubt that Nasty had looked at my files while removing the virus from my computer. And I'd been so thankful for her help, despite our past animosity, that I hadn't given it much thought. She owned a security company. What was she going to lift from me? The top ten colors used for design in 1958?

But Nasty knew things she shouldn't know. She knew about the email from Jane. And now she knew we were supposed to collaborate on a design for the VIP competition—a collaboration that not only hadn't happened, but wouldn't have happened, even if the falling out had never taken place. Nasty was feeling out the situation for her own personal benefit. I just couldn't tell what it was she was hoping to gain.

"Jane and I talked about submitting a co-design, but in the end, my application was strictly from Mad for Mod. That's not the same as what Sterling Webster did. This letter was written after Jane was murdered. He is using her death for his benefit."

"But that doesn't mean he's wrong, does it?"

It was the second time in one night that Nasty made me see

that the thing I was angry about wasn't what I was making it out to be. I tapped the newspaper page. "This doesn't seem sleazy to you?"

She shrugged. "It's totally sleazy."

"And he's going to win. You know that, right? That letter just swayed the judges in his favor. I can design the best apartment complex in the state and it's going to pale in comparison to that."

"Do you have a history with Sterling Webster?" Nasty asked.

I shook my head. "He's a glorified house flipper. He buys buildings cheap, demolishes or guts the place, and brings in a team to put a no-personality structure in its place. Sleek and modern, million-dollar jobs. He used to be based in San Antonio but opened a satellite office here last year. As far as I'm concerned, this town isn't big enough for the both of us." Accursed Pinot Noir. Now I sounded like Yosemite Sam. "No," I added. "our paths have never crossed."

"That seems odd," she said.

"It's not. Our work isn't about us, it's about the building or, in my case, the room. It's only recently that I expanded the scope of what Mad for Mod does with the Sweet Dreams pajama factory. That building gave me wider exposure, and because the DIDI committee was impressed, they invited me to submit to the VIP competition."

"And that was Jane's doing?"

"Pretty much."

"You're saying if Jane hadn't persuaded you to enter, this competition might have gone to Sterling Webster all along."

"It's possible," I said. "You're driving at something. Forgive me for not being at the top of my game," I said, cutting my eyes away from her to the empty Blendo glasses on the table, "but I can't help feeling like you know more than you should know."

Nasty pulled out her cell phone and tapped the screen a few times. "A whole bunch of businesses got hit with that virus today, so I got to see a whole bunch of hard drives."

I leaned forward. "Sterling Webster was hit too?"

"No, he wasn't. But someone else we both know was, and I

think you'll find what I discovered to be very interesting."

She handed me her phone. It took me a moment to realize I was looking at a copy of the VIP competition application. It took another moment to realize it was the application for Sterling Webster's building in the Arts District of downtown Dallas.

"If Sterling wasn't hacked, then how did you find this?"

"Keep reading, Madison. I'll let you get this one yourself."

I looked back at the application, using my fingers on the small screen to blow it up and move the image around for better clarity. The pixilation distorted the document, but when I saw the names of the investors in Sterling Webster's building, I gasped.

Now I knew why Tex wouldn't talk to me about the VIP competition. According to the picture Nasty had taken of Sterling Webster's application, Tex was one of his investors. Tex was on the opposing team.

FOURTEEN

"Where did you get this?" I asked Nasty.

"Where do you think?"

I was silent for a moment. I held up her phone and tipped it side to side. "Does Tex know you know this?"

"No."

"Why tell me? We're not exactly friends."

"You ever hear the expression 'the enemy of my enemy is my friend'?"

"Sure."

"It's something like that."

Nasty was being mysterious on purpose. It wasn't out of character for her to bait me or to use me for her own hidden agenda. In this case, I didn't know who her enemy was. It didn't really matter. I'd been mad at Tex earlier today because of Nasty, and now it turned out I was mad at him because of something Nasty told me. It was getting slightly hard to keep track of the reasons for my anger. The anger itself seemed to be self-renewing.

"Whatever your reasons, thank you for letting me know. I was encouraged to enter the competition, but I knew going in that my chances were a longshot. To be honest, just getting Mad for Mod listed on the press release as one of the participating design firms is a big boost to my visibility."

Joanie snored loudly, and then rolled over with her back to the table. I waited a few seconds to see if she'd wake back up. She didn't.

"How does a competition like this work?" Nasty asked, tearing my attention from Joanie's back. "Seems like an uneven playing field."

I thought for a second before answering Nasty's question, not because I didn't trust her, but because she was right. It was something Jane and I had talked about when we were friends. The boys' club feeling of many of Dallas's institutions and how we'd both come up against barriers before working out our own strategies to succeed.

For me, it was less a feminist battle than a course correction after establishing a small start-up decorating business when I first moved from Pennsylvania to Texas. For Jane, who'd spent years under the thumb of some of the most prolific designers in the state, it was an instinct to get back at the men who had kept her designing floor plan after floor plan lacking in originality. I'd always laughed when she went on a tangent about McMansions, writing her rants off as a way for her to disengage from her former life. But she'd been right. Whether we designed as a team or on our own, we were two women with more imagination than budget who believed we could hold our own against some of the most established talent in the state.

"The DIDI offices announced the contest last month. There's a tight application window. First step is to fill out their online application with credentials, upload photos from your portfolio, basically let them know what you're capable of pulling off. That allowed the organization to see how many entrants there would be and plan their promotional push accordingly. Remember, this isn't all about the work. It's about getting recognition on a national scale."

"What does 'DD' stand for?"

"Design in Dallas Initiative. It's a movement to shine a spotlight on the design talent in Dallas. To qualify, you have to have an office within the Dallas postal codes: 75201 to 75260."

"Does Sterling Webster?"

"Sure. He has offices throughout Texas." Nasty took a breath to speak and I cut her off. "There were guidelines for entry.

Maximum square footage, maximum investment by the designer. Meaning I can't dump a hundred thousand dollars into a property, but if I collaborated with five designers, we could each dump twenty-thousand dollars into it to have a hundred-thousand-dollar entry."

"You didn't know about this, did you?" she asked, shaking her phone. It had to be a rhetorical question. My reaction had said pretty much everything.

"I was surprised that Tex knew about the VIP competition. At least now I know *why* he knows about it. But now that he has a financial stake in the outcome as a silent partner of Sterling Webster, if he gets involved in the case—if he discusses it at all—he'll likely get his partner disqualified. Ooooh, this is good! It means his hands are tied."

"I didn't figure bondage to be your thing."

"You know what I meant." I jumped up and paced around the showroom. "It makes sense now. Sterling wanted to put more money into his design than he was allowed so he hoodwinked local investors. At least one that we know about—"

Nasty grinned unexpectedly. "I love that you just said Tex got hoodwinked." She tapped the screen of her phone. "Will you say that again while I record it?"

"No." I kept pacing. "Webster doesn't need to win. He already has a bigger reputation than the rest of us. So, what would he get from this?"

Joanie lifted her head from the pink pillow on the floor. "If it's not money or fame, then it's love. That's what makes the world go around." I stared at Joanie. She laid her head back down and tapped the floor to get Rocky's attention. He padded over to her and flopped down on the floor. She draped her arm over his body and fell back asleep.

"She's right, you know," Nasty said. "Money, fame, and love are the three big motivators in life."

"Give me your phone again," I said. Nasty stared at me. I held my hand out, palm side up, and curled my fingers repeatedly. "I'll give it back."

She pressed her thumb down to unlock it. "What do you want to know?"

"Find me a picture of Sterling Webster."

"Why?"

"Don't do it, then. I'll pull him up on my own computer." I stepped over Joanie and headed to the hallway.

"Madison, wait." I turned around and Nasty held out her phone. "Here he is."

I took the phone and looked at the picture, and as recognition hit, I felt the blood rush to my face and extremities. I knew this man. I knew him because just yesterday he'd met me at my apartment building in answer to a call to his office.

Sterling Webster, the house flipper and direct competitor for the VIP, had tried to pass himself off as the realtor, Kip Bledsoe.

FIFTEEN

I stared at Nasty's phone, not fully processing what this could mean. As possibilities danced into and out of my mind, I looked up and caught Nasty's eyes. "This man told me his name was Kip Bledsoe."

"The realtor?" Nasty asked. She took back her phone and tapped the screen and then handed it back to me. *"That's* Kip Bledsoe."

The man on the screen now was less pretty boy and more ex-football player. He had a short crew cut, and his neck was as thick as his head. His success in realty must have been driven by a need for custom made suits.

I handed her phone back to her. "I needed an apartment complex to use for my entry. I called Kip because he manages a lot of mid-century buildings around town. Today, I saw his name on my old building. I called him to see if I could buy it and he came out to meet me."

"Except he didn't come out to meet you. Sterling Webster did."

"Looks that way." I remembered something Kip had said. "Did Kip call you to work on his computer?"

"I was at Kip's office when he got a call about a property on Gaston," she said. "Sterling Webster was there too."

"You knew what they did?"

"I knew Sterling said he'd meet with Kip's client. I just didn't know that client was you. You already owned a building on Gaston. Why are you looking at another one?"

"Remember yesterday I told you I submitted an entry but needed a property? Jane and I were supposed to collaborate on a design. She had a building in mind. You already saw the email she sent me, so you know we weren't on the best of terms when she was murdered. I had enough invested in the competition that I wasn't going to just walk away. After I ran into her that morning, I spent the day at the library putting together my own concept. My proposal wasn't as pretty as Sterling's, but the contents were solid."

"How'd you know it paled in comparison to pretty boy Webster?"

"The designs didn't—I mean, I don't know what his designs were, but mine were inspired." I ignored her doubtful expression. "I meant his application. It was professionally bound, brushed steel cover, colored tabs probably breaking his concept down into categories like 'organic urban design' and 'seamless neighborhood integration'."

"Is that stuff for real? Sounds like PR mumbo jumbo."

"It's the kind of stuff that gets people's attention because it sounds like a thing that isn't a thing. If Sterling Webster cared about organic design, he wouldn't use so much polished chrome in his buildings. And if he cared about seamless neighborhood integration, he wouldn't knock down vacant buildings to make way for new ones."

"You really don't like this guy, do you?"

"I never paid much attention to him until I got involved with the design community," I said. "Until the DIDI appraised the pajama factory I converted into a shared workspace, I flew under everybody's radar."

Back in February, a few weeks before Valentine's day, I'd learned of the death of a friend. There'd been nothing suspicious about her passing. Alice Sweet had been eighty-six years old and in declining health, despite her good habits of swimming laps with other seniors each morning, but there's only so much you can do to slow down the clock. Shortly after her death, I'd learned that she left me a vacant pajama factory.

The interior of the building had been left untouched for forty years, which presented unique challenges and opportunities. It would have been easy enough to maintain seventy-five percent of the original design integrity of the building after restoring the hardwood floors, repairing the deteriorated window casings, and removing the abandoned bins of fabric, thread, and buttons that had sat untouched while the factory had closed. But my idea had been to convert the existing sewing stations into workstations in a shared office. The key was using fixtures I'd accumulated in storage over the years I'd been in business. Using pendant lamps, Danish modern desks, colorfully reupholstered diner chairs, and storage hutches, all items that were doing little more than taking up space in my garage, my storage locker, and my studio and could easily be installed. I implemented a variating color palette that matched the pastel conversation hearts in the company's signature pajamas to define each workspace, yet keep the entire floor cohesive. I'd even moved the sewing machines to the upstairs level, along with a painting studio, so creatives would have their own space to work.

The pajama factory had been called Sweet Dreams, and I'd left the name and logo mounted on the outside of the building. Lots of people had dreams they wanted to pursue. I'd taken what Alice had left me and done what I could to give entrepreneurs a helping hand.

"I've got storage lockers filled with furniture. I can't park in my garage because that's full too. I love mid-century design. I have no intention of branching out to the masses and taking a bite out of Sterling Webster's pie, but if I don't step things up a little, I'm going to drown in atomic fixtures."

"What's your growth factor?" Nasty asked.

"You're kidding me, right?"

"Your plan. Your projected profit. How much you plan to recoup of what you're putting into this."

"I know the definition of 'growth factor'."

"Good. You told me once you're a business woman just like me. I don't make a move without knowing what it means to my bottom line, what the potential immediate benefits are, and what the long-term impact will be. If you really are serious about leveraging the outcome of this competition into a platform for bigger jobs, then you darn well better know your growth factor."

The conversation had taken a weird turn, but like almost every other conversation I'd had with Nasty, this one was a verbal wrestling match, and there was no way she was pinning me to the floor. I crossed my arms. "Considering a sizeable portion of my inventory came from the street corners of Dallas on trash day, I've got low overhead. My twenty-thousand-dollar investment will go toward materials and installation: floors, counters, and paint. Five thousand in reserve for equipment rentals on my interior remodel and five for the exterior component."

"What's your concept?"

"Fully furnished short-term apartment rentals. Once the project is complete, I'll be able to keep the twelve units in constant rotation. One month of rentals will pay off the investment. From there, it's general maintenance."

Nasty stood up. "I want in."

"In on what?"

"Your entry. Sterling Webster has a private investor, now you do too."

Joanie stirred from the floor and sat up. Rocky did too. All eyes were on me to make what amounted to the most unpredictable decision I'd made in the past six months—and it didn't even involve Hudson or Tex or the decision-free zone I'd requested for my birthday.

"Silent partner, right?" I asked, with emphasis on the *silent*.

"You think I have an opinion on pink bathrooms?"

"Oh, what the heck," I said. I held out my hand and Nasty shook it. I couldn't help wondering what she was up to, but for one of the few times since we'd met, it appeared as though we were on the same side.

"The first thing I want you to do is distance yourself from this thing about Jane Spring."

"Strong," I corrected. "Jane Strong."

"Strong. Right. That visit from the detective earlier today was for one reason. You're on his short list of people with motive. And you can't win a contest if you don't find a way off that list fast."

"It's not like I invited him here for tea," I said.

"No, but think over the facts, Madison. A witness overheard you and Jane argue. You have no evidence that you were at the library when you say you were. The building was empty except for you and Jane—"

"It wasn't empty. Building security was there. So was her ex-husband, Gerry Rose. He's the head of the DIDI and the one who told me to get help while he stayed with her body. He didn't seem surprised or upset to find Jane unconscious. Before I returned, he carried her downstairs and said she was dead. Why aren't the police bothering him?"

"Surveillance shows Gerry Rose was in his office after you left DIDI. Your own statement lines up perfectly with when he found her. You're in trouble, Madison." She put her hands on my shoulders and stared directly into my face. While I was a lot soberer than I'd been when she arrived, I was exhausted, and the emotional turmoil of the day had left me feeling like I'd run a marathon. "Screw it." She dropped her arms and turned around, grabbing her handbag from the sofa.

"What are you doing?"

"I'm making sure you don't forget this conversation took place." She pulled a red lipstick out of her handbag, the same shade I'd seen on the invoice on Tex's nightstand. She uncapped the tube and wrote across the newsprint that was spread out on the table. *This document serves as a legal and binding contract between Donna Nast and Madison Night for the entry to DD competition.* She glanced up at me, and then looked back at the newsprint and signed her name with a flourish. She held out her lipstick to me. I took the proffered cosmetic and inserted two lower case "i's" between the DD and then signed my own name under hers. I handed the lipstick back.

"You'll have a cashier's check in the morning. If I were you,

Madison, I'd keep this between us girls."

Right. As if I wanted to advertise my pact with the devil.

I woke with a headache. Joanie was stretched out on the pink tweed sofa with Rocky by her thigh. Connie, who I hadn't remembered joining us, was nestled in a sleeping bag between a row of coffee tables. I seemed to have slept on the bean bag chair, proving the seventies advertisement accurate: it was so comfortable I didn't want to get up.

Outside the glass walls of my showroom, the sky looked cloudy. Dallas rain came in weekly showers, and from the looks of things, we'd only been given a temporary reprieve. Fat droplets fell, speckling the sidewalk. The reprieve was over.

I left Connie and Joanie sleeping and went to the office to make coffee. The mini fridge was stocked with food we hadn't had the night before, and I assumed it had been Connie who'd filled it. I pulled a premade breakfast sandwich out and microwaved it and then dropped into my chair to eat while I checked my email.

Sitting between the usual Yahoo group digests and eBay ending soon notifications was an email from Kip Bledsoe. The subject line said, "preapproved." I opened the email. He'd kept his update short and sweet: he asked the bank to prioritize my mortgage application and it had been approved, he'd contacted the property owner and made a bid on my behalf, and we should hear something this afternoon. Fingers crossed, I'd have keys in hand within twenty-four hours. A copy of the paperwork was attached to the email.

I hovered my mouse over the attachment. Did I trust Kip? Not after the Sterling Webster stunt. I called his cell.

"Kip, this is Madison Night."

"Great! I emailed you the documents. Good thing you have a clean credit rating. We pushed that mortgage approval through in record time. Just need your signature—"

I interrupted him. "Kip, did you or did you not send Sterling

Webster to meet me at the building? And to say he was you?"

"He told me he never said he was me. He said you assumed he was me and he didn't correct you."

"I asked you to make an anonymous bid on the property because it was for VIP. How anonymous could it be when I was talking to the competition?"

"You're the one who told Sterling why you wanted the building. Not me. And from what he told me, he made absolutely sure you knew what you were getting." He paused for a moment. "Does this mean you changed your mind about the building? I can keep looking, but I'm not sure we're going to have a whole lot of luck."

If Kip had been in front of me, it would have been awfully hard to hide my reaction. But he was right. I needed a building. And I'd already cycled through the necessary emotions to determine that the one I used to own was the right one. "I still want the building. I just don't appreciate the way you played me."

"It was meant to be a joke. Sterling said he's been hearing your name in a lot of design circles and wanted to meet you. Honestly, I was busy with the computers being down, so if he hadn't volunteered, I would have had to tell you no."

"These documents you sent me, are you sure they're free of viruses?"

"Scanned, scrubbed, and free as a bird. Your friend took care of our system herself."

I grumbled my thanks for the rush job on the documents and hung up. Real estate was a game of relationships, and for a person like Kip, making Sterling—a flipper with deep pockets and high profits—happy would be far more lucrative than catering to me. I navigated the mouse to the bottom right of my screen and checked that Nasty's firewall was still in place. The pop-up window said it was working and there were no threats detected on my computer. I clicked the attachment and scans of the paperwork opened. I sent the files to my printer, and then used the Save As function to file them to a folder on my hard drive.

That's when I discovered my hard drive was empty. My files, every last one of them, had been wiped from my computer.

SIXTEEN

No wonder Nasty's firewall indicated there were no threats on my computer. There were no *files* on my computer. None.

My internal hard drive was empty.

My external hard drive was empty.

My cloud storage was empty.

That can't be. I closed out of the save-as window and opened the file manager by clicking the small, beige folder icon at the bottom of my screen. Again, every place where I stored files on my computer was empty. The folders were there, but the digital contents were stripped.

No. No. No. No. No. No. It wasn't possible.

But it was!

It was like I was staring at a brand-new, fresh from the factory computer. Only there was nothing fresh or exciting about the circumstance. My brain refused to process the magnitude of the problem. Paralyzed from doing something that would make things worse—although what could make this worse?—I reached for my donut phone, and then for my cell phone, and then for the mouse to my computer. I felt like a robot controlled by an indecisive owner. Every one of my actions felt wrong and ineffective.

What I did was scream.

Okay, that felt better. It didn't accomplish anything, but it felt good.

Actually, the scream did produce two very specific results. It shocked me out of temporary paralysis, and it brought Joanie running to my office.

"What happened?" she asked.

"My files are missing," I said. I grabbed the mouse and clicked folder after folder. Nothing.

"You back up to the cloud, right?"

"Right." I opened the internet window and was met with a solid white screen. Slowly, words appeared in a reverse dissolve.

GOT YOU AGAIN! GOT YOU AGAIN! GOT YOU AGAIN!

The phrase increased in frequency until the words covered each other and blotted out the white backdrop. I slammed my hand down onto the power button and the screen went black.

I stood up and grabbed my handbag. "Can you lock up when you and Connie leave?" I asked. "I can't just sit here and right now, I'm afraid to turn my computer back on."

"Where are you going?"

I glanced down at my coveralls. "For starters, I'm getting a shower. Hopefully a little water therapy will help me focus on what to do after that."

I handed Joanie a spare key, collected Rocky, and left. I'd planned to spend the day working at the studio, but there wasn't much I could do without access to the internet. Right now, I needed to feel like *I* was in control of my business, not some green hat Robin Hood hacker intent to steal my files and my personality.

My first instinct was to call Nasty. Not only had she been the one to supposedly fix the computer yesterday—leaving me vulnerable and lulled into a false sense of security—but she'd wheedled her way into being my silent partner. In twenty-four hours, I'd agreed to terms I never would have agreed to under normal circumstances. Where was my common sense? As I idled at a traffic light on my way to Thelma Johnson's house, it occurred to me that Jane's murder had knocked me for an unexpected loop and I'd been off balance ever since. And what had Nasty said? Detective Henning was treating me like the most viable person of interest in his murder investigation, and if I had any chance of competing in the VIP competition, my top order of business was to get my name crossed off that list.

I drove home and stripped off soiled and smelly painting clothes on my way up the stairs toward my bathroom. As the water heated up, my mind raced. I climbed under the hot jets and scrubbed at the lilac paint stains on my hands with a loofah.

This wasn't the first time I was confronted with a jigsaw puzzle of evidence and the absolute knowledge that the picture on the puzzle wasn't what the police thought. More than once, I'd gone head to head with Tex when our opinions differed. I'd learned to respect him and know he had his reasons for interpreting the clues as he did, and I knew this was a time when I could benefit from talking out what I knew about Jane's murder.

Except for one thing. Tex wasn't just a police captain. And this had nothing to do with the six-month hiatus he'd agreed to give me for my birthday.

It had to do with the fact that he was competing directly against me in the VIP competition and hadn't said a word.

"Oooooooh!" I yelled. The scream bounced off the puce tiled walls of the bathroom until the relentless sound of gushing water drowned it out. Even when the man agreed to stay out of my life, he was in my life. He was infuriating.

By the time my shower was over, I had a plan. It was fraught with problems and potential emotional land mines, but it was something.

I flipped through the clear plastic garment bags from the oil baron's wife and settled for a dark brown pantsuit and ivory turtleneck. I added brown argyle socks and low heeled brown loafers with wide brushed brass buckles in the front, pulled an ivory felt hat with a chocolate brown and ivory polka dotted band over my quickly blown-dry blonde hair, and went downstairs to let Rocky out. It was warmer than the previous day, but still on the cool side. It took Rocky longer than usual to make his morning deposit on the flower beds, but when he was done, he charged right back into the warm house.

"Rocky, I have to go to work alone today. Can you be a good boy until I get back?"

He yipped. I ran my hand over his long fur and kissed him on top of his head. He nuzzled his pushed up black nose past my face toward my ear. I gave him fresh food and water, another kiss, and left.

What I didn't tell Rocky was that I was going to Hudson's house.

Kip Bledsoe's email had indicated that my mortgage papers were preapproved and that the seller of the apartment building had accepted my offer. I hadn't wanted Hudson to know the buyer was me, because I knew that would send signals I didn't want to send—signals of separation, of compartmentalizing my life, and of wanting to cut ties to him. That was the most troubling thing about this decision. I had never thought I'd be in a place where choosing one man meant I was saying good-bye to the other. But when two trains leave the station, whether or not they're moving at the same speed, unless they're kept separate, there's a point at which they'll intersect. And if I wasn't careful, that intersection would amount to a train wreck.

There was another reason I was going to Hudson's house and it was purely selfish. If Detective Henning was looking for me, he wouldn't look for me there. And if he asked Tex where I was, Tex wouldn't expect me to be there either. He'd expect me to honor the terms of our agreement like he was. In an unexpected way, it was Hudson, the formerly accused bad boy, whose house provided the safe, security I needed, not the officer of the law.

I parked my car on the street opposite Hudson's house. It was a modest white ranch that he'd inherited from his grandmother. She raised him and his sister before his sister married and moved to California. I climbed out of the car and approached the front door, not sure what kind of reception I'd get when he answered.

SEVENTEEN

Hudson opened the door before I had a chance to knock. "Hey, Lady," he said in his deep baritone drawl.

"Hey, Hudson." As we stood there, face to face, I knew my decision. It was as inconvenient as everything else in my life, but I knew. The clouds gathered overhead, and a clap of thunder sounded, followed by a flash of lightning. Pellets of rain started, first one, then two, then a downpour that plastered the oil baroness's ivory felt hat to my head.

Emotions overwhelmed me. Sadness, guilt, grief. I felt hot tears running down my cheeks but didn't know if Hudson could tell I was crying or if he thought I'd gotten caught in the downpour.

"Let's get you out of the rain," he said. He reached out for my arm and guided me into the hallway. The water that had accumulated on my blazer dripped onto the oriental carpet runner. I thrust my hands deep into the pockets and tried to figure out how to ask what I came here to ask without saying what I knew I had to say. Not yet. I wasn't ready yet.

"Can I get you some coffee? Tea?" he asked.

"Coffee," I said. I followed him into his kitchen. Packing boxes, some sealed, some open, sat in his dining room. I turned my head and noticed the paintings that used to hang in the hallway were now sitting on the shag carpet. When I turned back to Hudson, it was with unasked questions.

Hudson handed me a cup of coffee. "I already know why you're here, Madison. You're torturing yourself, and that speaks volumes. You say you haven't made a choice, but it's written all over your face. In a way, I've known all along."

"No," I said. I put my hand on his forearm. "That's not why I'm here."

A spark of hope appeared in his eyes, and he shifted his body toward me and put his other arm around my waist. I felt my body tense up. Hudson's hands dropped from me and he took a step back.

"Don't play games with me. That's all I ever asked. If you have any respect for me, then be honest and say what you came here to say."

I kept my hands wrapped around the warm coffee mug. "I'm the anonymous buyer," I said quietly.

Hudson stared at me. I tried to read the look on his face but couldn't. The words hung in the air until I couldn't stand the silence. "I should never have sold my old apartment building to you in first place and I suspect you bought it because you knew I'd regret letting it go. I asked the realtor to make an anonymous bid on the property for me because I was afraid of what you might read into my actions, but that doesn't feel right either. It's me, you know? And it's you. I wanted to be honest and tell you the truth."

"You're talking about the apartment building on Gaston," Hudson said slowly. This time I could read the expression on his face, and it wasn't relief.

"Yes. I need a property for the local design competition—"

"VIP, yes, I know all about it."

"Well, I was supposed to collaborate on an entry with Jane, but that didn't work out like I expected."

"That's right. You and she were close. I heard the news about her death last night. You must be taking it hard."

It was the one thing I didn't need to hear, because it made me feel like a fraud. The weight of pretending had left me spent, and I knew Hudson well enough to know he wouldn't judge me. I looked him directly in the eye. "Jane and I had a falling out the morning she was killed. I was there. I found her body. She sent me a nasty email that said in no uncertain terms she wanted nothing to do with me. We might have been friends for a short period of time, but by the time she was murdered, we weren't."

Hudson dropped into the chair. "What was in this email?"

"She pointed out my personality flaws. How I'm self-centered, I've embarrassed her in public, I think the world revolves around me..." Hudson's eyebrows went up. "What?" I asked.

"Well, you are a little self-centered." He smiled. "Look at this thing with me and Tex. All you have to do is make a decision and everybody moves on. But you didn't do that. You asked for six months, and we both gave it to you—not because it made sense, but because it's what you said you wanted. And now look at where we're at. You're in my living room, and you're decorating Tex's house."

"I agreed to decorate his house before any of this," I said. "It would have been unprofessional for me to back out of the job."

"Keep telling yourself that, Madison."

"Oh, come on, Hudson. Tex doesn't know what he wants. That's why he hired me."

Hudson's demeanor shifted from calm to thin on patience. "No, Madison, you're the one who doesn't know what you want," he said. The words stung.

The coffee had cooled, and the scent of freshly brewed dark roast invigorated me. I took a sip and set the cup back down. "I am self-centered, aren't I?"

He smiled. "I'm not saying it's a bad thing. It's part of what makes you unique. But I'd have to be blind not to see it."

"We've been together for a year and you never said anything about it."

"We haven't been that together."

I thought about that for a moment. "No, I guess we haven't."

Hudson's ornery black cat, Mortiboy, came into the kitchen and froze when he saw me. He stood still for a few seconds, and then resumed his path toward his bowl. Mortiboy and I had a history too, and I didn't think he'd ever forgive me for accidentally trapping him in my closet three years ago.

While Mortiboy crunched his food, Hudson and I lapsed into

silence. I drank more coffee. Hudson refilled his mug. They were the comfortable, lived in moments that I'd experienced when we were together in Palm Springs, the ones that made me feel like we'd been a couple forever. But today, an awkward weight hung over the moment, and it wasn't one hundred percent because of me.

"Why all the boxes?" I asked, trying to keep my voice light.

Hudson stared at the brown shipping containers stacked against the back wall. The outline of a star, tattooed on his neck, peeked above the collar of his long sleeved gray T-shirt. He appeared to be lost, trying to select the right words, and it was then that I knew he'd been grappling with his own sense of self in the middle of my drama. Hudson had left me once before. I'd been foolish not to suspect we'd find ourselves at this same intersection.

"My whole life, I made a living from what I could build with my hands," he said. "I paid cash for everything so I wouldn't go into debt. I don't even have a credit card. I know what people said about me, so I stayed away from places where they talked."

"That's your past, Hudson. That's all over."

He continued as if I hadn't spoken. "The thing is, I can't do that forever. There's going to come a point where I can't do contract work or construction or repair broken furniture. That time isn't yet, but it's soon."

"You're moving to California, aren't you?"

Hudson dropped back into the chair opposite me. He didn't say anything for a moment, and I wondered if he was thinking about everything that had led us here.

Twenty some years ago, Hudson had played Good Samaritan, only to find himself in the middle of a murder investigation. Lack of concrete evidence left him uncharged for the crime, but rumors around town closed a lot of doors in his face. When the dust settled two decades later and the truth came out, we all thought we'd move on. Enter a husband/wife team from Hollywood who negotiated with Hudson to buy the rights to his story.

"You know how I've been making trips from Palm Springs to Hollywood to meet with some studios about the pillow stalkings?"

"I knew you were, but you haven't mentioned it for a while. I thought maybe the deal fell through."

"The movie is in pre-production. Pretty soon the second unit director and his team are going to be in Dallas filming."

"They're filming here? Not on a backlot or in Vancouver? I heard all those movies were shot in Canada."

"The director went to school in Austin and he wants some local flavor. Establishing shots, location, etc." He studied his coffee mug for a moment. "Madison, this is my chance to change my life. To start over and be the person I could have been if things had been different back when I was twenty."

"You *are* that person, Hudson. Life didn't happen like you wanted, but you're still you. You've always been. You can move to California, but don't let that movie define you. You made a life for yourself by using your talent. Don't ignore that. Sure, you're getting older," I said. One side of his mouth turned up. "Oh, heck, we all are." Now I got a full-on smile. "But don't say you can't do what you do. You can. Start your own company. Train kids on woodworking and furniture restoration. Teach them your techniques. Be their mentor. That movie—that's not your legacy."

Hudson stared at his coffee mug, his thumb rubbing back and forth over a small, long-since smoothed over chip along the rim. His brows were pulled together, and I sensed he was wrestling with something difficult.

"Madison, there's something else I need to tell you," he said. I kept my eyes on his face. He looked up at me. "I didn't think it would be that big of a deal, but maybe I was wrong."

"What is it?"

"I sold the apartment building. Your apartment building. About a year ago, when I stayed behind in Palm Springs. I called a local realtor and asked him to find a buyer fast. My brother-in-law needed money to infuse into his development and that was the easiest way to get a lump sum."

"I don't understand. That was a year ago and there's a For Sale sign on it now. The realtor couldn't find a buyer?"

"The property sold before the listing went public. That's why I didn't say anything."

"But I put a bid on the property yesterday. The main reason I came here was to let you know so it wouldn't seem like I was doing it behind your back or avoiding you."

"Maybe the new owner changed his mind." Hudson shrugged. "I have to be honest. I thought he would have torn the place down by now."

"Who?"

"Sterling Webster. He's the guy who bought it from me."

EIGHTEEN

"Sterling Webster owns my apartment building?" I asked. I couldn't help feeling like I'd been played. Everywhere I turned, it was Sterling, Sterling, Sterling.

"You know Sterling?" Hudson asked.

"Oh, I know Sterling." I said. At his confused expression, I explained. "I mean, I don't *know* Sterling, but I know *of* Sterling. I know of his type. House flippers." I paused for a moment. "I can't believe my apartment building is just sitting there waiting for him to knock down."

"Technically it's not your apartment building."

"It *was* my building." Anger bubbled up inside me. I felt cheated by Hudson, but rationally I knew he didn't owe me anything. I'd sold him the building and from that point on he could do with it whatever he wanted. I just never expected he'd do whatever he did without telling me first.

"Well, like it or not, it seems as though I'm destined to do business with Sterling Webster," I said. It didn't matter if Kip had kept my name out of the offer. Sterling had known of my interest (and desperation) from the minute he'd shown up impersonating Kip.

I stood up. "I should be going."

Hudson stood too. He put his hand out and caught my forearm and, with a slight tug, pulled me toward him. There were a hundred small reasons that made me want to give in and be close to him, and one very big reason I resisted. My reaction told him what I wasn't yet willing to admit out loud.

We stood like that for a moment, Hudson's hand on my forearm and me maintaining the distance between us. "I don't think I can give you what you want," I said softly.

He smiled a bittersweet smile and hung his head a little lower. When he looked up, his amber eyes, flecked with gold under naturally thick black lashes, studied me. He said, "I don't think I can give you what you need."

"Goodbye, Hudson," I said. I put my own hand on top of his and squeezed his fingers and then turned around and left before the tears fell from my eyes.

I drove away from Hudson's house wondering if it was the last time I'd ever be there. There was no way out of my personal life drama without hurting one of two people who I cared about. Correction: one of the three people I cared about. Because in addition to Tex and Hudson, I cared about myself.

Which is why I pushed all thoughts of men from my mind and drove across town to Great American Hero for lunch. The sandwich shop had been a Dallas favorite since opening in 1974 and seemed to hold valuable the same love of the past that I did. I ordered a solid white albacore tuna hero and ate in a booth by the patio of plants. Less than a minute after I finished, the phone rang. I thought about ignoring it until I saw the caller was Hudson.

"Hey," I answered.

"Hey," he said. There was a pregnant pause, and then he spoke again. "Listen. You know how I said everything isn't about you?"

"Look, Hudson, I get it. I'm self-centered. Maybe I'm just not cut out for a relationship, okay? We don't have to do this."

"Madison!" he said sharply. "Listen to me. Two minutes after you left, somebody came looking for you. Detective Henning."

Pin prickles ran up my spine. "Why would he look for me at your place? Everybody who knows me knows we're on a break."

"Well, somebody tipped him off and I can guess who. It's probably the same person who wasn't all that happy to find me at your house two nights ago."

"Tex wouldn't."

"He would. It's a code of cops. If Detective Henning needed to find you and couldn't, he'd shake whatever trees he needed to shake to get the info, and Captain Allen isn't going to risk his job for that."

I didn't like what Hudson insinuated, but I had no evidence he was wrong. "What did Henning want?"

"He didn't say, but Lady, I got a bad feeling he didn't just want to talk." He was silent again. "Madison, are you in some kind of trouble?"

"I don't know," I answered honestly. I knew if I asked Hudson for help he'd give it, but that felt borderline manipulative and dependent, two things I didn't want to be. "Thank you for calling," I said and hung up.

Whatever Detective Henning wanted, he would have to wait. I didn't have any new information, and his need to keep checking up on me felt like a net was tightening regardless of the fact that I'd done nothing wrong.

I needed to work. Uninterrupted. This whole birthday thing had created a ticking time bomb and I needed a shelter where I could avoid being hit by the wreckage. I needed a safe zone where nobody could get to me, where I wouldn't be distracted by decisions and police investigations and computer viruses and vicarious friends and men.

Especially men.

And, oddly, I realized there was one place I could go where nobody would think to look for me. Jane Strong's business office.

Posh Pit was located in a small, converted post-war house in a part of town called Vickery Place. Sandwiched between houses that could accommodate a family, the small structure looked more like a dollhouse than an actual home. At less than a thousand square feet, with a low-pitched roof and prefab windows, it made more sense as an office than anything else.

Jane had converted the dining room to a desk for Vonda and used the living room for client meetings and design work. Her kitchen was outfitted with a juice bar and espresso machine, and her counter was lined with clear jars of colorful candies. The entire interior was done in shades of blue, red, and white, yellow, and black using a color blocked Mondrian-inspired aesthetic to give a cohesive feel. What not many of her clients knew was that, to save money, she lived out of the bedroom in the back instead of renting a separate property.

From the very first time I stepped foot inside Jane's office, I'd been taken by her overall color palette. Small spaces can easily be made to look even smaller by overcrowding walls and attempting to define open floorplans with varying paint colors and furniture choices. Jane's choice to decorate everything in primary colors unified the space. All the furniture, mismatched pieces from yard sales and thrift stores, had been painted with a high gloss white. Even the street-facing view reflected the theme with blue siding, shiny white trim, and red window boxes.

A long, narrow driveway led up to the attached garage on the right side of the house. As expected, the driveway was empty. I parked my car and approached the front door. A small pile of local newspapers was strewn across the yard, surrounded by dead brown leaves that had abandoned the branches on the trees overhead. I kept to the sidewalk and flipped through my keyring looking for the key Jane had given me months ago when we'd first exchanged them. The idea was that it would make things easier during our collaboration, and it had. It would also come in handy today.

Except, as it turned out, I didn't need Jane's key. The door to Posh Pit stood open. Odd, I thought.

I placed my white leather glove on the door and pushed.

"Vonda?" I called. There was no answer. I walked through Posh Pit to the back door. It, too, was unlocked, but there appeared to be no one here.

I returned to the studio portion of the building and sat behind Jane's desk. The studio looked like it was in use. A vase of purply-gray roses sat on the corner of the desk. Jane's Mondrian calendar was open to September. A white takeout coffee cup with Paxton's logo on it sat on the corner of the desk, and a recycled paper coffee cup holder sat inside the trash can under an accumulation of balled up yellow paper.

I hadn't thought through how to explain to Vonda why I'd come to Posh Pit, but her absence only solved one problem. If Jane's computer had been hacked like the rest of us, any attempt to work would be thwarted.

I switched on Jane's monitor and PC. The background, hex color #3399FF to match the blue Jane had used throughout the rest of the interior, glowed softly. Most people had a fair number of files saved to their desktops even if they backed up files elsewhere. On Jane's desktop, there was only one file folder, and it was marked "V-Day."

My memory flashed to what I knew about Jane. Not her decorating tastes or the jobs she'd applied for, not the posh vintage suits she wore or the signature color palette she used throughout her business. Her divorce from her overbearing husband Gerry Rose—which had taken place on Valentine's Day. Were these copies of her divorce papers? That had been eight months ago, before we'd met. Jane hadn't struck me as the sort of person who wanted to keep those files so accessible that she saved them to her desktop, especially when no other files were treated with the same level of importance.

Knowing full well that I was about to violate the privacy of a former friend, I clicked the folder. Inside was a file with my name on it, and inside that file were *my* files. The very same files that had been on my computer—and then missing from my computer.

It wasn't strange for Jane to have accessed my files. We'd set up a shared folder on cloud storage for the ease of collaboration. But these weren't in cloud storage. They were saved to her computer.

It took me a moment to realize there were far more files in her "Night" folder than we'd created. It took another moment to realize why the files I saw were so familiar, and it came from something Nasty had said when she explained how the personality virus worked. The virus duplicated the files on a computer and created a mirror image.

I was looking at a mirror image of my hard drive. And with alarm bells clanging in my head, the one thing I never considered became insanely obvious.

Jane Strong, recently murdered in the bathrooms of the DIDI offices at Republic Tower, was the person who had unleashed the computer virus on all other parties involved.

NINETEEN

I backed out of the copied computer files. I couldn't ignore the fact that Jane was behind the hackings of multiple businesses around town. I didn't know why, but that why might have been what had gotten her killed. Except the timing didn't make sense. The personality virus had been launched on my computer *after* she'd died. Had she hacked others before me? And one of them found out it was her and killed her? And if so, where were their files?

Before I could stop to think about what I was doing, I opened her browser and copied my files into the cloud storage we shared. I closed the windows and shut off her computer. As I was about to leave, I considered the open front door. The unlocked back door. The absence of Vonda.

Someone had been here. I glanced down at the terrazzo tiled floor. I'd closed the front door behind me, but a puddle of water had collected inside. Whoever had been here had been here recently.

Avoiding Detective Henning at this stage was reckless.

I pulled out my phone to call him. But first, I stood in the center of the room and made a video while slowly turning in a circle. It was a trick I'd incorporated in decorating jobs. Sometimes having a video of a room in the pre-renovation or mid-renovation stage could help me identify something that seemed out of place or if I were headed in the right direction. I made two full rotations while filming the room, just to make sure I got everything, and then switched to my keypad and called Detective Henning. "This is Madison Night," I said. "I'm at Jane Strong's house. The front door was open when I arrived, but nobody is here."

I heard tapping on a keyboard, and then the detective spoke. "The only address we have on Ms. Strong is Posh Pit in Vickery Place."

"Yes, that's it. She lives here. Lived. It's her home and her business."

"I'm on my way," he said and then disconnected.

There was no doubt that making that phone call had been the right thing, but I wasn't used to making phone calls like that to a cop I didn't know. Tex would have told me to leave, or to stay, or to do—or not do—*something*. But what now? I'd entered easily because the front door was open, and I'd gone so far as to use Jane's computer. In terms of evidence—

I was still wearing my gloves. There would be no evidence of what I'd touched or where I'd gone. Henning never had to know I'd been inside.

I waited in my car. I'd done nothing illegal. The downpour had stopped temporarily, but the color of the sky indicated the rain would be back before long.

And it did. The rain started back up about a minute later. I leaned back against the seats, watching fat droplets aggressively pelt the windshield. The world outside of my car faded to dull gray, a bland color that would never be used in the world of mid-century decorating. I closed my eyes and focused on the white noise of drops falling around me, but despite my desire for peace, my mind would not shut down.

I would never have the opportunity to ask Jane about the motivation behind sending that nasty email, or to give us enough time to one day put it all in the rearview mirror of life and become friends again. There would be no water under the bridge for Jane and me.

And when I thought about it like that, I saw things differently. The email had come from Jane's computer. The virus had come from Jane's computer. Maybe she'd been trying to distance herself from me, not because she'd been that offended by my actions, but for another reason. Maybe Jane had known she was in danger. And maybe, just maybe, she'd thought she could handle that danger herself. I'd certainly thought the very same thing about myself on more than one occasion.

And then it hit me, the person who Jane trusted more than anybody else. Vonda Quinn, her beleaguered right hand. Who had control of her computer, who had the keys to Posh Pit, and who knew about the email. Vonda had been in Jane's inner circle far longer than I had. But was I just grasping at straws? What possible reason could Vonda have for wanting to murder her boss?

The sounds of the rain drowned out all other exterior noises, which was why the knock on my window scared me as much as it did. I opened my eyes and looked out. A figure in plastic rain gear over a topcoat stood outside my car under an umbrella. I rolled the hand crank of my car window about a foot and recognized Detective Henning.

"Detective," I said.

"Ms. Night," he replied. "I wasn't sure if I'd find you here."

"I assumed you'd want me to wait."

He nodded. The wind shifted the rain, and I watched the now-diagonal drops pummel Henning's clear plastic poncho. He removed his hat and shook a buildup of water from the plastic covering and then put it back on. "I'd like to ask you a couple more questions. Will you stick around?"

"Sure," I said. "I'm happy to cooperate."

He nodded again and then headed toward the front door. I rolled up my window and called Effie.

"Madison!" she said. "I'm so glad you called me. Everybody is looking for you. What is going on?"

I wasn't yet sure it was a good idea to talk about what I'd seen on Jane's computer. I turned my back on Posh Pit and Detective Henning and focused on the conversation.

"After that greeting, I'd say that should be my question. Who's looking for me?"

"That detective was here. And Kip Bledsoe stopped by to turn over a set of keys to our old apartment building. He said the owner accepted your bid without any questions. And Nasty brought me a check, and the florist delivered a dozen roses, and the detective came by again—"

"Who sent me roses?" I asked. It was the least important part of Effie's rundown of the day's activities, but I'd already known or expected the other information.

"I don't know. Did you make your decision? Can I open the card? Ohmigod, this is so exciting. I hope you chose Hudson!"

This was getting out of hand. And when I thought about what might be written on that card, the only thing I was certain of was that I wanted to be the first (maybe only) one to read it. "Effie, I'm going to be tied up for the rest of the day. Do me a favor? Drop the roses off at Thelma Johnson's house. You can leave them on the porch if I'm not there."

"Okay," she said. The disappointment was evident in her voice.

We rounded out the conversation with a dictated list of what Effie needed to acquire before we could start working on the apartment building. Nasty's check, though completely unexpected, would make a big difference in our timetable. "We're going to need a lot of paint. Six gallons per apartment. Eleven apartments, so that's sixty-six gallons of paint and thirty-three gallons of primer."

"Hold on," Effie said. There was a *klunk*! And then she was back. "Sorry, dropped the receiver. You really need a speaker phone, Madison."

"I like my donut phone just fine. Call Mitchell at Paintin' Place and have him start mixing the colors." I stared at the water beating on the windshield and did the math. "We're going to use the four colors I endorsed for him. Get started priming and painting eleven of the units. Leave the front left one untouched."

"Why?" Effie corrected.

"I'm going to convert it into a clubroom for residents to use. That's going to involve some demolition." I wiped the condensation off the inside window and looked at the front door. There was no sign of the detective, but an unexpected stream of red water running next to the white siding of the building caught my eye. "Tell you what. I'll text you a shopping list."

"Sure, Boss," Effie said.

We hung up. I tapped out a list and sent it to Effie, and then rolled the window crank down and looked at the house. Initially I thought the water appeared red from the reflection of the window boxes, but that didn't make sense.

I opened the car door and ran to the overhang. As I shielded my eyes from the sheet of rain, I had a clear path of vision of the red stream coming from the opposite side of the building. While it was possible that there were window boxes there as well, I couldn't ignore the sense of unease. I stepped gently on the uneven wet soil, with one hand on the building, until I reached the other side.

And as it turned out, my fears were accurate. On the far side of the building, laying in a gully of mulch now saturated with inconvenient late September rains tinged with blood, was the body of Jane's assistant, Vonda Quinn.

TWENTY

I dropped onto the wet ground next to Vonda and pressed my fingers into her neck. There was a pulse! Faint, but present. But before I could feel relief, a dark, red substance transferred onto my hand. I lifted Vonda's head from the ground and found the wound behind her right ear. As the water dripped down from the gutter, it rushed past her, washing her blood away with it. I pulled off my now wet blazer and draped it over her head. "Detective!" I yelled. The shower drowned out my voice. "Detective Henning!"

"Ms. Night."

I turned around. Henning stood a few feet behind me. He quickly took in the body in front of me and then pulled me out of the way and dropped down next to Vonda. He pulled a white handkerchief out of the pocket of his coat and pressed it into Vonda's head to staunch the bleeding. With his other hand he checked her pulse like I did and then pulled out his phone and called for help.

Slowly, I backed away from both Vonda and Henning. My loafer sank into the wet ground and my footing was unstable. I almost lost my balance twice, wrenching my body and sending pain shooting through my formerly injured knee.

"Ms. Night, do not leave," Henning said. It was less request than command.

I nodded once. Vonda's body told me so many things I didn't want to know. She'd been struck on the head, just like Jane. Was it by the same person?

I waited in my car. A flood of uniformed officers and other

emergency personnel arrived at Posh Pit. Their rehearsed management of the crime scene was only mildly impeded by the rain.

Detective Henning approached the driver's side window of my car. I cracked the window. "Considering the circumstances, I'm going to need you to come with me to the stationhouse," he said.

"The circumstances..." I repeated, hoping he'd elaborate.

"Ms. Night, there are a few too many questions surrounding your relationship to Ms. Strong and Ms. Quinn. I'd like you to come with me so we can try to get some answers."

"I have my car. I'd be happy to follow."

The detective looked over my shoulder. "You're parked in."

I looked behind me. The narrow driveway was filled with emergency vehicles, police cars, and the detective's sedan parked. "I'd prefer if you rode with me," he added.

In that moment, I knew my circumstances were dire. "Sure," I said. "Let me get my handbag and lock up first." I rolled up the window and turned away from the detective. I felt trapped though I'd done nothing wrong. I sent a quick text to Effie asking her to get help moving my car back to Mad for Mod and then scooped my bag from the passenger-side floor mat and locked up. Henning had remained close to the car—a precaution in case I tried to get away? I forced a smile to my face and followed him to his sedan. He unlocked the back door and I climbed in.

Nothing about the circumstance felt friendly.

The door slammed. I tried to open it but couldn't. A barrier was in place between the front and back seats. Henning could pretend this was a technicality all he wanted, but in the span of five minutes, he'd made it clear that I had no choices in the foreseeable future.

I was silent on the drive to the police station. Henning hadn't said I was under arrest or in custody. He hadn't read me my rights. That meant something. It meant that, while he may have strong suspicions about my involvement in his case, strong enough to detain me, he didn't have the support of a judge or a warrant. He was inconveniencing me, which was well within the scope of his job as the investigating officer of a homicide, but unless he had concrete evidence against me, he could only inconvenience me for so long.

We arrived at the downtown Dallas police station. Henning parked and got out of the car and unlocked my door. I climbed out. I was thoroughly wet, thanks to removing my blazer to protect Vonda's body. The activity surrounding the new crime scene at Posh Pit had distracted me, but right now, I was cold to my core.

Henning led me through electronically controlled gates that were attached to fences topped with curly razor wire. We entered heavy steel doors that locked behind us. The interior of the police station was filled with officers in uniforms and men and women in suits. Curious glances came our way. I scanned faces quickly, hoping to read from their expressions what they were thinking about me.

They don't call it cop face for nothing.

A constant level of noise bounced off the walls and floor, crackling of police radios and arguments from rooms not visible. A man in an orange jumpsuit with CONVICT stenciled on the back in black letters mopped the floor by the outside of a small jail cell. I'd been to the Lakewood Police Department to visit with Tex numerous times and it had never felt like this. My senses were heightened, and the loss of my freedoms was palpable.

"Ms. Night," Henning said. "Officer Doyle will sign you in and hold onto your personal items." He nodded toward a fortyish woman behind a counter.

"Is that necessary?" I asked.

"Yes."

Alrighty-then. I handed my purse to the woman. She set it in a metal basket and pulled out a form. We went through a lightning round of name, address, and occupation before she took my purse and asked me to sign the form. The font was too small to make out without my reading glasses but the line for my signature was easy to spot.

"Detective Henning," she called out. "I'm all done."

Henning approached us and took a plastic package from Officer Doyle. With the slightest pressure on the back of my arm, he directed me down a hallway into a small, white room. Two chairs were facing each other next to a four-foot table. Henning set a stack of files on the chair closer to the door and I lowered myself into the other one. Even with the illusion of choice, there was none. He tore open the plastic package, pulled out a blanket, and handed it to me. I was too cold to pretend not to want it.

"Ms. Night," Henning started. "I know you aren't a stranger to police procedure. Do you understand why you're here?"

"I understand you want to talk to me about Jane Strong. I've been nothing but cooperative since I found her body. I'm happy to answer any lingering questions, but I've already told you everything I know."

He nodded along with me as if he understood how I felt. "How about we start with what I know?" he said. Before I could answer, he continued. "I know you and Jane Strong weren't as close as other people seem to think. I know you had no legal right to enter her place of business today. I don't know what it was you were looking for, but I'll figure that out."

"Me? I wasn't looking for anything," I said. "Jane and I were supposed to collaborate on a project. I went there to retrieve our files."

"Ms. Night, I think it's time I cut to the chase. I have witnesses that put you every place I need you to be in order to build a case against you for Ms. Strong's murder."

"There were no witnesses," I said. His expression changed, and I backpedaled. "What I mean is we were alone. The DIDI offices were closing for the night. The receptionist left right after I dropped off my application. When I went looking for help, there was no one."

"I have a witness that places you in the building," the detective said.

Immediately my mind flew to Delbert Manning, the security

officer.

"Talk to the security guard," I said. "He knows I left for a few hours and came back."

"Ms. Night. I have witnesses that places you on the twenty-third floor, in the powder room, at the time Jane Strong was murdered."

"Detective Henning, I appreciate the lengths you've gone through to put a scare into me, but whatever it is you expect to gain, you won't. You know what I know. Someone wanted Jane Strong dead and it wasn't me."

"I think you're lying," he said. He stood up. "I'm going to leave you alone to think about what you might know, and maybe when I come back you'll be ready to talk."

"And if I have nothing to say? You can't keep me here against my will, and you haven't read me my rights so I'm not under arrest."

"Actually, you signed away those rights with Officer Doyle." He leaned close and smiled. "It pays to read the fine print, Ms. Night."

TWENTY-ONE

There were no clocks in my little room. No indication of the passage of time. No offers of a cold soft drink or pop-in checks to see if I'd cracked. Whatever game Henning was playing, I was simply along for the ride. And sadly, since my knowledge of what was to happen to me at this stage in his game was limited to what I'd learned from movies and television, I knew my knowledge came at the expense of reality. So I waited. And waited. And waited.

When the door to my small room opened, it wasn't Detective Henning on the other side. It was Officer Clark. I'd forgotten that he transferred to this station but was overjoyed to see a familiar face. I stood up and threw my arms around him. Awkwardly, he patted my back until I let go.

"What's happening?" I asked. "Is Detective Henning coming back? Am I being booked for something? Henning wouldn't tell me anything. Can you tell me what's going on?"

"Come with me," Clark said.

I followed Clark through the hallway to the front desk. Officer Doyle had been replaced by another officer, this one a portly Mexican who looked about the size of Clark before his weight loss. His nametag said Martinez. He had my handbag next to him along with a copy of the paper I'd signed.

"Sign at the bottom," he said.

"I'd like a copy of that paperwork before I leave."

Martinez looked at Clark, who shrugged. "Sure," Martinez said. I signed the paperwork and Martinez pushed my handbag toward me. I pulled out my phone. Dead.

Martinez fed the paper through the copier behind him and handed me the duplicate. "Souvenir?" he asked.

I gave him a tight smile. "I doubt I'll need a souvenir to remember today. Good night, officer." I pulled the blanket from around my shoulders, dumped it onto the counter, and followed Clark out front. A small black Ford Focus with the Lyft logo on the inside windshield was idling in a visitor space by the front door. I turned to Clark, not sure what to say.

"That's my buddy. He'll take you home." He pointed to the car. "Henning went to the judge to get a warrant for your arrest, but the network is still sluggish from all the new antivirus software. Technically Henning can hold you for up to twenty-four hours, but if that warrant doesn't come in during that time, he blows any credibility he might have with a jury. You better leave while you can."

"I can just leave?"

Clark looked uncomfortable. "You were here voluntarily. You could have left at any time."

"That's not how it felt."

"That's not how it's supposed to feel." Clark looked down at his feet and then back up at me. "The hacker has everybody freaked out." He pointed to the police station over his shoulder with his thumb. "This whole place runs on computers now. Everybody does. If we get hit, who knows what could happen."

"But you use keys to lock the cells, right? It's not like the doors would pop open and the prisoners could walk out."

He dropped his voice. "We need every cell we have for convicted criminals. You got lucky tonight, but I don't know how long your luck is going to last."

"Detective Henning said something about a witness. There's no point denying that I was at Republic Tower, because I was, but who fingered me? I thought the building was empty."

"Building security was there. So was the head of the DIDI, Gerry Rose."

"He's the one who carried Jane down to the lobby. He's her ex-husband. Why is he without suspicion?"

"Surveillance camera in his office shows he was at his desk the entire time. The guy who owns the coffee shop under the store verified it too. Said he closed up early so he could deliver a decaf latte to Rose's office before he left."

"Paxton was there?"

"He didn't want to implicate you," Clark said. "You didn't hear this from me, but he mentioned seeing you on his way into the DIDI offices and Henning went after that detail. Paxton tried to backpedal but Henning didn't give him a choice."

"Yes, Henning does seem to have a one-track mind."

"It's not Henning. It's the way investigation works. There are a lot of clues pointing your direction."

"Do you think I killed Jane Strong?" I asked.

"No, ma'am." I smiled at that small victory and approached the black Focus. "Madison," Clark called out behind me. I turned and waited while he came closer. "There was somebody else."

"Who?"

"Henning's not saying. But he has a witness who placed you inside the ladies' room at the exact moment Jane was murdered."

I froze, my hand on the top of the car door, one foot on the floor board. The ladies' room had been empty, or so I'd thought. I'd written off the closed bathroom stall door to an out-of-order commode. I'd looked under it for feet and had kicked on the door to see if someone could have gotten help. There had been no answer. But if someone really had been in that stall, then she not only knew I hadn't killed Jane, but she very well might have been the one to do the deed herself. Which gave her a very good motive to lie about me.

The Lyft driver dropped me off at Thelma Johnson's house about fifteen minutes later. The ride had been conversation-free, something I hadn't realized I wanted. I thanked Clark's friend and climbed out. His taillights had faded into the darkness before I reached my front porch steps.

It was after eleven. I'd forgotten all about the flowers Effie had dropped off on the doorstop until I saw them. Soft, grayish lilac roses, splayed out in a cut crystal vase with ferns and baby's breath. I unlocked the door and Rocky raced outside. He bumped the vase and it tipped precariously. I bent down and caught it before it fell. The card jiggled loose and landed by the toe of my muddy brown loafers.

With the neck of the vase in one hand, I scooped the card up with the other. Rocky, who must have expected me home hours ago, ran directly to the corner of the garden and did what he needed to do. When finished, he took off into the yard and ran to the Japanese maple and back several times. He'd had the run of the house interior all day, but I didn't reign him in. Freedom felt more precious than usual tonight.

As Rocky raced around in the dark, I set the flowers down and opened the card. The message inside sent a splinter of cold fear directly down my spine.

Hope you decorate better than you negotiate – Sterling

I stared at the words on the card and then anger bubbled up within me. Sterling Webster, the cocky house-flipping jerk. The man Hudson had sold the building to without telling me. The man Tex was silently backing in a competition against me. The man who pretended to be Kip in order to play a joke on me. The man who'd written the manipulative letter to *The Dallas Morning News* about the tragedy of Jane's death that would sway the judges in his favor.

I snapped.

I screamed, the sound piercing the dark, still night. I picked up the glass vase with the purple roses and slammed it onto the patio. The glass shattered on impact. The violent act felt good but only took a slight edge off my anger. I needed to break something else.

Outside of Thelma Johnson's house was a set of storm doors that led down to a cellar turned fallout shelter. The house was built in 1925, and what had started out as a naturally cool place to store pickled jars of food had turned into possible protection from the threat of an atomic bomb. Texas soil was soft and didn't allow for the most stable of cellars, but when this house was built, the architect had seen fit to pour concrete in a level below the house and stabilized the space with thick, wooden beams.

None of that mattered to me tonight. What mattered was what I'd found the first time I'd explored that part of the property. Thelma Johnson liked, among other things, to grow and bottle tomatoes. And she'd done her work in the quiet cellar. When the house transferred to me, I'd inherited a wall of empty, dusty mason jars waiting to fulfill their tomato-storing destiny.

Screw tomatoes.

I flung the storm doors open and climbed down the concrete stairs. A single lightbulb overhead threw off enough illumination for me to find the wall of jars. I grabbed as many as I could and slammed them onto the concrete slab floor. *Crash! Crash! Crash!*

Before long, the shelves were more empty than full, and I was surrounded by sharp pieces of the wreckage. It was that moment that I realized I wasn't alone.

TWENTY-TWO

The silhouette of a man, backlit by the moon, stood on the stairs that descended into the cellar. Even with his face in shadow, I knew it was Tex. My anger was mostly spent, but he was the last person I wanted to see, and I told him in so many words.

"Get off my property," I said. "I've had a very bad night and I don't particularly want to talk to you."

"Too bad, because you don't really have a choice."

"Oh yeah?" I said. I moved toward him crushing pieces of glass under my feet and pushed him out of the way. Rocky sat on the porch step. I opened the front door and after the furry rascal and I were both inside, I locked the door behind me.

Tex pounded on the door frame. "Open up and let me in," he demanded.

"Why should I let you in? You're not even supposed to be here."

He rattled the door frame again. "I'm not playing, Night. Open up."

I glared at him through the glass. "No," I said. "I've had enough of you and your kind to last me a lifetime. You want things from me just like everybody else. Things I can't give you."

"Night, you're fifty. I figure the ship has already sailed on your virginity."

Oooooooh! I opened the door.

"I knew I could get you to let me in," Tex said with a grin.

"You're not coming in, but that comment deserves a response."

"What's that?"

I slammed the door in his face.

Tex opened the door and followed me into my kitchen. "There's a certain honesty in a slammed door. God knows I probably deserved more of them than I got."

"Go away, Captain. I don't want you here."

"Well, see, Mrs. Yoder called in a disturbance from next door. And it's my job as a cop to check it out and make sure everybody is okay." He set a large flat box on my kitchen table and knelt down to ruffle Rocky's fur. "Are you okay, little fella? The big mean lady in the funny outfit didn't tell *you* to go away, did she?"

Rocky yipped.

"It won't work, so just stop it. Stop being nice to me, stop being nice to my dog."

"You really want to be alone? Because I'll leave. I just came by to drop off your birthday present."

"You gave me six months of peace. That's what I wanted."

"I decided that was a dumb idea, so I got you something respectable to wear in public."

"You bought me clothes? Are you insane? Get out!"

Tex turned around and headed to the door. He appeared to think twice about leaving and turned back toward me. "I'm not looking for love in all the wrong places. I'm done with that. I have a life. I have a *good* life. I have Wojciehowicz and a cold beer waiting for me when I get home every night. Tell you the truth, I'm even learning to like the lilac and yellow spare bedroom."

We stared at each other. Everything Tex said was negated by the fact that he was a silent investor in Sterling Webster's VIP entry. I knew he was entitled to do whatever he wanted to do with his money, but tonight the battle of the sexes was too much for me to handle.

"I can't do this," I said.

"Night, I don't know what's going on with you. I don't know what triggered that outburst in your storm cellar, but I do know one thing. You have a darkness in you, just like me. A need for justice. I don't know if you had it before you moved here from Pennsylvania or not, but it's there. I'm a cop. On some level, I want to save people. And if I can save you from that darkness, then I'm good."

"I'm only one person."

"That's enough for me."

It was the most unexpected thing he could have said, and it broke my heart to say what I had to say next.

"I don't trust you anymore," I said quietly. I braced myself for Tex's reaction. Rocky, who seemed confused by the tension in the room, ran back and forth between our ankles trying to get someone to pay attention to him.

I raised my eyes from Rocky to Tex. The lines of his face were hard, his jawline rigid. He turned around and grabbed the box he'd set on the kitchen table and left, this time slamming the door behind him without my help.

I turned back in to the cheerful yellow kitchen and stomped through the living room to the stairs. I was halfway up when I heard the front door slam again.

Adrenaline from the fight with Tex mutated to fear. I ran the rest of the way up the stairs and secured Rocky in the bedroom. Footsteps sounded after me. I turned around as Tex advanced toward me.

"Sterling Webster sent you roses? Are you kidding me? You're supposed to be deciding between me and Hudson James, not entertaining a third option. This is like a bad episode of Moonlighting."

"What are you still doing here? Get out!" I said.

He reached the landing and pointed his finger in my face. "You owe me an explanation and I'm not leaving until I get it."

"I am so mad at you right now I could hit you."

"Assaulting a police officer." He shook his head. "Not a good idea, Night. That's the kind of thing that could get you arrested."

My eyes went wide. "What do you know about me being arrested? Hudson was right. You *do* have a cop code. You helped Henning. I can't believe anything you say every again!"

Tex's eyes flashed midnight blue, pupils dilated. "I don't know what you're talking about. I don't know why you won't trust me. What I know is there's a dozen sterling roses strewn about your patio. Only one person I know sends sterling roses to his conquests and that's Sterling Webster. That man is a player, Night. Don't let him play you."

I slapped his hand away from my face. "I bet you know all about Sterling Webster. Two peas in a pod, right? Just like me and Jane. Well, guess what. I already know the truth, Tex. You're *just like* Sterling. You're so like Sterling you're his silent partner! Well, I have a silent partner too and if you think I can't play dirty, just you watch me."

I did a one-eighty and went into the closed bedroom. Aside from the dent Rocky had left in the middle of the comforter, my bed hadn't been slept in for two days. The mere sight of it, quilted pink cotton coverlet with scalloped edges, gingham pillow shams, white pillows trimmed in lilac, yellow, pink, aqua, and mint green ribbons, was like being told I could have ice cream after I finished my homework.

Unfortunately, my homework followed me into the room. "What are you talking about?" Tex asked.

"Cut the innocent act. I know you invested in Sterling Webster's VIP entry. You're the competition, Tex. But you didn't tell me. You went behind my back and kept it a secret and I never would have known if your computer hadn't been hacked."

The expression on Tex's face changed from frustration and anger to confusion. "Where did you hear that?"

"It doesn't matter. All that matters, right now, is that I don't think I can do this. You and me. Every single time I think there's the tiniest chance we can find common ground, something like this happens. I'm too old, too tired, and too stuck in my ways to change, so just leave me alone."

"I can't do that, Night."

"Why not?"

"Whoever's been feeding you information just brought me into their game. You said you don't trust me, but who's your source,

Night? I have no ties to Sterling Webster other than a couple of bar tabs we split back in the nineties. I sure would like to talk to the person who told you I did."

TWENTY-THREE

"You swear on the graves of your family members in Greenwood Cemetery that you aren't a silent partner in Sterling Webster's VIP entry?" I asked Tex.

"Is that really necessary?"

"Considering the day I've had? Yes."

Tex pulled out his wallet and opened it up to his detective badge. He set the wallet face up on the corner of my bed. "I don't like swearing on graves. Bad juju." He pointed at his badge. "I swear on that and you of all people know what that signifies to me."

I sank down onto my bed and looked up at him. "Sit down, Tex. I have a lot to tell you."

His eyes moved from me to the bed and back to me. "Maybe we should move to a different room."

The adrenaline and the fight and the nervous energy that had kept me going for the past twenty-four hours eeked out of my system. A single fat tear formed in the corner of my eye and spilled onto my cheek. I kept my head tipped down because I didn't want Tex to see me cry, but when the droplet fell from my chin and landed on my rumpled cream turtleneck, I could no longer hide it.

He sat down and put his arm around my shoulders. "What's going on, Night?"

I stared at the floor. "When did life get so complicated? Every day, I do battle. I count on people and they let me down."

Tex turned me toward him and wiped the residue from my cheek. He put both arms around me and pulled me close and I rested my head on his shoulder. "I make a friend, she's murdered. I try to have a relationship and it fizzles out. I call the police to report a possible break-in at Posh Pit and I end up in an interrogation room while a detective tries to get a judge to issue a warrant for my arrest."

Tex's arms stiffened. He shifted his hands to my upper arms and separated us enough to see my face. "You were arrested?"

"I was taken in for questioning. It wasn't official, but it sure didn't feel like having dinner with a friend."

"Henning?"

I nodded. "He knows everything. He knows Jane and I had a fight, and he said he can't verify my alibi, and he has two witnesses who place me in that powder room with her when she died."

"Where did Henning find you? When he called me earlier today, he was out of leads."

"He called you? What did you tell him?"

"I told him I hadn't talked to you for the past five months and twenty-three days and couldn't help him out." Tex's eyes moved from my face to my clothes, rumpled from the rain saturation and subsequent air-dry-and-prison-blanket one-two punch. He looked back at me. "You were held in a police facility and you didn't call me."

"I was mad at you."

He stood up. "You said you don't trust me. When you think you're past that, let me know. We have a lot to talk about." He walked to the door.

"'Moonlighting'?" I said to his back as he was halfway through the door. "Ninety-five percent of the public wouldn't get that reference."

He turned around and grinned. "You did."

"I'm special." I smiled, my first genuine smile in days, while he stood in the doorway staring back at me. Neither of us said a word for several seconds.

"Don't worry, Night. It's going to be okay." He pulled the door shut behind him.

I'd hoped a shower would reinvigorate me, but it had the

opposite effect. I climbed out and dried off, wrapped my head in a towel and slipped on fresh undies and an Olympic blue track suit I'd acquired from the estate of Ingrid Vitalis. She'd been an alternate on the 1964 USA Olympic Track and Field team, and amongst her belongings, I'd found the blue zip-front track jacket with USA stitched on in red and white and matching elastic waist pants. My own style ran along more feminine lines. Thanks to a torn ACL several years ago and a string of follow-up injuries before the joint had a chance to heal properly, running wasn't part of my routine. But tonight, I wanted to channel the athlete's physical strength. Yet despite the best of intentions, I fell asleep on top of my pink coverlet before I had a chance to pull on a matching pair of tube socks.

I woke to bright, uninterrupted sunlight streaming through my bedroom curtains. I was under the covers and the towel that I'd wrapped over my hair was wedged under my neck. A vague sense of unease tickled at the fringes of my now-fading dreams, until I realized my dreams had nothing to do with it. The memories I'd hoped were nightmares were real. I flung back the covers and got up, pushed my feet into fluffy white faux fur slippers, and descended the stairs. Tex was on my sofa. Rocky was with him. My laptop was on the table in front of Tex and a stack of handwritten notes were taped to the wall. The two paintings that normally hung there were propped in front of an old, tube TV that still required rabbit ears to get acceptable reception.

"You came back," I said.

"I never left," he said. He glanced up at me and did a double take.

"What?" I asked.

"Nothing. Just never saw you do the Sporty Spice thing before."

"Just when you thought you knew me too." I went to the kitchen and poured coffee into an empty white mug that sat on the counter, carried an owl-shaped trivet and the electric pot into the living room, and refreshed Tex's cup. "What's all this?" I asked.

"I should ask you the same question," he said. He turned the laptop toward me. The screen was open to the cloud storage and displayed numerous file folders. I immediately recognized them as my own, the very same files that had been wiped from the computer yesterday.

I sat down next to him and, using the touch pad, opened and closed the folders. I turned to Tex. "These folders were empty yesterday. I thought the hacker wiped my hard drive."

"These are your files?"

I nodded. "Effie—you remember her, right? College girl who used to live in the apartment building I owned?" This time he nodded. "She's doing what she can to update the way I do business. Six months ago, she convinced me to move my files to the cloud and move my inventory to an online database. I would have thought you'd be impressed by my willingness to modernize." I wrapped my hands around the mug and took a tentative sip.

"Cloud storage is a good idea. That's not what I'm asking about." He tapped the screen. "I want to know how you got this."

"Hold on," I said. I stood up and scanned the room until I spotted a pair of reading glasses on the hutch. I retrieved them and pointed to Tex. "No cracks about my age."

Tex's lack of joke at my expense threw me off. I sat back down next to him and leaned closer to the screen, and that's when I realized why he wasn't cracking jokes.

The file Tex was looking at was in the folder I'd forwarded from Jane Strong's computer. Alongside client files and mood boards was a file marked "V-Day Is Coming." I double clicked the file. A spreadsheet opened. Along the top it said, "Viruses Launched." Below the title was a list of names and corresponding numbers, both mine and Tex's among them.

"Those are IP addresses, aren't they?" I asked Tex.

"Yep."

"A hacker needs an IP address to target a specific computer, don't they?"

"It's one way to get in."

"Which means that could be a list of the computers that were hacked. Right?"

"Night, at what point are you going to tell me why this list is on your computer?"

I stared at the screen while information clicked together. The reality struck me like the copper clapper of a church bell. "I copied those files from Jane Strong's computer at Posh Pit," I said. "But Jane was dead before the hackings started. And her assistant was attacked and is in the hospital. Somebody used Jane's connection to VIP to tag the rest of us and then they killed her."

"Back up. Jane's assistant is in the hospital? How do you know that?"

I sighed. "Make room for me. I've got a lot to tell you before we get to that, and I'd rather be comfortable." Now that I was back to trusting Tex, the idea of confiding in him felt cathartic.

He shifted to the right and I sat down. "I'm not sure where to start. I think this all connects back to the VIP competition. You said you already knew all about that, right?"

"Tell me why you thought I was Sterling Webster's partner. I want to know who's spreading rumors about me."

"It's not as simple as that."

"This is no time to protect your source, Night. Whoever told you that was lying to turn you against me and I want to know why."

I stood up and got my phone, and I tapped the screen until I found the picture Nasty had shared with me. "Brace yourself, because you're the one who sent this particular truth to my door." I handed him my phone.

He magnified the screen and moved the enlarged image around a few times. I saw the tips of his ears turn red and his jaw clench. "Nasty?"

I nodded. "She came to Mad for Mod to tell me why she was at your apartment. She said the note she left on your nightstand had to do with removing the virus from your computer, not...not what it looked like it had to do with." I took my phone back from Tex. "She took this screenshot. It's pretty obvious you gave Sterling Webster twenty thousand dollars to invest in his entry."

"Night, I haven't given that man a dime."

"Then where did this come from? It's a clear paper trail that leads back to you. Unless…"

"What?"

"Nasty told me the personality virus creates backdoor access to a computer. She explained how it works like this: the virus makes a mirror image of the computer's hard drive and then slowly steals the copies, not the original. So even if you detect the virus and get rid of it, the person who launched it still has everything they duped. But what if she was wrong?"

"Nasty's not usually wrong about stuff like that."

"That's not what I mean." I thought for a moment about how to explain my suspicion. "You know how in caper movies they show the criminals making a recording of the surveillance feed and then they patch it over the regular surveillance feed in a loop? What if whoever is watching the cameras thinks things are normal while really criminals are running around robbing a bank?"

"Those are movies. Nothing to do with real life."

"I'm not talking about the plot device, I'm talking about the principle. What if the virus did everything Nasty said it did, but it left the *copy* on the original hard drive so everything looked normal, while giving the hacker full backdoor access to the original files? That would let someone manipulate all sorts of things between computers, right?"

Tex looked angry. "Right."

"But why would somebody want to hack into a bunch of decorator databases? We're not known for our criminal tendencies."

"Speak for yourself," Tex said. He launched an internet window and accessed a police bulletin that under normal circumstances I'd have no reason to see.

The headline of the page said everything I needed to know.

Hacker's Interference in Police Database Corrupts Pending Case Files.

I looked from the computer to Tex. "Somebody connected to the VIP competition has something to hide."

TWENTY-FOUR

Tex handed me my phone. "Call Nasty and get her over here. I want to know what she knows too."

The last person I ever thought I'd invite into my house was Officer Nasty, but desperate times called for desperate measures. I picked up my cell phone and left the room.

"Where are you going?" Tex asked.

"You don't need to hear this conversation." I headed toward the door and Rocky got up from his spot by Tex's feet and followed me. I made him wait in the solarium, closing the storm door behind me. Yes, I wanted privacy to call Nasty, but I also wanted to deal with the mess of broken glass I'd made last night before Rocky's tender paws had a chance to come into contact with it.

But there was no mess. The broken vase I expected to find scattered about the patio, the thorny lilac roses, and the ferns and baby's breath had all been cleared. I approached the black trash receptacle and lifted the lid. Plastic bags, knotted off at the top, sat inside. I lifted the top one and heard glass shards shift against each other. Someone had cleaned up after me, and from the looks of things, that someone was Tex. I glanced up at the kitchen window and saw him watching me. I smiled my thanks and he nodded once.

My turn to return the favor. I turned my back on him and called Nasty.

"Big Brother Security," she answered.

"It's Madison." I waited for a response.

"I'm kind of busy here. What do you want?"

Yep, about the response I expected. "More hackings?"

"Yeah. At this rate I'll be driving a Lamborghini by Christmas."

"I wouldn't overdo it. Remember how you explained the virus to me? How it makes a duplicate of my hard drive and then slowly steals the duplicate files?"

"I didn't think you were paying attention."

I turned around and kicked my toe against the bottom of the storm cellar doors. "Would you shut up and listen to me for a moment?"

"Go."

"You were only half right about how the virus works. Yes, it makes a duplicate copy of the hard drive, but the copy is what's left on the computer, not the originals. Whoever's been doing this has backdoor access to every computer he's hacked."

Nasty was quiet. This, right here, was what I hated about phone conversations. Without the benefit of seeing her expression, I didn't know what she was thinking or how much else she knew. "You need to notify the police," she said.

"I already did. Tex is here at my house."

"The one on Monticello?"

"Yes."

"Wait there. I'm on my way."

Nasty arrived less than ten minutes later. I invited her in and turned my back on her before seeing her reaction to my newly renovated yellow kitchen.

"You got any coffee, or do you freebase sunshine?"

Grrrrr. "The coffee is in the living room with Captain Allen. I'll get you a mug."

We joined Tex. Whatever welcome I would have predicted he give Nasty, it wasn't the one she got. He stood up and approached her. She backed up. He was angrier than I'd ever seen him before and I'd had plenty of opportunities to see him angry.

"What did you do?" he asked, his voice a borderline growl. Rocky jumped on the sofa, turned himself around, and then faced Nasty and barked twice.

"I did my job," she said to Tex, ignoring his canine backup. "I engineered a patch that blocks the hacker's access to the IP in question. Madison was my guinea pig. I uploaded it to her system first and when it worked, I knew I had gold. Nobody else in the city of Dallas was ready for this."

"Why were you?" I asked. It was something that had been bothering me from the minute she'd claimed to fix my problem. Nasty turned her head and looked at me like she'd forgotten I was in the room. "According to everybody I've talked to, this is a brand-new breach. We all have some sort of firewall on our computers and the personality virus got through. How is it you were ready for a virus that nobody even knew existed?"

"Answer the question, Nasty," Tex said.

She put both arms up and flung Tex's hands off of her. She turned her back to him and took two steps away, and then turned back and looked at him first, and then me. "I got tipped off, okay? Somebody sent me a flash drive with the virus on it and said I stood to make a lot of money if I wrote the code to remove it."

I wasn't buying Nasty's act. "The way I see it, you're the one person with the most financial gain from what happened. How do we know *you're* not behind it?"

"Don't be stupid."

Tex stepped forward and I put out a hand and pushed him back. "I can handle this," I said. I turned back to Nasty. "Prove it. There's got to be something that shows you are as much of a pawn in this mess as we are, or else I call the detective who's trying to get a warrant for my arrest and I give him everything I know, including the photos you took of a police captain's files when you were mucking around inside his computer."

She looked at Tex. He pointed to me. "It's her game right now, Nasty, and if I were you, I'd play ball."

Nasty cursed and then walked over to the sofa. She pulled a laptop out of the messenger bag she'd worn slung across her body and ran a power cord to the wall. The computer powered on quickly. Her fingers flew over the keys, typing commands onto a root menu. She looked up at me and pointed at my laptop on the coffee table. "This one's yours?"

I nodded. She shifted and typed something on my computer. My heartbeat picked up, pounding solidly against my rib cage. Giving Nasty access to my computer felt a little like Fox Mulder working with Alex Krycek, but if the truth was out there, then this was what I had to do to find it. My eyes moved back and forth between the two screens, trying to make sense of what she was doing. She turned back to her own computer and hit the enter key several times. The screens were nearly identical.

Nasty leaned forward and appeared to compare the two screens. And then suddenly, she slammed her computer shut, flipped it over, and popped out the battery.

"What?" I asked. "Why'd you do that? What did you see?"

She looked up at me and leaned back against the sofa cushions. The bravado and confidence were gone. "You were right," she said.

"About what?" I asked.

"I'm behind the virus. Call Detective Henning and tell him I'll cooperate as best as I can."

"Hold on," I said. As much as I'd really, really love for Nasty to be the bad guy here, it didn't make sense. "How's that possible?"

"It's simple," she said. She pointed to her computer. "The code I wrote to counter the virus is the backdoor the hacker used to get in.

TWENTY-FIVE

"I'm not a techie," I said. "I'm going to need a little more than that."

"Me too," said Tex.

Nasty looked at us. She appeared to be collecting her thoughts before speaking. When she did speak, her voice was calm and steady. "The personality virus does two things. It takes a picture of a computer—mostly recent files—and builds a quickie profile of the sysop."

"The what?" Tex asked.

"The system operator. The person who manages the computer content."

"How?" I asked.

"Kind of like a word cloud. It scans your files and blows up the words that are used the most. That kicks off a customized screensaver that informs you your computer was hacked."

"The daisy," I said. "I got a daisy like my Mad for Mod logo, and one by one the petals dropped off and piled up at the bottom of the screen."

Nasty and I looked at Tex. "I got a baseball," he said. "The stitching unraveled one stitch at a time until the whole thing fell apart."

"How long did it take for the daisy to fall apart?" Nasty asked.

"I don't know. A minute? Two?"

"The baseball?" she asked Tex.

"Same."

"That must be how long it takes the program to duplicate the files," Nasty said.

"Okay, so now we understand how the virus worked, but I'm still unclear on your role in this whole thing," I said.

"My patch interrupts the command flow of the computer. It's like giving your computer the hiccups. It operates normally, but every seven seconds it jumps to a new setpoint. It's supposed to keep the virus from having enough time to grab hold of any new files."

"If Madison's right about the files on the computer being the copy and not the originals files, there wouldn't be anything new for the virus to grab," Tex said.

"There's a bigger problem than that," Nasty said. "The jump time creates a vulnerability. It's a nanosecond, but if someone recognized the pattern, they'd be able to get in."

"And do what?"

"Manipulate files. Make changes to the originals and replace the copy with the altered ones. Corrupt the hard drive permanently. Crash a system."

I looked at Tex. "You said you had nothing to do with Sterling Webster's entry to VIP."

"That's right," Tex said. "The only beef I have with Sterling Webster is that he gave guys like me a bad name."

"You said he was a player."

Tex raised one eyebrow.

"Slow down, cowboy," Nasty said. "I saw the evidence of your investment in his property myself."

I turned back toward Nasty. "If what you're telling us is true, then somebody could have planted that file on Captain Allen's computer, right?"

"Madison, whoever went this far to gain access to computers around Dallas probably has something bigger in mind than getting between you and your lover."

I stared at her. It didn't matter that Tex and I weren't lovers. Nasty said that for one reason: to regain control. But her words sent my brain on a course different from everything I'd considered all this time.

"That's just it. I found copies of my files on Jane's computer, but Jane was the victim."

"If Jane was the hacker, then this would have ended when she died," Nasty said.

"Jane wasn't the hacker," I said. "But somebody who knew her was. Somebody who was comfortable going to her studio, which was also her home. She was recently divorced, but there was someone in her life."

"Who?"

"She never told me. But if she was intimate with someone, she'd probably trust him enough to let him use her computer." I grabbed my phone and swiped through the recent photos until I came to the video I'd made of the interior of Posh Pit.

"What's that?" Tex asked.

I pressed play and watched the shaky video. "I took a video inside her place." I looked at him and Nasty and back at him. "It's something I do on decorating jobs, so I don't have to remember every single detail. My instincts kicked in and I thought it was a good idea."

"You came up with that on your own?" Nasty asked.

I nodded.

She looked at Tex. He grinned. "I told you she wasn't stupid."

I went back to watching the small screen. I watched it three full times before I spotted something I hadn't noticed on the first two viewings. The roses on the corner of Jane's desk were a familiar shade of purple-gray.

"There," I said. I paused the video and handed my phone to Tex. "The roses."

"I hate to tell you this, Madison, but lots of people display roses. Some people don't even have to buy them for themselves," Nasty said.

I ignored her and watched Tex. "They're the same color as the ones sent to me. Sterling. That means—"

"It doesn't mean anything," Tex said. "Sterling roses are everywhere. They're only in season until mid-October, so every rose grower in Texas is pushing them. Last week I saw them at the grocery store."

Nasty and I both looked at Tex. It was, quite possibly, the most unexpected piece of information he could have provided.

"Last night you acted like the color of those roses meant something."

"Last night?" Nasty said.

This time we both ignored her. "That's different," Tex said.

"No, it's not. Jane and I were in the same line of business. We both would have encountered Sterling Webster. Jane felt like she lost too much time in her loveless marriage and I know she was seeing someone. What if it was him?"

"It's too thin, Night. You need more."

I stared at the phone screen. "Jane's entire decorating aesthetic boiled down to red, blue, yellow, black, and white. If she were going to buy roses for herself, they wouldn't have been lilac." Tex kept watching me. "The screensaver on her monitor matched the exterior trim on the house! You think a woman like that doesn't think about things like purple roses not matching the paint job?"

"Tell me what you saw when you were there," Tex said. "Everything. Walk me through every moment from when you parked your car to when you called Henning."

"The door was open, but nobody was there. Somebody had a key. Maybe her killer was looking for signs of his identity, something that he'd left behind that would lead the police to him." I looked at Tex. "Whoever did this is tied to the design community. Think about it. Everybody we know that was hacked was involved in VIP."

"Except me," Tex said. "How do we find out who this guy is?" He looked at Nasty, but I answered.

"I don't know. But for the past six months, Jane was my best friend. I knew her better than most people. And If I can get a list of everybody she emailed the morning she was murdered, I can figure it out."

"Because the hacker wouldn't send the virus to himself," Nasty said, following my train of thought.

"That's right," I said.

Tex cut me off but said what I was already thinking. "Access the sent files, Nasty. I want a list of everybody who got an email from Jane that didn't include an attachment."

Not one to let either of us have the final word, Nasty pointed to her mug. "More coffee." And then she went to work.

I picked up the empty pot and carried it to the kitchen. I was counting teaspoons of coffee when Tex joined me. I held up a finger and kept counting until the basket was full. I filled the pot with water and pressed the on switch.

"Okay," I said.

"Not okay. You have a problem."

"Considering I'm making coffee for Nasty, I'd say I have more than one. Which are you talking about?"

"The competition. You've got less than a week to renovate a twelve-unit apartment building or Sterling Webster wins. If he's a part of this, then I'll get him. But if he's not, you can bet he's out there doing what he can to beat you. That video you took, that was a good thing. Between that and the files you sent yourself, we've got a lot to work with. You can't afford to waste time babysitting Nasty."

The absolute last thing I wanted to do was leave Tex and Nasty alone in my house. They had a history. One that included his house, though I'd never gotten a straight answer on the conditions of their short-term co-habitation. But if Nasty ended up being the reason I lost to Sterling Webster, I'd never forgive myself.

Plus, she had given me twenty-thousand dollars to make it happen.

I pushed Tex out of the way and went back into the living room. "You said you wanted to be my silent partner because the enemy of your enemy is your friend. Who's your enemy?"

"Him," Nasty said with a nod to Tex.

"You knew I was mad at Tex because of the invoice you left on his nightstand. You used that anger to get onto my team. You wanted me to be mad at Tex."

She didn't even look up. "You already were mad at him. I just threw fuel on the fire."

The back of my neck got prickly and I was more aware of my breathing. Nasty had manipulated me, and I'd fallen for it. While the rest of us were worried about a murder investigation, a crazy hacker, and a design competition which, in the balance, lay my professional future, Nasty had played a prank to keep me away from her ex-boyfriend.

"Why was it so important to you that I take your money?" I asked.

"None of your business."

"You signed a legal and binding contract that made it my business."

She glared at me.

"Nasty, answer Madison's question," Tex said.

She tossed her long hair. "Sterling Webster has been buying properties all over this city. I want his business, but he's not interested. He thinks he's covered. If I want to get his attention, I need to know enough about him to show him where he's vulnerable. You were never going to beat him on your own, but if you beat him now, with my money invested, I can use that to show him I'm a player too."

"You used me."

She shrugged. I felt Tex watching me. I crossed the room to Tex and put my hands on his face. I pulled him close and kissed him full on, tongue and everything. I felt his hands on my waist pulling me closer.

Nasty cleared her throat. I slowly pulled away and dropped my hands to my sides.

Tex spoke in a low voice. "Go do your thing. Nothing's going to change by the time we're finished."

Oh, how I wish Tex had been right. Because by the time Nasty found the answers we needed, I was in a holding cell waiting for someone to bail me out.

TWENTY-SIX

Tex was right. The priority of finding out what happened to Jane shouldn't have been as important as completing my VIP entry. I waited while Tex sent my video file to his phone and then left Tex, Nasty, and Rocky at Thelma Johnson's house. Instead of gunning it to the apartment complex, I pulled over and called the hospital where the medical technicians had taken Vonda Quinn after finding her outside Posh Pit. My entry in the competition had absolutely nothing to do with Vonda's condition, but until I knew if she was going to be okay, I wouldn't be able focus on work.

My call yielded one thing: Vonda Quinn was not allowed visitors. Which told me she was alive but not out of the woods yet.

I reminded myself that Henning was just doing his job. Vonda had been assaulted in the same manner as her boss and that alone looked suspicious. Add in the unlocked doors at Posh Pit, the virus originating from Jane's computer, and any other evidence that I hadn't known to look for, and Henning would have more questions than answers. Protecting Vonda had as much to do with her safety as his chance at her untainted statement.

I pulled back into traffic and drove to my new-old apartment building. Of the five cars already there, the only one I recognized was Effie's Ford Escape.

She met me by the back door. "Hey, Boss!" she greeted me. "Ohmigod, the paint looks soooooo good. We did three apartments in Lemon Twist, three in Cherry Rocket, three in Cool Cat, and two in Beach Party. We left the front apartment unpainted like you said."

"Who's 'we?'"

"Connie, Joanie, Mitchell, and me. Ned's still out of town. I thought maybe Hudson would help, but—"

"Don't worry about Hudson. We have a good team."

"But you said you wanted to demo a wall and convert the new space into a clubroom."

"That's right." I entered the back door and walked through the hallway toward the front apartment.

"Won't we need an experienced contractor to knock down the wall?"

I picked up a sledgehammer that was propped outside the unit and went inside. The room was empty and half painted, renovation mid-progress by one of the previous owners. If I were to convert this apartment to a clubroom, the wall between the living room and the bedroom would have to come down. I already knew there were no outlets on the wall from when I'd owned this building the first time and managed it as the landlord. I raised the sledgehammer over my shoulder like a baseball bat and swung. The hammer punched a hole into the middle of the wall. Drywall crumbled and fell to the floor, leaving the left side of a two by four exposed.

"I'm pretty sure I can handle the demo myself," I said.

"Alrighty then. I'll tell the team."

There is nothing like good, old-fashioned physical labor to take your mind off your troubles and give you an outlet for aggression. Demolition wasn't usually part of my job. Mad for Mod was more about decorating than design, and frankly, most people who owned mid-century houses weren't looking to knock walls out of the existing floorplans. But the requirements for entry into the VIP competition were that you had to not only design and decorate, but demo. Your final entry had to be structurally different from how it started to illustrate each team's ability to see both what was there and what wasn't. Come to think of it, that might be why preservationists tended not to enter.

As good as it felt to use the sledgehammer, I knew that wasn't the proper way to bring down an interior wall. We were lucky to be working on an unoccupied building, but with fresh paint going into the remaining eleven units, there was a need to contain the dust from my destruction by hanging plastic over the doorway.

There were other considerations as well. The wall wasn't a load bearing wall. The gaping hole I'd created left fluffy pink fiberglass insulation visible on the other side of now-crumbling drywall. I could grab the broken drywall pieces and tear them off with a combination of brute force and determination, but that would only create more potential problems down the line.

No, this wasn't the time to go nuts.

I moved the six-foot ladder to the corner of the room and climbed up with a sharp utility knife in my hand. I scored the intersection of the wall and the ceiling with a horizontal line, a five-minute task that would potentially save us hours by not tearing through the joint tape. Back down to the floor. I picked up a drywall saw and slowly cut from my sledgehammer opening at waist-height, across the crumbling surface, with the saw at an angle. Every once in a while, I felt resistance from the studs behind the drywall and shifted the angle of my drywall saw to a diagonal. This part of the job wasn't about getting down the interior structure. It was about cutting through the outer layer. Like nibbling off the frozen chocolate coating to a Dove Bar but leaving the ice cream and wooden popsicle stick intact for later.

It took the better part of an hour, but by a process I'd first learned on a YouTube video, I pulled off the drywall, hammered the exposed nails to the side, used the reciprocating saw to cut through the center of the stud wall, and pulled the beams out as well. The hardest part of the process was prying the beams up from the floor. When I finished the demolition portion of the job, I set the tools down and set out on the first of multiple trips to the dumpster out back. On my third trip, Joanie set down her paint roller and joined me. Two more trips covered the biggest of the pieces. When we went back inside, Connie ducked into the apartment across the hall and brought out an industrial vacuum. It was connected to a long electrical cord that was plugged into one of the recently painted units that still had power. I took the vacuum from her and switched it on, getting up the dust, debris, and chunks of gypsum that had dropped onto the floor.

Two years ago, I'd had the idea to pull out the carpets and refinish the hardwood floors underneath. Today, I was actually happy that a deranged killer had changed up my priorities. I'd long ago learned to work on a room renovation from top to bottom—ceiling to floor—and Sterling Webster's team must have been instructed to do that here as well. The texture of the ceiling was freshly painted, and I'd have to drywall the new gap in the ceiling where I'd just taken down the wall, but Sterling's team hadn't gotten much farther than that. The apartment grade carpets that I'd wanted to tear out were still in place, protecting the building's original wood floors that I now had the opportunity to refinish when the rest of the room was done.

Small miracle.

"What's the plan, Mads?" Connie asked when I switched off the vacuum. "Paint?"

"No. Drywall the gap in the ceiling where I removed the stud wall, mud it, then panda paw it. When that's dry—"

"Panda what it?"

I pointed up at the ceiling. "Panda paw. That's what we called the tool that makes the circular texture in the ceiling."

"Who's we?" she asked, and then, almost instantly, answered. "Oh, Hudson."

"Actually, Hudson calls it a slap brush. Same thing, different name. I first learned about it from Brad."

This time Connie was quiet. I rarely talked about Brad Turlington, the man who'd first noticed my uniquely trained mid-century modern decorator's eye, refined through years of watching the Doris Day movies my parents had gifted me every year on the birthday I shared with the actress. They'd died in a car crash when I was twenty-one, and the collection of movies had gotten me through the grieving process. Over twenty years had passed since their deaths, but every time I decorated a room, I was reminded of Mom and Dad.

The memories of Brad were less welcome. He'd been my teacher, my co-worker, and my lover, until one day he wasn't. Lately unwanted memories of Brad had been surfacing. I pushed them back down. I needed to hold on to my anger toward him, because it was the protective device that kept me from ever allowing myself to get hurt again.

It occurred to me that Jane may have done the very same thing. She'd briefly talked about her divorce but had told me there was another man in her life. She hadn't wanted to jinx it by telling me who he was. Had she kept quiet for reasons other than superstition? Had this been an affair that happened at the right time—that delicate window after she'd already known her marriage was over but before she'd worked up the courage to legally end it?

And if that was the case, who would be angrier, the divorced husband or the new guy? And what would that anger propel one of the men to do when he found out?

I surprised Connie by continuing. "Brad taught me a lot about this world, and if I were mature enough to get past my anger, I'd give him credit for that. But I can't. There's a lot of rage inside of me because of him. Sometimes I wonder if that's what happens. If people get burned by one relationship and ruin the next one by trying to course correct."

"Are you talking about you and Hudson?"

I pushed the industrial vacuum out of the way. "I'm talking about Jane. She had a secret, and I think it got her killed. If only she'd opened up to me, confided in me instead of fighting with me, maybe I could have helped her."

"You guys fought? When? Joanie said you called her your bestie."

"Actually, Joanie came up with that, not me."

"So?"

"Connie, Jane and I had a fight the morning she was killed."

"Do the police know?"

"I don't know. Detective Henning listed a bunch of things that made me look suspicious, but that wasn't one of them."

Connie studied me. "Why did you lie in the first place?"

"Because it made me look like a pretty crappy friend." I studied Connie's expression. She was nervous. "In hindsight, I should have told the truth from the beginning, and I know that now."

"Madison, the police came to my house. They know I used to work for you, and they were asking lots of questions. They asked how well I knew you and if you had any reason to lie about your relationship with Jane."

"I'm sorry to have put you in that position. I don't know why the police are looking so closely at me for Jane's murder. Nobody knows about that fight, and if we both keep quiet about it, nobody will."

Connie's eyes shifted from my face to over my shoulder and then back to me. Her eyes were wide. "I'm sorry, Madison."

Slowly, I turned around. Detective Henning stood in the hallway with two uniformed officers. I recognized Officer Martinez and Officer Doyle from the police station last night. The familiarity of their faces did little to alter the sense of impending doom established by their presence.

"Ms. Night," Detective Henning addressed me, "I'm going to ask that you come with us."

"Detective, I've already lost too much time on my entry in the VIP competition, and if it's all the same to you, I'd much prefer talking in one of the vacant units here."

"I'm afraid we're beyond that." He reached into his suit jacket and pulled out a folded set of papers. "The computers came back online, and I was able to get that signature from the judge."

"No," I said. I stepped away from Martinez and Doyle. Doyle looked at Henning, who tipped his head toward me. "You're wasting your time talking to me. You need to talk to Captain Tex Allen of the Lakewood Police Department. He's working with an independent computer expert who has evidence that will lead you to the real killer."

"I already spoke to Captain Allen and he's agreed to cooperate with me."

"Did he tell you about the sterling roses at Jane's business? And their link back to Sterling Webster? Sterling sent the same ones to me—"

"Sterling Webster has an alibi. He was signed out of Republic Tower before the murder took place."

"Did you ask Captain Allen about the computer virus? That's evidence. Whoever killed Jane hacked into her computer and sent out the viruses that corrupted all our computers. They might even be the person who took the security cameras offline. Find the person Jane *didn't* send an attachment and you'll have the one person who wasn't targeted. That has to be the killer."

"That's exactly what Captain Allen told us before he turned his information over to me."

"And? Did you follow the email trail and find a suspect?"

"Funny you should ask. The only person Jane didn't send an attachment to that morning was you."

TWENTY-SEVEN

The fact didn't fit with reality. "That's not possible," I said. "Jane did send me an attachment. She sent a copy of our collaborated design files."

The detective studied me. "We've been over your computer, Ms. Night. We've been over the sent files from Ms. Strong's computer. There was no attachment."

I wanted to argue the point, but I already knew if the hacker had been able to falsify files on Tex's computer and delete the files on mine, he would have been able to manipulate this as well.

"Assuming you are telling me the truth, why would Ms. Strong send you those files? Wouldn't you already have them?" the detective asked.

"I did, but they were erased."

Henning looked at the uniformed officers and nodded. Doyle stepped toward me. Henning spoke. "Ms. Night, it's not necessary for us to handcuff you if you come with us voluntarily."

A rebuttal of assumptions was on the tip of my lips, but the train had already left the station and Henning was driving it. Earlier today, Tex and Nasty had been intent on reverse engineering the sent emails from Jane's computer to determine who was to blame. If the found evidence pointed to me, that only said one thing: the hacker was still in control of the game.

I turned to Connie. "Keep working on the design. Effie can get a copy of my application from the DIDI offices," I said. "Tell her, and this is very important, to sign *in* and sign *out* and to look for any familiar names on the registry. Don't stop working—don't let anybody stop working—and don't use my computer for *anything*."

"Do you want me to call anybody for help?"

"Absolutely not."

I left the partially demoed room and walked with the officers through the hallway and out the back door. A standard issue police cruiser with the slanted words *DALLAS POLICE DEPARTMENT* in all caps was parked in the middle of the lot. In front of it was a dark gray sedan. Henning got into the sedan and the officers led me to their marked car. I waited by the back door while Martinez let me in. He didn't make eye contact.

I hadn't realized how much time I'd spent working on the demolition inside the apartment building, but it now struck me that I must have been at it for at least a few hours. The sun was high in the sky, hitting the peak temperatures for a late September day. The recent rains had let up indefinitely, replaced by a post-storm glow. It was as pretty a day as any I'd experienced recently, with the exception of the black cloud over my head.

For all the good the physical labor inside the apartment building had done, giving me an outlet for pent-up frustration, it had lulled me into a safe zone where I hadn't seen the possibility of this particular outcome. I'd left Tex and Nasty in control of finding out what had happened to Jane.

I was never collaborating with anyone again.

My tumultuous thoughts kept me distracted from the ride to the police station. The process of arriving, walking past the gates topped with razor wire, hearing the heavy doors clank shut behind me, and taking in the faces of the officers inside were only slightly less intimidating thanks to their now (unfortunate) familiarity. I'd left my belongings at the apartment complex, so I had nothing to check in with the desk sergeant. Detective Henning was mildly annoyed that I had no reason to sign the paper being thrust at me. I smiled sweetly—for now. The way things were going, I suspected a different waiver of rights would be in front of me shortly.

I was led to a small desk. Officer Martinez moved to the computer behind it. He clicked the mouse a few times and then asked me a series of questions: name, address, birthdate, social security number. As uncomfortable as I was reciting the personal information to him, the environment around me left me feeling like I had little choice.

"What happens next?" I asked him.

"You don't know?"

"How would I know? I've never been arrested before."

"Once I finish the paperwork, I'll turn you over to Officer Doyle for a drug test and cheek swab. Then Detective Henning will get your statement. You'll go into a holding cell until arraignment."

The officer talked like I had no choice of participation in those activities, and as long as I was pulling out my cooperative, nice lady act, it seemed wisest not to challenge him on that. Yet.

"Arraignment is when the judge sets bail, right?"

He nodded. "Dallas uses a standard bail schedule. You're a first timer, no history of criminal behavior. Your bail will be two million dollars."

"Two million dollars?!" I exclaimed. Several people standing around the interior of the police station looked my direction. "Two million dollars?" I repeated in a quieter voice. "How am I supposed to get two million dollars on a Thursday afternoon?"

He glanced at the clock on the wall. I followed his stare. It was going on three o'clock. "Circuit court closes at five, so you'll probably spend the night here and see the judge tomorrow."

Of all the times I could have used a friend on the police force, this one shot to the top of the list. But there was no way I was calling Tex, not now. I had no idea how things had gone so wrong after I left him and Nasty, but whatever he and Nasty told Henning had led to me sitting right here, right now.

I finished up with Martinez and followed a petite female officer named Fields to a door marked Women. She had mostly brown hair that was slicked back into a tight bun at the nape of her head. Her roots had gone a few weeks past acceptable for a touch-up and gleamed silver under the harsh interior light. She unlocked a cabinet on the far wall and pulled out a sealed plastic bag that held a cup, a large Q-tip, and an assortment of other items.

"What happens now?" I asked.

"You submit for a voluntary drug test and let us swab your cheek for DNA."

"Your use of the word 'voluntary' suggests I have a choice. It doesn't feel like I have a choice."

"Ma'am, this is standard procedure. You're innocent until proven guilty. These are the tools that can do that." She handed me the plastic cup. "Bathroom's over there."

I hadn't done anything wrong. I knew that. Whoever killed Jane knew that. But so far, that person had orchestrated things to put me where I was. Officer Martinez had led me to believe I wouldn't have a chance to approach the judge until tomorrow, but there were two hours left before the courts closed. I wasn't about to fritter them away with an argument I probably wouldn't win.

I gave them the requested samples, submitted to the cheek swab, and had my fingerprints recorded by Live Scan. (When that last part came back with a hit, the officers all looked a bit surprised.)

"Your prints are already in here," she said. "I thought you didn't have any priors."

Not willing to eat up the clock with unnecessary explanations, I simply said, "It's a long story."

Officer Fields led me to a small room. "Detective Henning will be in to take your statement."

And when Detective Henning showed up about twenty minutes later, I gave him the only statement I was prepared to make. "Detective, you've arrested and booked me. The only statement you're going to hear out of me is the one I intend to say to the judge."

"You sure about that?"

"I am. And I believe we have enough time to see the judge about bail before the courts close for the day."

"Under normal circumstances, you'd be right."

"What do you mean, 'normal circumstances'?"

"Computer systems went down again. Right after I got your warrant. Unless you change your mind and give me a statement, there's nothing left to do but take you to lockup."

TWENTY-EIGHT

Things to check off my bucket list: spending the night in jail.

Officer Clark, who had obtained a better-fitting uniform since the last time I saw him, escorted me to my visit with the judge. He handed me a bar of soap, a white towel that smelled faintly of bleach, and a can of Pepsi.

"I'm sorry, Madison, this was the best I could do."

I took the proffered items. "Why are you handling me?" I asked. "Henning knows you know me. He seemed surprised by it the morning I found Jane, but by now he's had plenty of time to uncover the details. Isn't that a problem for him? Or for you? Or for me?"

He lowered his voice. "Henning wants to make you feel comfortable."

Now I understood. Henning was using my familiarity with Officer Clark in the hopes that I'd confide something I wasn't willing to tell Henning directly. If I'd done something wrong, it might have worked.

I took the items from Clark and went into the ladies' room. Any hope I'd had of appearing fresh as a daisy in front of the judge were out the window. My appearance was like my mental state: dull as mulch. I did what I could with the soap and the sink water, downed half of the Pepsi, and returned to Clark who was waiting for me in the hallway.

The judge, a sixty-year-old woman with brushed steel glasses and shoulder-length, highlighted hair, didn't seem bothered by the way I looked. "Ms. Night, I'd like to apologize on behalf of the court for detaining you overnight. I have had a chance to review your case and ties to the community. Based on your history, I've reduced your bail to two hundred thousand dollars. See the bailiff for your court date."

"But I don't have two hundred thousand dollars," I said.

There were a few snickers around the room. The judge looked at me over the top of her glasses. "For someone with as colorful of a history as you, Ms. Night, I'm surprised you're not better acquainted with how the legal system works. Once bail is set, you're only required to pay 10 percent of the bond. You're free to leave. Next," she said.

I turned to Officer Clark. "Twenty thousand dollars is still going to be a problem."

"Your bail was paid, Madison. You're free to go."

There was no one in the world who owed me a twenty-thousand-dollar favor: not friends, not lovers, not enemies. But there was one person who had recently given me twenty thousand dollars, and I hated knowing it was Nasty's money that had bought my freedom.

I found Effie standing in the lobby. "I'm sorry, Boss, I didn't know what else to do."

"You cashed Nasty's check, didn't you?" I said.

She nodded.

It was only then that I realized the black man standing a few feet away from Effie was listening in on our conversation. And despite the fact that he wore a suit and tie in place of the security uniform issued by Republic Tower, I quickly recognized Delbert Manning.

"Delbert?" I asked. "What are you doing here?"

Delbert held a tweed cap in his hands, though his nervousness appeared to be taken out on the fabric by balling the cap into a wad.

"Boss," Effie said, "I cashed Nasty's check, but this man paid your bail."

"Thank you," I said to Delbert. "But why? And how did either of you know I where I was?"

"Miz Madison, I think we need to sit down and talk and I'd really rather it not be anywhere near here."

That made two of us.

The neighborhoods surrounding the Dallas jail were filled with bail bondsmen and liquor stores. I wasn't dressed (or deodorized) for anything fancy, so Effie dropped Delbert and me off at a small coffeeshop on Commerce Street while she went in search of parking. The older security guard remained quiet until we were seated.

"Miz Madison, I can't tell you how sorry I am," he said. His blue eyes were watery but clear. He seemed troubled by something and I wanted to put him at ease.

I put my hand on his forearm and said, "I don't know how you came to bail me out of jail, but I owe you a huge thank you. You have nothing to apologize for."

"Oh yes, I do." He let his coffee go untouched while I drank mine. After a few awkward minutes of silence, he spoke. "I'm the reason the police arrested you for Miz Strong's murder."

"Delbert, I know you were just doing your job."

"Miz Madison, I lied about something on my application when I applied for the security job at Republic Tower. It was 1970, before background checks like they do today. Times were different then and I got the job because my uncle vouched for me. I was fresh out of jail and at a crossroads. Straighten up my act or die young."

"Delbert, I'm getting the very strong feeling you have something to tell me. Something you need to unburden yourself from and something I need to hear. You just bailed me out of jail with the kind of money it would take anybody some effort to get, so whatever it is you have to tell me, I'm not going to judge you."

He looked up at me. "I assaulted a woman when I was eighteen. I'm ashamed of my past, but I did my time. When I got my second chance, I didn't want to screw it up. Got a job, got married, and got a family now. I've been on the straight and narrow since then and retirement with a pension is something I never dreamed would happen to me. But somebody found out. Somebody knew I lied about my past when I applied for this here job. And that somebody was your friend, Jane Strong."

TWENTY-NINE

"Delbert, are you saying Jane blackmailed you?" I asked.

"I don't know what else to call what she did," Delbert said.

"She confronted you? At work?"

"Not exactly."

I was starting to have my doubts about the truth versus Delbert's perception of the truth. Not because I didn't trust him—although after his admission, I needed a bit more information before I made my determination on that. "Tell me what happened."

"I had just turned eighteen, and I spent a lot of time on the streets looking for money. Handouts and easy jobs. That's what we did in my neighborhood."

I tried to put myself in Delbert's shoes, but our backgrounds were so disparate that I couldn't begin to imagine what it was like for an eighteen-year-old black man in Dallas in 1970. "Go on."

"I did a job for a lady in Oak Cliff and she caught me—" he looked down at his hands and refolded them a few times "—she caught me going through her purse. She said she was calling the police and I got scared. When she turned around, I hit her with a lamp. I got picked up by the police later that same day."

I shivered. His story wasn't a pleasant one and painted a very different picture of the jovial security guard. He'd admitting to lying about the incident to get the job at Republic Tower, and I knew he would have had to lie to even be considered.

"What happened with Jane?"

"About a week ago, I got a package at work. Now, I don't get much mail at work. I get a couple of magazines, you know, ones I don't want my wife to know about." He looked up at me, embarrassed. "She doesn't share my interest in woodworking, and sometimes things get quiet in the lobby. There's only so many times you can flip through one of those Neiman Marcus catalogs."

I stifled a smile. Not what I'd been expecting! "Go on," I said.

"Well, I got a package, and I was curious, so I opened it up. It was a printout of my arrest record and a note that said if I didn't look the other way, the same files would be sent to my employer. Later that day, I got an email that said the same thing."

"You say this was from Jane?"

"That's what it said."

"But Jane's the one who ended up needing help."

"Yes, ma'am."

This time we were both silent. I considered what might have happened. The killer knew he was going to strike. He threatened Delbert not to get involved but used Jane's name as misdirection. Delbert would have been torn between helping Jane and not—jeopardizing his future or protecting his past. It explained the look I'd seen on his face when he heard what had happened on the twenty-third floor. By the time Jane was dead, Delbert had no idea he'd been distracted from a murder in progress.

"You didn't verify my alibi," I asked. "I left Republic Tower and went to the library to work. You said you'd sign me out, but you didn't, did you? To the police, it looked like I'd been in the building the whole time."

"Miz Madison, I sure am sorry. I didn't know. And then, I was scared, and I kept my mouth shut. I was afraid if they knew I let you come and go without signing in and out, they'd wonder how I got my job in the first place and they'd do some digging and I'd be back out on the streets."

"What happened to make you tell the truth?"

Delbert looked nervous. "A lady called me yesterday. She said she represented a private security company and was verifying that I received an email from Jane Strong the day before she was murdered. I'm supposed to be security for Republic Tower. If they hired a private company to look into me, that means it's only a matter of time before they let me go."

What I knew that Delbert didn't was that Nasty owned the private security company, and when I'd left her and Tex, they were hard at work tracking down the recipients of any emails that had come from Jane's computer. Detective Henning claimed that the outcome of those efforts was what led him to my door.

I took another sip of my coffee and considered things from Delbert's perspective. He'd been living with the knowledge that his employment was based on a lie. And now, weeks away from his retirement, the secure future he thought he'd earned was threatened by someone who knew his secret. On one hand, that kind of threat might lead someone down a murderous path. On the other hand, I already knew the murder victim in this case wasn't the person sending the emails. Someone knew about Delbert's past and had played him just like they'd played me.

Delbert had also paid my bail, which did not seem like the sort of thing a murderer would do. Knowing the police had enough on me to get a warrant for my arrest would be what the murderer wanted. Delbert's actions, sacrificing his secret to save me, was the last thing a guilty person would do.

Effie joined us in the coffee shop. "There's more, isn't there?" I asked.

He nodded. "The secret was tearing me up, so I told my wife. She smacked me upside the head. She said, 'Delbert, you go get that nice lady out of jail or you'll be spending the rest of your life in the dog house."

"Does your wife know the truth about you?"

"She does now." He held my stare. "I've been counting on that pension to make retirement easier, but without my wife by my side, it's just not worth it."

"You tell your wife I said thank you."

"I'd rather tell her you said you'll pay us back."

"You drive a mean bargain." I said. "Effie, give the man his money." And then I gave him the biggest hug I could manage under the circumstances.

Effie dropped Delbert off at Republic Tower and drove to Thelma Johnson's house. On the way, she caught me up on the status of the apartment complex. "I got your designs from the receptionist at DIDI, just like you suggested. She wasn't all that happy about having to make a copy, but I bought her donuts and coffee from Paxton's coffeeshop and she softened up a bit."

"Did she say anything? About the competition, or the entries, or the judges?"

"Apparently their computers were hacked just like everybody else. You were smart to drop your entry off in person. She said four of the application files were corrupted and they had to bend the rules to allow them entry."

"Did she mention names?"

"No, but that Sterling Webster showed up while I was waiting. He said it was cute how you assembled your entry like a high school paper."

"What was he doing there?"

"He had an appointment with the head of the DIDI."

"Gerry Rose?"

"Yes. The two of them went to a conference room while the receptionist made the copies."

"That's fine. Let him think he's going to breeze into the prize. I like being the underdog."

"You're funny, Boss. Nobody would know you have a competitive streak by looking at you."

I glanced down at the Olympic track suit I'd worn for the past thirty odd hours. "Today they would."

Effie parked behind my Alfa Romeo. Neither Tex nor Nasty were at my house, but Rocky was. I thanked Effie for the seventy-third time and let her play with Rocky while I went upstairs for a shower and change. More than just about anything I wanted in life was to climb into bed and sleep. Two things exceeded that in priority: finding Jane's killer and winning the VIP competition. After everything that had happened this week, I wasn't going to say

I'd sleep when I was dead, but I'd certainly sleep well when this current set of circumstances were behind me.

After a night in a jail cell, I was desperate to reclaim my sense of self. I fluffed up my blonde hair, applied tinted moisturizer, powder over my freckles, and a sheer tomato glaze over my lips. I dressed in a light blue and ivory tweed dress with three quarter sleeves, nude hose, and the white Courrèges boots I wore the day Jane had been killed. I stuffed an oversized gray sweatshirt into a bag and pulled on a tall blue cone hat. It had oversized daisy petals on the side fashioned out of polka dotted fabric. The back of the hat flipped up above my ponytail. Inside the hat were two tags: one indicating the designer, English milliner James Wedge, and the other indicating the original owner, Jan Randall. I hadn't known enough then to ask her family members to tell me about Jan's life, so she remained a mystery woman with a fabulous collection of wigs and hats and footwear. (Jan was the original owner of the white Courrèges boots too). I pulled on a pale blue wool cape that buttoned by my neck and met Effie downstairs.

"Wow, Boss, you look pretty good, all things considered."

"Thanks. That's exactly the response I wanted."

She looked confused. "Is that smart? Wearing a good outfit to work on a renovation?"

"It's not smart at all. Let's head toward the apartment building and I'll tell you the plan."

On the short drive to Gaston Avenue, I brought Effie into my current list of problems and how I intended to solve them.

"Everything started the morning Jane sent me that email, right? I went straight to Republic Tower to confront her."

"Yeah, that was a bad idea," the usually more tactful college grad said. "If you just got mad at her like a normal person, you'd never be involved in this."

I'd had a fair amount of time to think things over while in a jail cell, and I'd reached the same conclusion. "Jane sent that email for one reason: to get me to stay away from her. She knew something was going to happen. Severing ties from me was an act of self-preservation."

"You think?" Effie asked. The light ahead of us turned yellow and she floored the pedal instead of slowing down. If I weren't so eager to get to work, I might have questioned her driving.

"I don't just think, I know. It's what I would have done."

"So why didn't you do what she wanted and leave her alone?"

"That's the irony. I would have wanted her to leave me alone, but I couldn't do that for her. On one hand, it makes me a hypocrite."

"And on the other?"

"It means I'm in a very good position to figure this out. This is about Jane. It's about someone from her life. I've only been in her life for six months, and I met her after her divorce."

"That makes you valuable how?"

"I don't know how to explain this part, but there's something about that time after a serious relationship ends that's euphoric. It's a time of self-discovery and empowerment. That's where Jane was when I met her. She left her job, cashed out her 401K to start Posh Pit, and set out to make a name for herself. Jane wasn't at all interested in fading into the woodwork and quietly going away. She wanted to be her own person."

"But why would someone go after her assistant?"

"If the killer wanted Vonda dead, she would be."

Effie's expression changed. Dimples appeared on her cheeks, not because she was smiling, but because she was pressing her lips together. Their natural pigmentation all but disappeared with the pressure. Her eyes were wide, blinking repeatedly like an eyelash was irritating the surface of her contact.

"What is it?" I asked. "Is there news about Vonda?"

Effie nodded. "She never woke up. She died at the hospital last night."

THIRTY

I hadn't realized how much I'd clung to the hope that Vonda would survive the attack until Effie told me she was dead. Not because I wanted to know what Vonda knew, but because she was a person who had gotten caught in the crosshairs of Jane's life. And now, she was gone, and with her passing, so was my last tendril of hope that she could provide a clue. I had only myself to rely on now. I wouldn't pull anyone else into my nightmare.

The first stage of my plan was simple. Effie drove us to Gaston Avenue and parked out back. I got into my recognizable Alfa Romeo and moved it from the parking lot out back to the sidewalk out front. I wanted to make sure anybody watching knew exactly where I was.

I adjusted my tall, blue cone hat and walked halfway up the sidewalk that led to the front door. It had been awhile since I'd assessed the building's curb appeal. When I first owned the property, I'd bought it as equal parts investment and residence. None of my tenants knew I was the landlord, and rent checks were dropped off in the box in the lobby and picked up either under cloak of darkness (by me) or by Hudson, who was often on the premises to do minor repairs. But this new incarnation of the building was about more than earning a quiet, steady income. I was forced to acknowledge that the exterior of the property was as important as the interior, and my exterior was sorely lacking.

It struck me that less than an hour ago, anyone could have said the same thing about me. After a night in the temporary holding cell at the Dallas police station, I'd been grungy. Exhaustion marks showed in undereye circles, limp hair, dry skin, and a rumpled outfit. A shower, some makeup, and a change of clothes had transformed me back into the person I was.

I could do the exact same thing for the house: power-wash the white brick exterior, repaint the shutters and trim, and add in decorative breeze block walls to make the entrance more majestic.

The bad news: my night in jail had cost me in both time and money.

The good news: I had everything I needed in storage just waiting for the appropriate project.

I flipped the cover back on my notebook and made a quick list. When I finished, I walked the rest of the way up the sidewalk and inspected the light fixtures that flanked the door. Yep, they'd have to go too. As I bent down to test the moisture level of the empty flower beds under the front windows, someone cleared his throat behind me.

I straightened and whirled around. Kip Bledsoe, in an athletic-cut gray suit that accommodated his football-player build, stood on the landing behind me.

"I saw your car out front and thought I'd check in. You sure didn't waste any time starting work on the building," he said.

"I don't have time to waste."

He looked confused, and then understanding dawned on his boyish face. His eyebrows relaxed, and he smiled, but the smile didn't quite reach his eyes. "Now I get it. It's okay, Madison. We all do what we have to do for money. Nobody's going to think any less of you for getting into the house flipping game."

"I'm not a house flipper!" I exclaimed. And then the more important aspect of Kip's unannounced visit to the property struck me. I forced my face into a smile to match his. "I'm glad you stopped by. My employee gave me the keys you dropped off, and so far, so good. We have a lot of work to do, but that's the fun of a project like this, right?"

"Right."

"You saved me a phone call. I need some additional

information on this building for the VIP competition, information that was lost when my computers went down. Could you access it from the MLS database and send it to me?"

"Most people ask about a building's history before they buy a property."

"I'm not most people."

"Yeah, I guess most people wouldn't have plowed ahead with their own entry after their original partner was murdered."

I studied Kip. His arms were crossed over his linebacker chest and the fabric of his jacket strained across his biceps. "What do you know about Jane and me working together?"

"Don't be naïve, Madison. The whole design community knows you and Jane were going to work together on an entry. People talk. Jane's death shook a lot of us up. But not you. It is a little weird how you submitted your own entry under the wire the day she died."

To explain my actions would have been defensive. Plus, I couldn't tell what Kip knew. Was he aware of the rift? Or did he think Jane and I were still on the same team? Where had his knowledge come from, local gossip or first-hand?

"How well did you know Jane?" I asked.

"Better than most."

"Oh? She never mentioned you."

His face reddened. "We were...discreet. For obvious reasons."

It wasn't what I expected, and the idea that Kip and Jane had been involved in what sounded like more than a professional manner caught me by surprise. "Kip, where were you the day she died?"

"I was outside Republic Tower. She told me she had to talk to Gerry and I gave her a ride, but she was going to call when she was done so I drove in circles around downtown."

All thoughts of the apartment building faded into the background. "You're the witness," I said slowly. "You told the police I was there."

"I'm sorry, Madison. I had to. I saw you two argue through the glass and when the police started asking questions, I didn't have another choice."

The witness had placed me on the twenty-third floor, in the ladies' room, at the time Jane died. That wasn't what Kip had seen. If his statement ended with a few loops around the block while Jane and I fought in the lobby, he wouldn't know about the rest.

But there was one way he could know details about what had happened and inserted me into the timeline. If he'd been there himself.

I needed to find out if Kip's IP address was on the V-day list I'd found on Jane's computer. "Back to the MLS listing, do you think you could get me the details on this building?"

He appeared to consider my request. "I guess I owe you one. Our systems are back online, and nothing was lost. I'll print out the history and drop it off later today."

"You don't have to make a special trip. Just scan the document and email it to me."

"No can do. With this recent hacking, we're not sending any attachments. Not worth taking a chance and alienating prospective buyers."

"You emailed my paperwork to me. You said it was scrubbed and sanitized."

"Some issues have come up since then and we're being more cautious."

Kip appeared to sense my mood toward him had changed. He said good-bye with something about an appointment across town and left. As soon as his car drove off, I went inside. I wanted to think about what he'd said, but I needed to check on the interior progress.

The hall was painted in Beach Party, a soft taupe-beige. Mismatched atomic-era wall sconces of similar sizes had been repainted with a highly reflective Dupli-Color chrome spray paint and mounted to the walls at four-foot intervals. Connie came out of the last apartment on the left. She wore a white hardhat with the Mad for Mod logo on the front.

"Hey, Mads!" she called out. "Nice hat."

"You too," I said.

"Effie and I made them last night. Bought the hats at Paintin' Place and printed out stickers from my home computer. We're not only going to have the best entry, we have the best-looking team too."

"How's it going?"

"Great. Your instructions made a huge difference. We painted and installed all the light fixtures. We just have to tear out the carpets, refinish the floors, and load in the furniture and then we're done. Plenty of time before the judges show up on Monday morning."

"Not exactly. I have a new plan for the exterior." I tore the top page out of my sketch pad. "It's going to be all hands on deck until the deadline."

"All hands on deck?" said Joanie from the hallway behind me. "Then my timing is perfect."

"What are you doing here? Shouldn't you be at your store?"

"Joanie Loves Tchotchkes is closed for the day."

I met her by the back door. "You shouldn't take a loss in business because of me," I said.

Joanie grinned. "Yesterday some hipster bought out my entire collection of Daileyware. That's almost four hundred pieces of melamine. Sold. I can afford to close for the day and help you."

"What did she want with four hundred pieces of melamine?"

"He, not she. He and his partner are opening a mid-mod ice cream parlor on Garland Road past the lake."

The lake in mention was White Rock Lake. As various pockets of Dallas underwent turns toward the trendy and then not trendy, I'd watched buildings and businesses change hands with alarming regularity. Joanie's store was out that way, and her kitschy business had benefitted from White Rock Lake being labeled the hot new spot to live. Many of the old, rundown businesses had changed hands and gotten face-lifts. As the apartment buildings flipped and underwent the most basic of remodels, new residents moved in and quickly populated the restaurants, coffee shops, and bakeries in the area.

Hudson's house was on the northwest side of White Rock Lake. After my recent visit to his house and our resulting conversation, I suspected I'd want to avoid that side of town.

"This guy didn't even try to undercut my prices. Just bought it all. Pink, blue, yellow. That's a lot of melamine. And he paid cash, which was perfect since I'm afraid to rely on the computers these days."

"So you're happy."

"Not only am I happy, I'm flush. And that means you have a new investor."

I held my hands out in front of me. "Joanie, I can't."

She jabbed her finger at me. In her bowling shirt, ratted hair, and tight jeans, she looked like someone I'd rather not mess with. "No way, José. You don't get to say 'yes' to Nasty's money and 'no' to mine."

"It's not that easy, Joanie. I listed you as part of my team. Investors can't be part of the team. I'm the designer, Effie's the project manager, and you, Connie, Ned, and Mitchell are the team. If we violate the conditions of our application, I can be disqualified, and I'm not losing this competition because of a technicality."

Joanie looked uncomfortable. "Um, Mads, when Effie went to get you last night, we weren't sure how soon you'd be back. We made an executive decision to add a member to your team. Ned's still out of town and it seemed like we could use the help, and all things considered, I didn't think you'd mind all that much."

"You didn't," I said.

"I did."

"Where is he?"

She twisted at the waist and pointed toward the room from which I'd knocked down the interior wall. I went back down the hallway. A cloud made up of freshly-sanded mud hung in the room, making it difficult to make out the figure on the ladder.

Difficult, but not impossible.

I picked up a pair of safety glasses and a particle mask and crossed the room. The man's back was to me, and he operated a sander with one hand and the Shop-Vac with the other, making it loud enough that he didn't hear me yelling. I pulled the power cord out of the wall and crossed my arms. "What do you think you're doing?"

Tex glared down at me. "You have a lot of nerve."

"Me? What did I do? You're the one sanding my ceiling. Why?"

"Hudson James isn't the only guy who can sand your ceiling."

"I don't need Hudson to sand my ceiling. I can sand my ceiling all by myself!"

"Oh yeah?" he said. He set the sander on the top of the ladder and climbed down. "Then why didn't you? You're running out of time, Night. You're supposed to be working around the clock. That mud was dry. You could have sanded it last night."

Several retorts sprung to my lips, everything from euphemisms about sanding my ceiling to witty banter to the kind of language you'd never hear in a Doris Day movie.

"You are not seriously asking me why I wasn't here working on my entry, are you? Are you the most insensitive man on the planet? Or is your ego so big that you honestly can't deal with me not calling you for help?"

"Hey, Boss," Effie called from the hallway. I turned toward her. "Um, I need to talk to you."

"Not now, Effie."

"But—"

"Fine." I headed toward the door and then, not willing to just drop it, turned back to Tex. "Has anybody ever told you that *you* have a lot of nerve? *You're* the one who's responsible for me not sleeping in my own bed last night."

Tex's face turned red. "You made your decision?"

"I have now. I don't want either one of you!"

"Real mature, Night."

"Sorry if my *maturity level* is on the fritz. I'm a little off my game after spending the night in *jail*."

"You were where?" Tex asked.

"Don't act all surprised. I already know you and Nasty contacted Henning. I would have thought, after all this time, I'd at least earned a heads up that the police were on their way to arrest me."

We glared at each other. I was so angry it took longer than it should have for Tex's reaction to compute. And, full disclosure, it was Effie who made it perfectly clear.

"Boss?" she said. "I sort of lied to Captain Allen and told him you asked him to work with you here last night."

"Why would you do that?"

"It was the only thing I could think of that would keep him from finding out the truth."

THIRTY-ONE

My first instinct was to storm out, slam a few doors, and put distance between me and Tex and the situation. On the immaturity meter, that would have broken the device. And considering the four walls around me were all ones that needed to remain intact, grabbing the sledgehammer was also out of the question. I balled my fists up and considered my options. None held the satisfaction I wanted.

I kept my back to Tex and addressed Effie. "I was allowed a five-person team. I turned in five names. Theodore Rexford Allen was not one of those names."

"Who's Theodore Rexford All—" Effie's eyes grew wide. "That's Captain Allen's name?" She looked past me. "Did people call you Teddy?"

Tex didn't answer, and I didn't turn around to see his expression. "Effie, did you or did you not put our application in jeopardy?"

"Hear me out, Boss. When I went to Republic Tower to get a copy of your designs, they asked me how it was going, and I said fine, because I wasn't going to tell them the truth, you know?"

I nodded and spun my hand toward me in a small circle to indicate I wanted the rest of the story.

"But while I was there, Sterling Webster showed up and said he needed to file paperwork for a team member substitution. And then Captain Allen called to find out where you were, and I knew you did *not* want him to know what happened, so I said you were going through inventory and you'd be working here on the apartment complex all night."

And Tex had shown up to help. Not knowing the only inventory I'd been doing was of the recent decisions that had led to me peeing in a cup for a drug panel.

"It's okay, Boss," Effie said. "You just have to file paperwork with the DIDI office to let them know you're swapping out a team member. You can make the substitution until midnight tonight. Sterling was doing the exact same thing. It's totally legit. It's in the rulebook and everything."

I turned around and glared at Tex and then turned back to Effie. "Show me," I said.

Effie led me to the front, street facing unit where we'd set up a makeshift desk by propping a piece of plywood on two paint cans. She sat on a five-gallon drum of drywall mud, clicked through a couple of computer screens, and pointed at the monitor. "See? You have forty-eight hours before the end of the competition to change your team."

I pulled out my phone and dialed the number. A man answered. "Dallas in Design Initiative, Gerry Rose speaking."

I was surprised to have gotten the head of DIDI on the phone, but I didn't let that derail my mission. "Gerry, this is Madison Night of Mad for Mod. I'm participating in the VIP competition. One of my initial team members hasn't been available to work on our entry. Do I understand correctly that I can swap out a new team member in his place?"

"Sure," Gerry said. "Just fill out the team member substitution form and drop a copy off at the office."

"I can't email it as an attachment?"

"These computer hackings have knocked us out twice so far. We're not taking chances on any more attachments until this contest is over. If you don't have a blank copy of the form, you can pick one up here, but you'll need to come with the new team member because we'll need her signature. We do require verifiable evidence that the original team member had no involvement. Is she sick or couldn't get the time off?"

"She's a he, and he was called out of town."

"A copy of his hotel bill should be sufficient."

"Okay." I thanked him and hung up. Immediately, I called Ned's cell phone and got his voice mail. I left him a brief message outlining my need for a copy of his hotel bill and why. "See you when you get back." I hung up. Effie vacated my chair and I dropped into it. "I'll take care of this," I said to her. "You keep working."

"What about Captain Allen?"

"Officially, he's not a member of our team until I get this paperwork filled out and delivered to Republic Tower." I held a pencil between my thumb and forefinger and tapped the eraser end on the surface of my desk. "Unofficially, you put that man to work."

"Okay, Boss," Effie said. She saluted her hard hat and left.

While waiting for Ned to call back, I studied the screen. An assortment of company logos was displayed on the contest page alongside the Mad for Mod daisy. I recognized most of them as belonging to various designers around Dallas. The same stylized rose from Sterling Webster's brushed aluminum cover I'd seen the day I dropped off my application was the opposite of the simple daisy that I'd designed myself. The contrast told any prospective client what they needed to know about the two of us: my designs were pure, simple, and organic, and Sterling's designs were overworked and overdesigned. His inflated client prices were needed to offset expenses like aluminum binder covers and dye-cut business cards.

I really wanted to beat him at his own game. I wanted the in-crowd of the design community to acknowledge that one woman's vision was as good as a conglomerate. I wanted to win for all the little people out there.

A stack of file folders from Mad for Mod sat on the corner of Effie's makeshift desk next to a portable printer. I found the file with the VIP paperwork. I didn't have a blank copy of the form, but it would be better time management to keep Tex working while I dropped off the paperwork than to take him with me to Republic

Tower. As I flipped through the contents of the folder, I discovered a note on Jane's Posh Pit stationary.

Von—Here's what I'm sending Madison. Too harsh? –Jane

The note was paperclipped to a printed out copy of an email. *The* email. The note that I'd received from Jane that had gotten me upset enough to confront her face to face.

For the past week, I'd been entrenched in Jane's murder. I'd convinced myself that she'd had some ulterior motive for sending that email, that she hadn't really wanted to cut me out of her life. I'd started to remember her as the friend she was and not the antagonistic woman I'd encountered in the lobby the morning she was killed.

But there was no denying the truth anymore. This note was the proof. I didn't know why Jane had been killed, but now I knew the email was real. If Jane could speak from the dead, she'd probably tell me to butt out of the investigation into her murder.

Fine. Everything I'd done to try to get answers had led to my worst night ever, and I had no reason to stay involved. Jane had made it clear she didn't want me in her life. I balled the email and the note in a wad and threw them into the empty box we'd been using for trash. I never wanted to be reminded of that email exchange again.

I crossed out the original information on the form and wrote in Tex's name. I was annoyed by the mundanity of the task, but until I received Ned's hotel reservation bill, there was nothing else I could do.

After completing the paperwork with still no word from Ned, I went in search of Connie. I found her on the second floor, sewing café curtains at a makeshift sewing station in the middle of my old apartment.

"Hey, Mads. What do you think?" She held up a curtain panel. My storage facility had been bursting with vintage fabrics acquired from various estate sales, and they'd been sorted into four piles to coordinate with the four different paint colors we'd been using. Connie's curtain panel-in-progress was a turquoise bark cloth with a Polynesian print.

"They look great. I don't want to interrupt you, but you haven't heard from Ned, have you?"

"No. He said he'd be on the road today, so I don't expect to hear from him until tonight. Why?"

I explained the situation. "I have until five to drop the paperwork off at Republic Tower, and I'm afraid if I don't have proof that Ned's been out of town, we're going to either be disqualified or we won't have enough people to get the job done."

"No worries," Connie said. "He booked the trip on our credit card. I'll print out the bank statement. That'll work, right?"

"You're a lifesaver," I said. Connie switched off the sewing machine and headed downstairs. I heard her voice on the back stairs. "Are you coming?" she called.

"I'll be down in a second. Go ahead and use my computer."

I wasn't worried about Connie needing me to log onto my computer. Before she'd started her surprisingly successful Etsy business, she worked for me part time. She knew my filing system, my passwords, and my preference for yellow highlighters. She also knew I hadn't been in this apartment unit for a long time, so she'd understand my need to get reacquainted with the four walls.

My design had opted to use one solid color throughout the furnished rental, and in this apartment, the walls had been painted Cherry Red, a pinkish red hue that immediately lifted my spirits. Using Effie's new sortable inventory database, I had easily accessed the furniture, appliances, knickknacks, and objects d'art to use based on color. The hardwood floors in this one unit had been exposed before I'd moved out but had benefitted from a recent buffing and glowed brightly against the white trim. When we placed rugs, loaded in the pink sofa, added Danish Modern furniture, framed floor plans, and other knickknacks, the unit would be a thing of beauty. I'd probably never be able to live in the space without remembering everything that had happened there, but that was just me.

I peeked my head into the pink bathroom and then left the

apartment and returned downstairs. I heard Connie yelling before I reached my office.

"I can't believe you lied to me," she said "Don't bother coming home. There is no home. We're through!"

I rounded the corner in time to see Connie throw her phone against the wall.

"What's wrong?" I asked. "What happened?"

She could barely get the words out between irregular breaths. "There's not a single charge on our credit card which is weird. I called the office and found out Ned didn't go on a trip to promote a new band. He went to Shreveport with his secretary. And it's not the first time. He's been cheating on me for who knows how long."

Immediately I thought of the faked computer files and corrupted databases. "Connie, this virus has been doing some crazy things. Give Ned a chance to talk. I wouldn't trust something you saw online."

"I just gave him a chance to talk," she said. She kicked the file cabinet behind my desk and then looked up at me. "The office connected me to the emergency number Ned gave them. He confessed to everything: the affair, the lies, and the fact that our marriage is over."

THIRTY-TWO

"Ned wouldn't cheat on you," I said.

"He has. He is. He didn't deny it." She pointed to the computer. "I know how important it is for you to have proof, so when I couldn't get him on the phone, I logged into his business account and I saw the credit card statements. I just talked to him and it's all true."

Her use of the plural of 'statement' broke my heart. Ned and Connie Duncan had been the kind of clients who become friends and confidants. Ned had befriended my ex when Brad had come to Dallas to win me back, and I hadn't thought much about the easy friendship that had sprung up between the two men. Now, knowing the lies Brad had told me, I wondered if it weren't possible that the two men had other similarities I'd never wanted to see.

None of that mattered right now. I put my arms around Connie and held her while her shoulders shook with sobs. "It's going to be okay," I said.

"No, it's not," she muttered into the shoulder of my blue tweed dress. She pulled away from my hug and wiped her face. "I put a hole in the wall."

"That's not a crisis. We've got a five-gallon drum of drywall mud and a team of experts to fix it."

Connie smiled. "Can I use the sledgehammer now?"

"Let's not get carried away." I leaned against the front of my desk. "Do you want to get out of here?"

She shook her head. "No. I want to help you win."

"At this stage, that's not likely."

She stood erect and stared me straight in the face. "Renovation hath no motivation like a woman scorned."

"That's embroidered on a pillow collection at the Jonathan Adler store, right?" I said with a smile.

She forced her own smile to match mine. "I don't want to think about this right now. I know I have to soon, but if something can take my mind off the fact that my marriage is over, then sign me up."

"Okay," I said. "But if you change your mind, I'll completely understand."

She pointed to the portable printer. "You don't have a lot of time, Mads. You better get to Republic Tower. The credit card statement is right there."

"How about you relax for a moment while I round up the team?" She nodded and sat down on the drywall bucket.

I found Effie and Joanie in the new (and empty) community room. "Where's Captain Allen?" I asked.

"I gave him the list of supplies we needed to do the exterior. He left to go let Wojo out and then get the power washer. That was okay, right? Did you get what you need to add him to the team?"

"I still need his signature." I dropped my voice. "We have another problem. Connie just got some bad news about Ned, and I don't know if she wants to talk about it. I don't want her to be left alone, okay? Joanie, you take over the sewing machine. Effie, work with Connie to load in the furniture. When Captain Allen returns, get the interior finished and start working on the exterior design. I'll be back as soon as I can."

I collected the necessary paperwork and left. I hated knowing my professional needs had led to Connie discovering the worst about her husband, but I also believed it was far more powerful to know the truth than to live in the shadows of lies and willful ignorance. Connie's near future was going to be dark and cloudy and horrible, but she'd emerge like I had, like Jane had, into a stronger version of herself. More equipped to handle the curveballs the universe threw her way.

It troubled me how quickly I'd lumped Connie in with Jane, and again I found myself wondering about Jane's recent past, the past she didn't talk about because she was so focused on her new independence. Why hadn't I thought about that before? There is always darkness before a storm. Jane would have been no different. The fact that I'd met her after her storm didn't change reality. And now that she'd been murdered, maybe no one would know her darkness.

It was shortly after lunch time, and traffic was light. I quickly covered the three miles between the apartment building and Tex's townhouse and found curbside parking. I didn't have time for a long confrontation, but I needed Tex's signature to file the paperwork. My hope was that he'd understand.

The doorbell went unanswered, as did the pounding. I let myself in with his keys and climbed the stairs. "Tex?" I called. "It's Madison. I need your signature."

No reply.

I reached the landing. The box Tex had with him at Thelma Johnson's house sat on the counter next to a box marked Dog Poop bags. I must have just missed him taking Wojo out.

How long could it possibly take for a Shi Chi puppy to poop? I stared at the box next to the Dog Poop bags. Wojo better hurry up, because I was running short on restraint.

One peek. I deserved a peek, right? Tex had broken the rules by getting me a present. I could break the rules and see what it was. He claimed he'd gotten me something to wear. The idea was equal parts amusing and scary. Tex knew I was my own woman, and the thought of him trying to make me over in Nasty—or anybody else's—likeness was unwelcome. I was going to have to pretend to like whatever was in that box, and it was going to be a whole lot easier if I had time to prep for that moment.

I lifted the corner of the box and saw cream wool with red pinstripes. Immediately I knew the fabric was old.

The door between the garage and the kitchen opened and Wojo and Tex came in. I was so startled, I jumped, knocking the box onto the floor. The lid fell off. The garment, a vintage baseball jersey, fell out and landed on the black leather bar stool, dangling inches above Wojo's water bowl.

"Night," Tex said. His eyes moved from me to the empty box on the counter to the uniform and back to me. Wojo took off into the townhouse and up the stairs. "What are you doing here?"

"I need your signature."

With shaking hands, I opened the folder and pulled out the sheet of paper. I handed it to Tex. He signed it and handed it back.

"Thank you," I said. I felt stiff and awkward. I knew I'd seen the contents of the box. Tex knew I'd seen the contents of the box. Yet neither one of us mentioned the contents of the box. "I'm in kind of a hurry."

He nodded.

I got as far as two steps down the staircase before I turned back around. "Is that for me?" I pointed to the box.

"What do you think?"

"I think it's the box you brought to my house. I think it's a vintage Philadelphia Phillies uniform from the sixties."

"And?"

Not many people in Dallas knew I used to play baseball. Somewhere along the way I'd told Tex. He knew I was from Philadelphia. He knew I'd left everything behind. With an itchy wool uniform from the decade when we were both born, Tex had given me that common ground I'd been hoping to find.

"And...I think it's just about the most personal present anybody's ever given me." I climbed back up the stairs and lifted the jersey from the barstool and held it up. That's when I saw number "15" with "ALLEN" on the back.

I lowered the shirt. "Allen? Are you kidding me?"

Tex grinned. "Richie Allen was Rookie of the Year in '64. I couldn't resist."

I was swimming in emotions. "When this VIP stuff is over, I'll come back and finish your bedroom."

"No rush. Let's call it a work in progress."

"Deal."

I put the baseball jersey back in the box and carried it to my car. Tex's Jeep was in the garage, which I would have known if I hadn't parked on a side street. I was eager to get back to the work on the apartment building. For the first time in six months, I felt my future was tangible and exciting and not something to dread.

I parked under Republic Tower in a space near the coffeehouse. The impact of my sleepless night in jail was hitting me, and a boost of caffeine would help. The bell over the door announced my presence to the otherwise empty cafe. Paxton popped up from behind the counter and smiled. "Hey, Madison," he said. "Long time no see."

"Is a week a long time in your world?"

"In a store where my regulars come in three times a day, yes."

"Point taken." I ordered a large coffee. Paxton's expression shamed me into revising my order. "Scratch that. Tall vanilla latte."

"You got it."

I stood off to the side and browsed the baked goods while he set to work. The process of making elaborate coffees was an art I'd never learned to appreciate. For me, coffee was more about caffeine than taste—necessity over satisfaction—but I supposed there were those who viewed interior design the same way. I shifted my focus from the trays of miniature Bundt cakes and scones to the paintings that hung on the exposed brick walls. I'd seen the paintings before on each of the countless times Jane and I had met here to work on our collaboration but had never taken time to inspect them up close. What I'd first seen as paintings I now recognized as black and white photographs of nondescript architecture that had been digitally printed on canvas and then painted to capture their former glory, or what they could be if someone paid attention to them now.

Paxton joined me by the wall and handed me my beverage. "I can tell a lot by a person based on how they react to the art. Most people don't look twice."

"Until today, I was one of those people."

"What changed?"

I held up the cup. "You forced me to wait for my drink."

He smiled and turned back toward the wall. "I've always loved this series. The longer you look at them, the more you see. Jane was a genius at including details in her paintings."

"Jane?"

Paxton gave me a funny look. "Jane. Your friend. These were hers." I stared at him for a few seconds, not processing. "She made them. When she worked for that big design firm, she had access to their library of floor plans. She used to say the floor plans were the purest part of the house. No matter what the building ended up looking like when it was done, the plans were a thing of beauty."

There was something about the tragic way Paxton spoke about Jane, about her belief in the purity of something as simple as floor plans that told me he knew Jane better than I thought.

"Jane was more to you than a customer, wasn't she?"

He nodded. "Jane was everything to me. When she was married, she was safe. But now, she's gone and it's all because of them."

THIRTY-THREE

"Who?" I asked.

"The men in her life. She had a revolving door on her bedroom and one of them killed her."

"Jane wasn't happily married," I said. "Her divorce granted her the freedom to make those decisions. She wanted to make up for lost time."

"For twenty-five years, Jane played it safe with a guy who took advantage of her talents and ignored her as a woman. Their divorce was the best thing that happened to her. When she came in here after it was final, she was like a lit candle. Bright, passionate, and wide-eyed, like she was seeing the world for the first time. I actually thought—" he stopped talking and shrugged. "Doesn't matter. Sterling Webster got to her first. Scene and curtain."

I glanced at the clock on the wall. As much as I wanted to find out how many of Jane's secret relationships Paxton knew about, I had to get upstairs and turn in my paperwork in the next twenty minutes or be disqualified from the competition.

"Paxton, I'm sorry to be abrupt, but I have to get to DIDI before they close. Can we talk tomorrow?"

"Sure. I'll be here all day."

I left the coffee shop and climbed in the elevator. While it climbed the twenty-three stories, I sipped my beverage. The latte had cooled considerably, and I gulped down several swallows to quickly get the effects of the caffeine. The doors pinged open and I got off, tossed the remainder of the beverage in the hall trash, and entered the DIDI offices.

The front desk was vacant. I hadn't gone to all this effort to leave my files in an inbox, so after about twenty seconds of looking around the lobby, I ventured down the hall toward the sound of male voices. I discovered two men conversing in a conference room with glass walls. One was Gerry Rose, the older gentleman who had carried Jane's body to the lobby the day she died. He was sartorially appointed in a chocolate brown and ivory wool three-piece suit with a bold windowpane pattern that recalled the flamboyant style of one of the appraisers on *Antiques Roadshow*. The other man was the blond and blow-dried Sterling Webster. I hadn't responded to his flowers, and as much as I didn't want to talk to him, I didn't see a way around it.

I tapped on the glass door. The two men seemed to notice me for the first time. Sterling flashed a grin. Gerry waved me in.

"Madison Night. We haven't been formally introduced, but I'd recognize you anywhere. Gerry Rose." He held out his hand. "I was just explaining to Sterling here that I was expecting you." He pointed to the folder under my arm. "I assume that's your paperwork?"

"Yes." I looked from him to Sterling and back. "I would have left it with your receptionist but she's not at the desk."

"I told her to leave early. Republic Tower needed an isolated window of time to conduct tests on the computers, make sure the security systems are all functioning properly after the recent hacking. I let everyone go at three." He turned to Sterling. "I appreciate your concerns, and I'll get back to you after I've had a chance to consider your proposal. If you don't have anything else for me, I'm going to help out Ms. Night."

The two men left the conference room and I followed them to the front desk. I watched Sterling's back until he disappeared around the corner by the elevator wells.

"How's the entry?" Gerry asked.

"It's slowly coming together."

"Last minute team member substitution two days before the deadline—you cut that awfully close." He signed the document with a flourish and set his pen down. "It's official. The judging panel will be on site at five a.m. on Monday morning, and it won't look good if you're still working."

"I'm confident that we'll not only be done, but that we'll knock your socks off."

He smiled. "You know, Madison, you've made a real splash around here. Your portfolio is relatively small—a kitchen here, a living room there—but everyone at DIDI is impressed by what you've accomplished on your own. If you ever decide you'd like an influx of cash to scale your business, you just let me know. Standing offer."

I was surprised by the words of praise. "Thank you," I said. "But if I've learned anything from my short involvement with DIDI, it's that I like my independence."

He lay my paperwork face down on a scanner and pressed a button. Lights came on and out chugged a duplicate copy. "You were a good influence on Jane," he said. "Too bad she lacked your confidence and vision."

"What do you mean?"

"She was a technician. She could research design elements and follow instructions, but she lacked ideas. It's one of the reasons she was more successful working for me than she ever would have been on her own."

"Jane had vision," I said immediately. "She was one of the most determined women I've ever met. She wanted to make up for lost time. That's why winning VIP was so important to her."

"Jane had no chance of winning VIP, and if the two of you hadn't had a falling out, you would have had no chance of winning either. The designs she submitted with your name on them weren't hers. She stole them from my company when she left and thought I wouldn't catch on."

"How do you know about our falling out?"

"Madison," he said gently. "When I discovered the design theft, I contacted Jane immediately. You were to be my next phone call. She insisted I let her tell you yourself. We all heard about your fight in the lobby the day she died. I don't like encouraging the gossipmongers, so I didn't say a word, but I was personally thrilled when you submitted your own design later that day."

"That's not what we fought about," I said. "She didn't say anything about being disqualified. Your receptionist said she was here to drop off her entry, and her email to me had nothing to do with VIP."

"Oh?" He looked interested.

"It was about something personal."

Gerry looked like he expected more, but I chose not to elaborate. "That's too bad," he finally said. "All this time, I thought you knew the truth, but it sounds to me like she was embarrassed by the truth and wanted an easy way out." He shook his head. "That's the thing about character. It either speaks for itself, or it doesn't."

In the ensuing silence, I laid the signed paperwork on the desk and took a picture and then texted it to Tex with a note: *Get back to work.* I slid the paper into the outside pocket of my white laptop case and turned toward the door and then turned back.

"Gerry, perhaps I'm mistaken, but just now I got the impression you expected me to accept your offer to invest in my business. If you really do believe everything you said about me, why would you think I'd say yes?"

He shrugged. "Your clientele is dedicated, loyal, and hates everything my company stands for. If you said yes, I would have succeeded in eliminating my competition while providing you a platform for your own expansion." He locked eyes with me, and I saw the shrewd businessman who had built his own company from the ground up and had gone on to help the Design In Dallas Initiative. "Times are tough for everyone, Madison. Taking money from me would not be the worst decision you made."

"But you just said—"

"I said *Jane's* entry was disqualified. That's why she was here the day she died. I notified her by phone and she came here in person to confront me. When it became clear I wouldn't change my mind, she tried to pressure Sterling Webster to add her to his team. I can't say they were a fit, but it was the only way she was going to participate in VIP." Gerry seemed pensive. "I can't say for certain that Sterling's team isn't better off without her."

"You think he has a better chance of winning without her than with her?" I asked.

"He has a solid reputation and an established design aesthetic. Jane hated designing unimaginative properties when she worked for me. They would have butted heads out of the gate."

"Then why would he have said yes?"

"Madison, even you must know how hard it is to say no to a lover."

THIRTY-FOUR

"But Jane was married to you at the time," I said.

"Yes, she was. Unfortunately, to her, our marriage vows were neither a promise nor a guarantee of fidelity. Jane had more than one affair while we were married, and Sterling was one of them," Gerry said.

"That didn't bother you?"

"I'm twenty years older than her. I looked the other way because I valued her companionship. Her affairs started hitting too close to home, but they allowed me to see the writing on the wall."

"She told me she asked you for a divorce," I said. "If you knew about her indiscretions, why didn't you divorce her?"

He sighed. "I wanted the woman to be happy. I thought in my own way, I was giving her that. I just wish—" he stopped abruptly.

"What?"

He stared at the papers on the desk. "Once the divorce was final, her future was her choice. There wasn't anything I could do to stop her from making mistakes."

The thought of Sterling Webster taking advantage of Jane's vulnerability made me sick to my stomach. Sterling was the worst kind of predator, the kind who wanted to own people. If there was anything positive to say about Jane's murder, it was that she was free of people like him. I couldn't begin to understand why she'd slept with him or even why she'd signed on to be part of his VIP team.

And then it hit me. Sterling had a history with Jane. A history nobody else knew about. Gerry said Jane and Sterling had different design perspectives and that Sterling's team was better off without her. But he'd also said that her affairs hit too close to home. *Affairs.* Had Gerry known about more than one? I already suspected Kip Bledsoe as being a notch on Jane's bedpost. How many men in the design community had Jane been entangled with aside from her husband?

I'd recognized the bloom of independence in her, the same one I'd felt when I first moved to Dallas. Jane's divorce from Gerry had given her a sort of power. It must have been why she felt comfortable confronting Gerry about his decision to disqualify her face to face. She wouldn't have backed down, not easily, not without analyzing everything she stood to lose.

But there was that night that she'd called me in tears. She refused to tell me who the man was who had hurt her, but that night I saw Jane's vulnerability. I remember thinking that maybe the vulnerability was what I lacked—what kept me from fully entering a relationship with hopes for the best. I didn't want to get hurt again. Jane, fresh from her divorce, had allowed herself to be hurt too soon and it had been what killed her. Perhaps it was Sterling who hurt her. Perhaps it was her ex-husband. Perhaps it was someone else.

As my suspicions grew, so did my fears. Already this competition, that I'd entered to expand the horizons of Mad for Mod, felt like a rugby scrim with me in the center. There was a reason I'd chosen to play baseball and not more of a contact sport. I liked playing the field.

Scratch that thought. People like Sterling Webster played the field. I was nothing like Sterling Webster. Or was I? We were both here on the last possible day to make changes to our team roster. That had to mean something. And right now, it meant less about any similarities between me and the cocky designer and more about his ability to know where I was and what I was doing. All information he could get by hacking into my computer.

In fact, every single thing Sterling knew about me could have come from my computer. The personality virus had generated a profile, but my designs, my team, my timetable, and my inventory were all there for the picking. Any privacy I'd thought I had behind a firewall had been more like a smokescreen, and where there's smoke, there's fire.

A flush of heat climbed my neck under my cape and crawled up to my hairline. Angry righteousness was even less welcome now that I'd experienced the occasional hot flash. I left the DIDI offices and made a quick trip to the ladies' room.

I entered the room, shaking off the memory of Jane's body on the cold, tile floor, and held my hands underneath the stream of cool water for several seconds. When I looked up at my reflection, I noticed the stalls behind me. Two of the doors were open and one was out of order. The same one that had been closed the day Jane died.

And then I remembered, in a series of fragmented memories, that Jane had been sick before she'd died. Her shoes, under the neighboring stall, pointing the wrong direction for normal bathroom business. The sounds of her nausea. Tapping on the door to see if she was okay. Her tossing her cookies when she opened the door.

I'd thought we were alone, but a witness had come forward and claimed to have been in the bathroom with us. And the only place that witness could have been was in the closed stall.

Feeling foolish, I said out loud, "Come out of that stall."

The door swung open and Sterling Webster's reflection stared back at me.

"Shhhhh," he said, with one finger held up in front of pursed lips. "Don't make any noise. It'll be okay."

"Stay away from me," I said. I put a hand out in front of me and stepped back.

"Madison, wait. I need to talk to you." It was five o'clock, the same time Jane had been in here. The DIDI offices closed at five. The rest of the building would be on skeleton staff as well. I didn't know what the protocol was for checking the restrooms before locking up, but with Delbert home for the day, and the staff being sent home early, it was best to assume I was on my own, just like Jane had been.

Was this what Jane's final moments had been like? A man coming out of a stall in the bathroom, bludgeoning her and then hiding while I went for help? Had Jane trusted him? Or had she passed out and not been aware of his presence?

None of that mattered, because I wasn't Jane.

Sterling came out of the stall and put his hand on my arm. "Hear me out," he said. "I know who killed Jane."

It was the one thing he could have said to make me want to listen. The identity of the real killer was what I needed to be out from under Henning's suspicions. But I didn't trust Sterling Webster. Not enough to chance my life.

The water was still running. I cupped as much as I could catch in my hands and flung it at Sterling's face. It was enough to startle him. I kept my hands on the sink edges and then the wall, and then the door, and then the hallway, half stumbling and half leaning against the textured wallpaper until I reached the elevators. I slapped the buttons, up and down, not caring which arrived first. Two cars arrived within seconds of each other. I sent the Down car down and jumped into the Up hoping to create a diversion and buy myself some time. The doors closed, and I hit the buttons for the higher floors. I'd get off and find help.

The adrenaline rush left me alert. When the elevator car slowed onto the thirty-third floor, I got off. "Help!" I called out. There was no answer. I moved through the halls. The offices were empty.

Was the building really conducting tests of the computer systems? I didn't know. I didn't care. I had to get out. As I returned to the elevator wells, the bell announced a car arriving on my floor. I ducked into the stairwell and pushed the door closed behind me. How long until Sterling found me in here? I didn't know, and I didn't wait to find out. I grabbed the banister and moved down the stairs as quickly and quietly as I could. My bad knee screamed out in pain after four flights. I had twenty-nine to go. This definitely wasn't the time to whine about being a victim.

I kept moving down, down, down until the pain leveled me at the seventeenth floor. I sat on the top step and pressed my hands around my swollen knee joint and then stood back up and tried the door. It was locked.

As was the door on the sixteenth, fifteenth, and fourteenth floors. I was thankful the architect and builder hadn't put in a thirteenth floor. One less flight of misery.

By the time I found an unlocked door on the fourth floor, my knee was the size of a cantaloupe. I stumbled into the hallway and toward the elevator. The Up and Down buttons both glowed and, according to the display above them, the cars were in motion on the floors high above me. A security camera in the corner was aimed at where I stood. Despite my choice of powder blue dress and boots, cape and cone hat, I knew I looked a fright. I faced the camera and said, "Help me."

I looked back at the elevator indicators. The car to my right started a rapid decent through the floors. The bell dinged. The doors opened in front of me.

I wanted to get on. I wanted to get out of the building. I wanted to get as far away from the threat of Sterling as I could. But I couldn't. Because Sterling was face down in the elevator car, and even more scary than the sight of his unconscious body was the open laptop next to him that flashed the words YOU'RE NEXT.

THIRTY-FIVE

Everything about the scene screamed trap. The elevators I had previously considered my way out seemed too predictable. What if Sterling was faking being hurt and was waiting for me to get in so he could kill me? My mind jumped to crazy conclusions and the only thing I knew was that I didn't know anything.

But if Sterling was hurt, if there was a chance he was alive, I had to help him.

I kept one foot wedged next to the elevator doors to keep them from closing and bent down to feel for a pulse on Sterling's neck. He grabbed my ankle. I screamed.

I kicked his hand off. The elevator doors jerked. I pulled away and they started to close. No! I grabbed the laptop and rolled out of the elevator in a sideways somersault favoring my knee as best as I could. As soon as I was on the other side of the elevator doors, I crawled directly under the surveillance camera—the one place I figured I'd be invisible.

I rested the laptop on my thighs and hit the ESC key. Nothing happened. I hit Alt and then Tab to see if there were any other open screens.

There it was. It was a split screen that showed the position of each of the four elevators. I checked the screen and then looked at the display above the elevator bays on the floor where I sat. They matched. Whoever was behind this—the murders, the computer hackings, the building evacuation, and now the destination of the elevators—was the owner of the laptop. I didn't know how to find out who it belonged to, but I knew one person who would.

I pulled out my cell phone. My battery was below ten percent. The police would have been the smart call, but I needed more specific help.

"Nasty, this is Madison."

"What do you want now?" she asked.

I rushed ahead. "I'm trapped on the fourth floor of Republic Tower. I found a laptop that I think belongs to the hacker. Is there a way to find out who owns it?"

Her tone changed. "Where did you find it?"

"Planted in an elevator next to Sterling Webster. I thought he was dead or injured but he grabbed me—"

"Get out of that building."

"I'm trying to! The laptop is monitoring the elevators. Can you help me?"

"Maybe if I had the serial number or could find a way to get deep inside the computer—hold on. You said the laptop was overriding the building elevators?"

"Yes."

"Listen to me carefully. If this guy has that kind of control from a laptop, then he's close. You need to shut down the computer to sever his connection to the network. The elevators will return to the first floor for an automatic reset and then they'll operate as normal."

"And I can just walk out of here?"

"Well, there's a catch." She paused. "As soon as you sever the connection, the hacker is going to know what you did. You won't have a lot of time."

"I already don't have a lot of time."

"Just remove the battery and get out of there." She hung up.

Normally, I would have chalked Nasty's abrupt sign-off up to her Nasty personality. This time, she sounded scared. And while I could say a lot of things about her, the one thing I couldn't say was that she was easily scared.

I slammed the computer shut. I flipped it over and popped out the battery and threw it into the trash. I was about to make a break for the stairs when I realized if my phone died, the laptop might be my only way to call for help. I lifted the lid from the trash and reached inside, past old newspapers and coffee takeout cups and pulled the battery out. It was as I was wiping my hand on my now soiled dress that I realized what I'd just seen.

Coffee cups. Paxton. He was in his shop in the subbasement. The employees of Republic Tower had been told to leave the building, but Paxton's shop was attached. He had no idea something was going on in the building above him. I had to get him out too.

I watched the elevator indicator lights as each car dropped down to the first floor. I could wait for them to land, reset, and then come up to my floor, but I'd have to come out from under the security camera to push the button. But as soon as I called an elevator to the fourth floor, the hacker would know that's where I was.

I unfastened my cape. It was almost a full circle, light blue double-knit polyester backed with ivory. The color mattered less than the size and density of it. With the flair of a bullfighter in training, I flung it over my head and let go. It caught on the back of the security camera, slid a few inches, and rested on top.

I stumbled back to the stairs. I made it down the remaining flights and burst through the doors into parking level one. My car was where I'd left it, next to the coffeehouse. I went inside and looked for Paxton. When I didn't see him, I went behind the counter to the storage room where he kept the coffee.

Except it wasn't a room filled with coffee.

Paxton Brannigan sat facing a table filled with computers. Multiple screens monitored everything from the elevators to the front entrance to the lobby.

"What is all this?" I asked.

Paxton swiveled his chair toward me. "What are you doing down here? You were supposed to get on an elevator and leave like everybody else. Get out!"

Reality dawned on me and I realized how wrong I'd been.

"You," I said. "You're behind the hackings," I said. "But you're not connected to the design competition."

"Jane made a mistake. I had to fix it."

"What did you do?"

"I hacked into the DIDI computers and replaced her entry with files from her husband's company. They disqualified her."

"You destroyed her chances of success. What could you have wanted to gain?"

"I needed her to need me. If she made it on her own, she never would have come back to me. I would have lost her to that world." He slapped his hand on the counter. "I've been a very patient man. I was there through her marriage and her flings. It was my time. I could have been anything—anybody—she wanted me to be."

That's what the personality virus had done. It combed through a person's computer and built a profile. The way Paxton spoke made it sound like that's what he was doing with himself. Trying to be what Jane wanted him to be instead of seeing the value in who he was.

"Why did you hack the police department?"

"Diversion. When they thought their hacked files were connected to Jane's murder, this investigation became priority number one."

"And the other local business?"

"Wasn't it obvious? Every hacked computer was related to the design community. Keep the police focused. At first, I wanted Sterling or Gerry to take the fall, but you were too perfect. You're just like her, but you're not her. You'll never be her."

I heard the weight of Paxton's emotions for Jane in his voice. This wasn't a spontaneous plan or a temporary crush. He'd imagined an alternate reality of his future with Jane, and when she hadn't cooperated, he'd killed her as easily as if he were terminating a computer program. "How did Delbert fit in?"

"It pays to know people's secrets. Once I knew about Delbert's past, I knew I could get him to do anything I wanted. Maybe he would have felt loyalty toward Gerry or Sterling, but he wasn't going to go out on a limb for you."

"How long have you felt this way about Jane?" I asked softly.

"Since college. We met in the computer lab. That was my major. I wrote her programs to design interiors and she—" he blushed. "She paid me back in other ways."

It was then that I noticed the smallest of the laptops on the desk. The images on the screen showed Jane. A younger Jane than I'd known. Like me, she'd maintained her youthful appearance while aging. If she'd been wearing clothes, I'd bet they would have identified the decade as the eighties. But instead, she was wrapped in a bedsheet, with tousled hair and a smile.

"She should have been with me. But after we graduated, she met Gerry Rose and married him. Twenty-five years I've waited. For twenty-five years, I've made her vanilla lattes and listened to her talk about her unfulfilled dreams and desires. It was my turn. Mine. When she finally asked for a divorce, I thought we'd be together."

"But you found out Jane hadn't been faithful to her husband. She'd been with other men the whole time. Only never you."

Paxton's face contorted, and tears streamed down his cheeks. "She told me she married him for security. I had to let her know I could take care of her too. I needed her to need me. She had to cut all ties from the design world and she wasn't willing to do it. Once she felt like she had nothing left, she'd see I was willing to give her anything she needed."

It was the most twisted proclamation of sacrifice in the name of love I'd ever heard. Paxton decoded was the worst kind of villain, one with an agenda that wouldn't be assumed or understood by rational people. He murdered the woman he claimed to love and, in his mind, he'd done her a favor.

"But she went straight to Sterling," I said softly. "She didn't try to fight the disqualification. She didn't turn to you for help."

"I was going to be there to help her find a new life. I could have shown her that I was all she needed."

"Jane's coffee. She had a cup of coffee that day. You

intentionally poisoned her."

"Not enough to kill her. Only enough so she'd need me." He kept using the words. Need me. All she needed. Anything she needed. Need wasn't a part of love.

"And Sterling Webster?" I pointed up toward the ceiling. "He's unconscious in an elevator. Or is he dead by now? And how did you get the laptop in there with him?"

"I left laptops in each of the elevator wells. That message was programmed to come up as soon as someone powered it on."

"So Sterling was alive when he got onto the elevator? Or did you use enough poison to kill this time?"

"Jane needed more than someone like Sterling could give."

There was that word again: need. He couldn't stop using it. "The only thing Jane needed was time. She could take care of herself. For the first time in more than half her life, she experienced what it felt like to be on her own."

"She needed *me!*" He slammed his hand down on the counter. "She wouldn't listen. I tried to make her understand. I didn't want to hurt her. And then—it was an accident. She should have listened. She should have believed in me." Slowly, his body crumpled into his chair.

I imagined the events as they must have unfolded. Paxton poisoned Jane's coffee and followed her upstairs. Hid in a ladies' room stall, knowing she'd eventually come in. Waited. And in the moments between me leaving her to get help and Gerry Rose coming in, he bashed her head against the tile floor and killed her.

And then ran away.

I thought about the interior of Posh Pit. I'd been distracted by the roses and hadn't thought twice about the takeout coffee tray in the garbage. Paxton had used Posh Pit to unleash the virus on all of us. Vonda must have caught him, and he'd killed her too.

Whatever role Paxton imagined he could play for Jane, it wouldn't have worked. He would never have been there for her. At his core, he was a coward.

"You tipped off Donna Nast to write a program to counter the virus. Why?"

"Don't you understand? The virus was what I left behind. I needed someone to hide my tracks. That's what her program did. She removed any traces of the virus and that removed any clues that would point back to me. Donna Nast was my secret weapon."

Paxton stared at the ground. He appeared overcome with guilt and sadness over the result of his actions, but he wasn't taking ownership of the role he'd played in that outcome. It would have been easy to only see the obvious grief and pain he suffered from, but there was more to this situation than Paxton's grief and pain. Jane had died in the ladies' room twenty-three floors above his coffeeshop. His choice to hide behind that Out of Order stall before attacking Jane was the definition of Malice Aforethought.

No, Paxton didn't deserve my empathy. Not just yet.

"Jane needed time to heal," I said. "Twenty-five years is a long time to be married. No matter what she said—what she told you— she needed time to recover from her emotions. You pressured her when she wasn't ready."

"Jane said Sterling Webster was her future. He took her from me. He should be dead, not her."

"What about Vonda? What did she do to you?"

"I used Jane's computer to track the virus. Vonda shouldn't have been there. She had no reason to go to work after Jane died. I left out the back and was going to hide until she was gone, but she started snooping around. I knocked her out and dragged her to the side of the house."

"You didn't knock her out. You killed her. Vonda must have known it was you."

"I knocked her out and left. She didn't know it was me."

"Sterling was Jane's professional future. Jane was going to join his design firm."

"No! The reason I hacked into the VIP database was to destroy him. After Sterling Webster had nothing to offer her, she would have come to me."

I thought about Sterling, barely conscious in an elevator car.

I'd been so sure it was a trap that I'd kicked away his hand and ran. Nasty had said the elevators would return to the main floor. If Sterling didn't make it, I would be complicit in his death.

My eyes swept the desk behind Paxton. Aside from the computers, I saw no weapons. No gun. Nothing that he could use to stop me from saving myself except possibly an ability to overcome me with physical strength.

And what did I have? A messenger bag filled with tinted lipstick, SPF, a preowned wallet from the oil baron's wife—

—and the laptop I'd grabbed from the elevator.

I hadn't put the battery back into the laptop, but I didn't need it to work. I just needed it to be heavy.

And I needed a distraction.

For the six months of our friendship, I'd gotten to know Jane well. I'd watched her talk to Paxton every single time we came here for coffee. Now I knew why she had a coffee cup permanently attached to her hand, and more than that, I understood how that could help me.

"Paxton, Jane didn't want to need anybody. She wanted to be whole. But she did want you. She wanted the best for both of you."

"How do you know?"

"She told me." I thought back to that night when Jane had cried over two gallons of ice cream. "She knew your relationship was moving too fast and she wanted to slow things down. Not break them off. She knew what you two had was special and she wanted to protect it."

He considered my words and while he thought, I slowly slipped my hand into my bag. "Jane told me she was seeing someone and—"

Paxton snapped to attention. "Someone?" he said. "She didn't say me?" His eyes focused more intent than they'd been moments before. "You don't know that she wanted me, do you?" He noticed my hand in my bag. "What are you doing? What are you holding?" He stood up and charged me.

My hand closed around the computer battery. I pulled it out

and swung. The battery connected with his head. His neck twisted. He fell against the table. He reached for something I couldn't see. I raised the battery a second time, prepared to bring it down on the back of his skull.

"Madison, don't."

I whirled around and swung the battery out of self-defense. Nasty stood in the doorway. She grabbed my wrist with her outstretched hand and wrenched my arm the opposite direction. A sharp slice of pain speared my shoulder. Nasty looked past me. A gun fired. She let go of my arm, and I fell to the floor.

THIRTY-SIX

The coffeeshop was quiet. I looked up at Nasty. She held a gun aimed at a spot on the floor behind me. I turned away from her and saw Paxton Brannigan's body. In his hand was a shotgun. If Nasty hadn't killed Paxton, Paxton would have killed me.

"Can you walk?" she asked.

I pulled myself up with the help of a chair. "Yes."

"Go to the first floor. The police are on their way. I'll wait here with him."

"Sterling Webster is—"

"Sterling made it to the lobby. You're the only person left. Go."

My blue dress was stretched, shredded, and stained. My matching hat was who knows where. I hobbled two steps toward the exit and then turned back around. "Thank you," I said. They were two of the hardest words I'd ever spoken.

"Madison, I saw the way you swung that battery. I have no doubt if I hadn't shown up, you still would have walked out of here." She shook her head as if not believing what she'd seen. "I never thought you'd be the one to last."

It was a small victory. I managed a smile and joined the police in the lobby.

The shotgun was registered to Paxton Brannigan for the protection of his coffeehouse. It had been stored in the back room, behind the table where he'd set up his computer hacking station. It had never been fired. Had he gotten off a shot at me, it would have been a first for both of us.

Nasty was a hero. After I'd called her, she contacted Republic Tower security and learned the building network had been shut down for tests. When she arrived and discovered the coffeehouse had an open network, she went to investigate. Paxton Brannigan's only connection to DIDI and VIP was proximity, but he'd used that proximity to manipulate everyone involved in the competition in a twisted effort to win Jane's heart.

Paxton hadn't lived to tell us that much, but it was pieced together based on information a team of computer specialists pulled off his network. The origins of the personality virus were there as well, as were floor plans for all thirty-four floors of Republic Tower.

The technicians found one more thing: instructions for how to build a bomb that would level the building. Paxton's plans involved more than just hacking into a design competition and manipulating Jane's chances at success. He wanted to destroy everything she valued so the only thing left would be him. Steel girders wouldn't have stabilized his instability.

The lilac roses I'd seen on the desk at Posh Pit had been sent by Sterling Webster. When he regained consciousness, he told police to look for an accompanying card that welcomed her to his team. He hadn't known of Jane and my falling out, and when she agreed to work for him, he had hoped I'd fall in line. The flowers he sent me were his way of softening me up.

Clearly, Sterling didn't know me at all. I'm more of a daisy kind of gal.

Sterling made one more confession. He didn't think the police were on the right track. Jane had been murdered in the ladies' room, and despite the sign on the door, he wanted to see it for himself and try to establish a theory. He hid when I came in and would have left after I left if I hadn't confronted the closed door.

*   *   *

A week had passed. In light of Paxton's actions, the DIDI offices postponed the judging of VIP for one week, allowing all of us a chance to finish what we started. It was the first week in October, a week that, six months ago, felt far in my future. It was my deadline for making a decision between Hudson and Tex, though when I drove past Hudson's house and saw the For Rent sign in the yard, the decision felt anticlimactic. I'd be lying if I claimed not to care.

Even though I'd made my decision, neither Tex nor I (nor the rest of my VIP team) spoke of it. I spent one night in the hospital and another in my bed while Rocky bunked with his pal Wojciehowicz. When I showed up at the apartment building on Gaston Avenue, to help put the finishing touches on the Mad for Mod entry to the Very Important Projects contest before the judges arrived, I knew we had a real shot of winning.

And we did.

The front yard had been assembled per my sketch. Yellow stones, blue-green grass, and cherry-red impatiens created a patchwork quilt to set off the newly power-washed building exterior. The white brick was accented with colorful shutters in the same colors—all of which matched the interior rooms. White decorative breeze blocks had been mortared into four-foot tall walls on either side of the front door, behind which were beds of turquoise sand that closely matched the Cool Cat paint inside.

I stood back on the sidewalk while my team celebrated. One member was missing, but only because the police force waits for no one. As Effie popped a bottle of champagne and filled the latest round of mid-century modern glassware the Bickners had sold me before heading out on their anniversary cruise with their family, one overriding thought filled my mind.

Maybe collaborating with friends wasn't so bad after all.

Epilogue

One week later, dressed in a red turtleneck, red pull-on stirrup pants from Thelma Johnson's own closet, and the vintage baseball jersey Tex had given me, I stood in the security line outside the Texas Rangers' stadium. An employee waved me forward. I walked through the security scanner and an alarm bell rang on the other side.

I'd anticipated as much. My knee had been injured and healed too many times to ever make a full recovery, and the metal knee brace under my knit pants was a part of my life. Nerves over a date with Tex had made me forget about my handicap until now. I turned back toward Tex, who was standing on the other side of the scanner.

"I'm not perfect," I said. I knocked on the metal brace. "I'm part bionic. And the part that's not bionic is equal parts angry and afraid. Are you sure about this?"

Tex held my stare for a moment. Was he seeing the reality of dating me for the first time? He pulled his shirttails up to expose his chest and stomach. His abdomen held a four-inch horizontal scar and a six-inch vertical scar. There was a small cluster of puncture wounds over his left pec.

He pointed to the scar on his right side. "Appendix. Fourteen years old." He pointed to the vertical scar. "Knife. Twenty-first birthday."

I left the scanner and pointed to the cluster of scars on his chest.

"Badge and medals on my uniform. Sometimes people like to

hug cops."

"Are you saying I'm weird because I'm not a hugger?" I asked.

"I'm saying you're not the only one here with battle wounds." He put his hand behind my neck and kissed me. Stadium security and fellow baseball fans all melted away into the background, and for the tiniest moment, I had absolutely no idea where my future was headed.

It felt great. Like a bright, sunny day.

Diane Vallere

After two decades working for a top luxury retailer, Diane Vallere traded fashion accessories for accessories to murder. *The Pajama Frame*, #5 in her Madison Night Mad for Mod Mystery Series, came out February 2018. She also writes the Samantha Kidd, Lefty Award-nominated Material Witness and Costume Shop, and Sylvia Stryker Outer Space mysteries. She started her own detective agency at age ten and has maintained a passion for shoes, clues, and clothes ever since.

**The Madison Night Mystery Series
by Diane Vallere**

Henery Press Mystery Books

And finally, before you go...
Here are a few other mysteries
you might enjoy:

PROTOCOL
Kathleen Valenti

A Maggie O'Malley Mystery (#1)

Freshly minted college graduate Maggie O'Malley embarks on a career fueled by professional ambition and a desire to escape the past. As a pharmaceutical researcher, she's determined to save lives from the shelter of her lab. But on her very first day she's pulled into a world of uncertainty. Reminders appear on her phone for meetings she's never scheduled with people she's never met. People who end up dead.

With help from her best friend, Maggie discovers the victims on her phone are connected to each other and her new employer. She soon unearths a treacherous plot that threatens her mission—and her life. Maggie must unlock deadly secrets to stop horrific abuses of power before death comes calling for her.

Available at booksellers nationwide and online

Visit www.henerypress.com for details

THE DEEP END

Julie Mulhern

The Country Club Murders (#1)

Swimming into the lifeless body of her husband's mistress tends to ruin a woman's day, but becoming a murder suspect can ruin her whole life.

It's 1974 and Ellison Russell's life revolves around her daughter and her art. She's long since stopped caring about her cheating husband, until she becomes a suspect in Madeline Harper's death. The murder forces Ellison to confront her husband's proclivities and his crimes—kinky sex, petty cruelties and blackmail.

As the body count approaches par on the seventh hole, Ellison knows she has to catch a killer. But with an interfering mother, an adoring father, a teenage daughter, and a cadre of well-meaning friends, can Ellison find the killer before he finds her?

Available at booksellers nationwide and online

Visit www.henerypress.com for details

BONES TO PICK

Linda Lovely

A Brie Hooker Mystery (#1)

Living on a farm with four hundred goats and a cantankerous carnivore isn't among vegan chef Brie Hooker's list of lifetime ambitions. But she can't walk away from her Aunt Eva, who needs help operating her dairy.

Once she calls her aunt's goat farm home, grisly discoveries offer ample inducements for Brie to employ her entire vocabulary of cheese-and-meat curses. The troubles begin when the farm's pot-bellied pig unearths the skull of Eva's missing husband. The sheriff, kin to the deceased, sets out to pin the murder on Eva. He doesn't reckon on Brie's resolve to prove her aunt's innocence. Death threats, ruinous pedicures, psychic shenanigans, and biker bar fisticuffs won't stop Brie from unmasking the killer, even when romantic befuddlement throws her a curve.

Available at booksellers nationwide and online

Visit www.henerypress.com for details

PUMPKINS IN PARADISE

Kathi Daley

A Tj Jensen Mystery (#1)

Between volunteering for the annual pumpkin festival and coaching her girls to the state soccer finals, high school teacher Tj Jensen finds her good friend Zachary Collins dead in his favorite chair.

When the handsome new deputy closes the case without so much as a "why" or "how," Tj turns her attention from chili cook-offs and pumpkin carving to complex puzzles, prophetic riddles, and a decades-old secret she seems destined to unravel.

Available at booksellers nationwide and online

Visit www.henerypress.com for details